P9-DGN-809

RENDELL--Going wrong   ENT'D

WITHDRAWN
BEAUMONT
DISTRICT LIBRARY
125 EAST 8th ST.
BEAUMONT, CALIFORNIA 92223-2194
(714) 845-1357

GOING WRONG

Also by Ruth Rendell

The Bridesmaid
Talking to Strange Men
Live Flesh
The Tree of Hands
The Killing Doll
Master of the Moor
The Lake of Darkness
Make Death Love Me
A Judgement in Stone
A Demon in My View
The Face of Trespass
One Across, Two Down
The Secret House of Death
Vanity Dies Hard
To Fear a Painted Devil

Chief Inspector Wexford novels:

The Veiled One
An Unkindness of Ravens
Speaker of Mandarin
Death Notes
A Sleeping Life
Shake Hands for Ever
Some Lie and Some Die
Murder Being Once Done
No More Dying Then
A Guilty Thing Surprised
The Best Man to Die
Wolf to the Slaughter
Sins of the Fathers
From Doon with Death

Short stories:

Collected Stories
The New Girl Friend
The Fever Tree
Means of Evil
The Fallen Curtain

GOING WRONG

RUTH RENDELL

THE MYSTERIOUS PRESS
New York • Tokyo • Sweden • Milan
Published by Warner Books

 A Time Warner Company

Copyright © 1990 by Kingsmarkham Enterprises Ltd.
All rights reserved.

 Mysterious Press books are published by
Warner Books, Inc., 666 Fifth Avenue, New York, NY 10103

 A Time Warner Company

Printed in the United States of America
First Printing: September 1990

10 9 8 7 6 5 4 3 2 1

Library of Congress Cataloging-in-Publication Data

Rendell, Ruth, 1930–
    Going wrong / Ruth Rendell.
        p.   cm.
    ISBN 0-89296-389-1
    I. Title.
    PR6068.E63G63   1990
    823'.914—dc20   90–40421
                                                                              CIP

Book design by Giorgetta Bell McRee

For Fredrik and Lilian

GOING WRONG

CHAPTER ONE

She always had lunch with him on Saturdays. This always happened, was an absolute, unless one of them was away. It was as certain as that the sun would rise in the morning, sparks fly upward, and water find its own level. He found comfort and reassurance in it when things were bad. Whatever else might happen to bring him doubts and make him afraid, he knew she would have lunch with him on Saturday.

Usually, when he went to meet her at one o'clock on Saturday, he was optimistic. This time he might persuade her to have dinner with him one evening in the week or let him take her to a theatre. She might agree to see him before next Saturday. One day she would, she was bound to, it was only a matter of time. She loved him. There had never been anyone else for either of them.

When he repeated those words to himself as he walked to their meeting, he felt a tremor of apprehension. His heart misgave him. He remembered what he had seen. Then he told himself for the hundredth time that it was all right, he was worrying unnecessarily. He held up his head and braced himself.

He was on his way to a wine bar quite near to where he had first met her. She had chosen it, knowing he would have picked somewhere expensive. If he arrived in a taxi she would remind him of his wealth, so he was on foot, having got out of his cab at the top of Kensington Church Street. He was wealthy by the standards of all but the really rich, and seemed a millionaire in the eyes of most of the people she knew. Lefty, "green" do-gooders, who thought there was something morally proper about not having a freezer or a microwave, about going on camping holidays and riding a bike. He could have given her anything she wanted. With him she could have a beautiful life.

She would come to their meeting by walking along the Portobello Road. Its picturesqueness appealed to her: the Saturday stalls, the hubbub, the people. That was what he disliked, it reminded him too much of the bad parts of his childhood and youth, of what he had left behind. Instead he took the long, austere Kensington Park Road, the wide impersonal avenue that led northwards. The trees were dark green and dusty with high summer. It was hot, the sun white on the pavements, the air above the tarmac distorted into dancing glassy waves by the heat. She disliked his sunglasses, she said they made him look like a mafioso, so he would take them off when he came into the darkness of the restaurant. He was hoping they would meet this side of the restaurant, she coming from the west, from where she lived on the other side of Ladbroke Grove. Then she would see he hadn't come in a cab.

He glanced down the mews on the left. He couldn't help it, though it hurt him rather, bringing a sweet and bitter nostalgia. In one of those pink-painted, window-boxed doll's houses she had lived with her parents, the one with the balcony like a fire-grate and a front door white as whipped cream. It was as if she had chosen this place for their lunch today to torment him. Only she was not the kind who did things like that. The point was she had no idea it would torment him, she no longer understood how he felt, and he had to make her understand. He had to make her feel the way she used to feel about him when she passed the block of council flats where *he* had grown up, a few streets away in Westbourne Park. For a moment he wondered what it would be like to know that she yearned for him as he did for her, that the mere sight of a place where he had lived would bring to her a rush of memories and tenderness and longing for the sweetness of the past. He thought stoutly, I can make her feel like that again.

When he was fourteen and she was eleven they had wandered these streets. His gang. Not innocent children at all, tough kids, white and black, big for their ages, most of them, brilliant shop-lifters, inveterate smokers of marijuana. Those were the early days of his dealing and very well he had done at it, made a little fortune leading schoolchildren astray. They were rich, some of those school-kids, with parents living on the "right side" of Holland Park Avenue. His mother had never known or cared where he was so long as he didn't bother her, and why would he? He was five feet ten and shaving, taking a girl of eighteen about, still going to school most days, but rich enough to forget about all that. Taxis were what he used for transport when he wasn't driving his girl-friend's car.

But she . . . He had loved her from the first, from the moment she came down Talbot Road and stood there on the corner watching them, four of them sitting on the wall having their first joint of the evening. She was small and very young, with a grave face, hungry for experience. The others weren't interested but he went on looking at her and she went on looking at him, it was love at first sight for both of them, and when the joint came round to him he stuck it on a pin and handed it to her and said, "Here—don't be shy."

Those were the first words he had said to her. "Here—don't be shy." So gently he'd said them that Linus had given him his long Muhammad Ali look and spat in the gutter. She took the joint and put it to her lips, made it wet, of course, they always did the first time. But she wasn't sick, she didn't do anything

3

stupid, just gave him that heart-breaking smile of hers that ended with a small giggle.

Her parents stopped it a month later. They stopped what they called "playing in the street." It was dangerous, anything might happen to her. Of course they went on meeting, he and she, after school, on the way to school and the way back. There had never been a time since then when he hadn't known her—gaps, of course, three and four months long, when she was at college—but never a real separation. No separation of her from him was possible, he told himself as he came into the wine bar and went down the spiral staircase.

He paused to take off his sunglasses. The place had a thirties theme and the music they were playing was a selection from Astaire-and-Rogers movies. All around the walls were photographs of old film stars like Clark Gable and Loretta Young and long-forgotten people that meant nothing to him. She was there already, sitting at the bar with an orange juice talking to the French boy who was the barman there. He wasn't jealous—or at least only when it was reasonable to be jealous. He liked looking at her when she was unaware of being watched.

She was a very dark girl in the way Celts can be dark, which is not at all the way of Indians or Middle Eastern people or even the Spanish. Her skin was always brown, summer and winter, but now in a hot summer she was deeply tanned. None of her features was beautiful, except her dark blue eyes, but they added up to beauty, to something entirely pleasing and satisfying. They made you say, "This is how a nice, good, intelligent, interesting woman of twenty-six should look." Her face in profile was what he saw now, the small straight nose, the chin that was slightly too big, lips that were a red rose petal, and its mirror image, the eyebrows that flew off into her hairline. Her hair was like a page's in a Rossetti painting. Her mother had once said that, her *mother*. It was the darkest that brown can be without being black, hanging just below her ears like a metal bell, a fringe cut across her forehead. She was in white, white shorts to the knees, white shirt with big sleeves

4

rolled up, a belt that was red, white, and blue joining them up but slack on her tiny waist. Her brown legs were very long, long enough and shapely enough to wear thick white socks and running shoes and still look beautiful. Those absurd earrings! Black vases with double handles, like something out of the mummy's tomb. They moved him, those earrings, to an unbearable tenderness.

The barman must have whispered something to her. She turned round. He would have given anything to see delight dawn on her face, to have seen her face as his would be when he saw hers. If only he could have deluded himself that her expression was not—dismay. Gone at once, wiped away by duty and politeness and the decent goodness that was so much a part of her character, but there first of all. Dismay. Disappointment that he was there already, that he hadn't been late or sent at the eleventh hour a message that he couldn't come. It felt like a long thin pin going into his heart. Then he deluded himself. He was imagining it. She was pleased to see him. Why else make and keep these regular Saturday arrangements? Look at her smile! Her face was suddenly radiant.

"Hallo, Guy," she said.

When first he saw her, even when she had spoken to him, he found it hard to speak. For a moment. He took her extended hand and kissed first her left cheek, then her right. As he might kiss any woman friend. And he felt her lips move in the accepted way against his left cheek, his right.

"How are you?" He had managed it. The ice that held the back of his tongue frozen was broken.

"I'm fine."

"Will you have a real drink now?"

She shook her head. Wine she would drink sometimes, spirits never, and she mostly kept to fruit juices and fizzy water. It was a long time since the days when, after school, they had sat on a gravestone in Kensal Green Cemetery drinking the brandy Linus said had fallen off the back of a lorry. You can drink a lot of brandy when you are eighteen and fifteen. Your heads are strong and your stomachs made of iron.

He asked the barman for another orange juice and a vodka and tonic. Somewhere in the world there must be perfect sun-ripened oranges without seeds, oranges as big as grape-fruits and sweet as heather honey. Those were the ones they should have here to squeeze for her into a tall crystal glass, frosted white all over from a freezer, a glass from Waterford, precious, chased with leaves and flowers, which would be smashed when she had drunk the contents. Thinking of it made him smile. She asked him what amused him and began frowning when he explained.

"Guy, I want you to stop thinking about me like that. Stop thinking of me in those terms."

"What terms are those then?" he said.

"Romantic fantasy. It has nothing to do with the world we actually live in. It's like a fairy story."

"I don't only think of you like that." He looked deeply at her, spoke in a slow, measured, and reasonable way. "I believe I think of you in every possible way a man can think of the woman he loves. I think of you as the nicest girl I know and the most beautiful. I think of you as unique, as clever and gifted, and everything a girl should be. I think of you as my wife and the mother of my children, sharing everything I have and growing old with me, and me being as much in love with you in fifty years' time as I am now. That's how I think of you, Leonora, and if you can tell me any other ways a man can think of the brightest star in his heaven, well, I'll do those too. Does that satisfy you?"

"Satisfy me! It isn't a question of satisfying me."

He knew she had heard that speech of his before, or something very much like it. He had composed it long ago, learned it by heart. It was none the less true for that, and what else could he say but the truth? "Please you then. I want to please you. But I don't have to say that again, you know that."

"I know I'm not going to be your wife, I'm not going to be the mother of your children." She looked up when the orange

6

juice came, gave the barman the smile that should have been his. "I've told you enough times, Guy. I've tried to tell you nicely. I've tried to be honest and behave properly about this. Why won't you believe me?"

He didn't answer. He raised his eyes and looked sombrely at her. Perhaps she took this heavy look of his for a reproach, for she spoke impatiently.

"What is it now?"

It was hard for him but he had to ask. If he didn't ask now, he would do so later. If not today, he would ask tomorrow on the phone. Better ask now. Better to know. He had to know what he must fight against, if he had an adversary. His throat dried a little. He badly didn't want his voice to be hoarse.

"Who is he?"

His voice *was* hoarse. He sounded as if someone had him by the throat. She was surprised. He had caught her off guard.

"What?"

"I saw you with him. Walking along Ken High Street. It was last Tuesday or Wednesday." He was pretending, in a breathless voice, a casualness he didn't feel. It was not only the day that he knew, indelibly, but the hour, the precise time to the minute, the precise spot. He could find it if he were to go there now, as if their footprints were engraved in the pavement. He thought he could find it blindfold or in his sleep. And he could see them, the two of them, images petrified in his memory, their happy faces—no, not that, he was inventing that—outside the Kensington Market.

"A little runt of a fellow," he said, and now he was savage. "Ginger hair. Who is he?"

She hadn't wanted him to know. That gave a scrap of comfort. Her cheeks reddened. "His name's William Newton."

"And what is he to you?"

"You've no right to ask me these questions, Guy."

"I have a right. I'm the only person on earth who has a right."

He thought she might dispute that but she only said sulkily,

"Okay, but don't make such a big thing of it. Remember, you did ask, so you have to accept the answer." Did she know how that made his heart fall through his body? He looked at her, holding his breath. "I've known him for about two years, as a matter of fact. We've been going about together for a year. I like him very much."

"What does that mean?"

"What I say. I like him a lot."

"Is that all?"

"Guy, this is very hard for me to talk about when you look at me like that. William is becoming important to me and I am to him. There, now you know."

"Is he your lover?"

"Does it matter? Yes. Yes, of course he is."

"I don't believe it!"

She tried to say it lightly. "Why not? Aren't I attractive enough to have a lover? I'm only twenty-six, I'm not bad-looking."

"You're beautiful. I don't mean that. I mean him. Look at him. Five feet six, sandy-haired, a face like a zebra without the stripes—and what's a zebra without stripes? What does he do? Has he got any money? No, don't answer that. I could see he hasn't. A poverty-stricken ginger dwarf—I don't believe it. What do you see in him? For Christ's sake, what do you see in him?"

She said equably, looking at the menu, not even looking up, "Do you really want to know?"

"Certainly I want to know. I'm asking you."

"Conversation." She lifted her eyes. He thought she sighed a little. "If he talked to me all day and I never heard another person talk as long as I lived, I'd never get bored. He's the most interesting man I ever knew. There, Guy, you did ask."

"And I'm boring?"

"I didn't say that. I said that to me you're not as interesting as William. Not just you, no one is. You asked me why I go about with him and I told you. I fell in love with William for the things he says and—well, for his mind, it's as simple as that."

"You fell in love?" Oh, the horror of uttering those words! He would have expected to die before he spoke them, or that speaking them would kill him. He felt weak and his hands went out of control. "You're in love with him?"

She said formally, "I am."

"Oh, Leonora, you can say that to *me*?"

"You asked me. What am I supposed to do? Tell lies?"

Oh yes, tell lies; tell me any lie rather than this awful truth. "And you go to bed with him for his conversation?"

"You want to make it sound ridiculous, I know that, but, yes, oddly enough, in a way I do."

She ordered melon with prosciutto without the prosciutto, followed by pasta. He had gambas and tournedos Rossini. He made an effort to speak, to say anything, and succeeded only in sounding like some scolding chaperon. "I wish you'd have a decent meal for once. I wish you'd have something expensive."

He could tell she was relieved he had changed the subject, or she thought he had. The truth was he couldn't bear to go on talking about it. The words hurt. Her words stayed in his ears, pressing and drumming: *I fell in love with him.*

"As it is," she said, "I don't like you paying. I don't belong in a world where men pay for women's food just as a matter of course."

"Don't be absurd. It's not a question of sex, it's a question of me earning about fifty times what you do." He shouldn't have said it, he knew that as soon as he had. It was a fault with him, which he recognized, to be unable to resist expressing pride in his success as a self-made man. The frown was back on her face, drawing together those winged eyebrows. He began to feel angry as well as miserable. That was the trouble; when they were together, on these rare occasions, always in the glare of noon, always in public, he was unable to keep his temper.

"I know you hate what I do for a living," he said, staring at the two frown lines, the steady blue eyes. "It's because you don't understand. You don't know the world we live in. You're an intellectual and you think everyone's got your taste and knows what's good and what isn't. It's something you can't understand, that ordinary people just want ordinary pretty things in their homes, things they can look at and—well, identify with if you like, things that aren't pretentious or phony."

" 'His position towards the religion he was upholding was the same as that of a poultry keeper towards the carrion he feeds his fowls on: carrion is very disgusting but fowls like it and eat it, therefore it is right to feed fowls on carrion.' "

Guy felt himself flush up to his eyes. "I don't suppose even you made that up."

"Tolstoy did."

"I congratulate you on your memory. Did you learn it on purpose to come out with it today? Or is it one of the things *he* says in his marvellous conversation?"

"It's a piece I like," she said. "It's appropriate for lots of the terrible things that people do to other people today. I don't like any of the things you do for a living, Guy, but that's only part of it."

"Are you going to tell me the rest?"

Her melon came and his prawns. He asked for a bottle of Macon-Lugny. He was a long way from an alcoholic but he liked to drink every day, to drink quite a lot, an aperitif and wine at lunch-time, two or three gins before dinner, and a bottle of wine with dinner. If the person he was with wanted to share another bottle or two in the evening, that was all right with him. Even for Leonora he wasn't going to pretend he didn't like a drink or deny himself the cigarette he would have after his steak.

"You never have actually told me, you know. You've said why you fancy the ginger dwarf but never quite why you don't fancy me. Any more, that is. You did once. Fancy me, I mean."

"I was fifteen, Guy. It was eleven years ago."

"Nevertheless. I was your first, and a woman always loves her first best."

"Antiquated sexist rubbish, that is. And I must tell you, if you call William a ginger dwarf, I shall get up and go."

"I'm not going to sit here and be insulted," he jeered in a cockney char voice.

"As you say. I'm glad you said it; saved me the trouble."

He was silent, too angry to speak. As was often the case at these meetings of theirs, he became too angry or too unhappy to eat, in spite of the hunger he had felt a few minutes before. He would drink instead and end up reeling out of the place, red in the face. But he wasn't red yet. He could see himself in the black glass panel opposite, next to the still of Cary Grant in *Notorious,* a very handsome man with strong classical features, a noble forehead, fine dark eyes, a lock of dark hair falling casually over his tanned brow. He put Cary Grant in the shade. His looks paradoxically made him angrier. It was as if he had everything already—looks, money, success, charm, youth—so what was there left for him to acquire, what was there he could find to sway her when everything was inadequate?

"I don't want a sweet," she said. "Just coffee."

"I'll just have coffee too. D'you mind if I smoke?"

"You always do smoke," she said.

"I wouldn't if you minded."

"Of course I don't mind, Guy. You don't have to ask with me. Don't you think I know you by now?"

"I shall have a brandy."

"Go ahead. Guy, I wish we didn't quarrel. We're friends, aren't we? I'd like us to be friends always, if that's possible."

They had been through that before. *I fell in love with him.* The words buzzed in his ears. He said, "How's Maeve? How're Maeve and Rachel and Robin and Mummy and Daddy?"

He knew he should have said, "Your mother and father," and he wished it didn't give him pleasure to see her small wince when he referred to her parents like that. But he went on, he compounded it, he couldn't help himself, "And their appendages," he said, "Step-mommy and Step-daddy, how are they? Still in love? Still making mature second marriages now they're old enough to know their own bloody minds?"

She got up. He held her wrist. "Don't go. Please don't go, Leonora. I'm sorry. I'm desperately sorry, please forgive me. I go mad, you know. When you're as unhappy as I am, you go mad, you don't care what you say, you'll say anything."

She prized his fingers off her wrist. She did it very gently. "Why are you such a fool, Guy Curran?"

"Sit down again. Have your coffee. I love you."

"I know that," she said. "Believe me, I don't doubt that. You'll never hear me say I don't think you love me. I know you do. I wish you didn't. God, I wish you didn't. If you realized what a hassle it is for me, how it blights my life, the way you go on and on, the way you never leave me alone, I wonder if you'd—well, if you'd give up, Guy?"

"I'll never give up."

"You'll have to one day."

"I won't. You see, I know it isn't true, all that. You say you fell in love with what's-his-name, but it's infatuation, it's a passing phase. I know you really love me. You'd hate me to leave you alone. You love me."

"I've said I do. In a way. It's just that . . ."

"Have lunch with me next Saturday," he said.

"I always have lunch with you on Saturdays."

"And I'll phone you tomorrow."

"I know," she said. "I know you will. I know you'll phone me every day and have lunch with me every Saturday. It's like being sure Christmas will come round."

"Absolutely," he said, raising his brandy glass to her, sipping it, then drinking it as he might wine. "I'm as reliable as Christmas and as—what's the word?—inexorable. And I'll tell you something. You wouldn't come if you didn't really love me. The ginge—this William, you're not in love with him, you're infatuated. It's me you love."

"I'm fond of you."

"Why do you keep on seeing me then?"

"Guy, be sensible. I only do it now because—well, I needn't go into that."

"Yes, you need go into that. Why do you 'only do it now because'?"

"All right, you asked for it. Because I know how you feel, or I try to know how you feel. I want to be kind, I don't want to be rotten. I did make promises and whatever to you when we were kids. No person in their right mind would call those promises binding, but just the same. Oh God, Guy, you're on my conscience, don't you see? That's why I have lunch with you on Saturdays. That's why I listen to all this stuff and let you insult my father and mother and my friends and—and William. And there's another reason. It's because I hope— well, I *hoped*—I'd make you see sense; I hoped I'd convince you it was hopeless—sorry about all those hopes—and you'd come to see there wasn't a joint future for you and me. I had this idea I'd convince you we could be friends and that's how it'd have been by this time, you agreeing to be my friend— well, *our* friend, William's and mine. Does that explain it now?"

"Quite a speech," he said.

"It was as short as I could make it and still say what I meant."

"Leonora," he said, "who's turned you against me?" It was a new idea. It came to him as a revelation might, enlightenment vouchsafed to a faithful believer. Her face, guilty, wary, on guard, showed him he was right. "I can see it all now. It's one of them, isn't it? One of them's turned you against me. I won't do for them, I don't match up to their idea of what's good for you. That's it, isn't it?"

"I'm grown-up, Guy. I make up my own mind."

"You wouldn't deny you're a close family, would you? You wouldn't deny they've got a lot of influence on you." She couldn't deny it, she said nothing. "I bet they're over the moon about this William, I bet he's first favourite with the lot of them."

13

She said carefully, "They like him, yes." She got up, touched his hand with hers, giving him a look he couldn't understand. "I'll see you next Saturday."

"We'll speak first. I'll phone you tomorrow."

She said in an even cheerful tone, "Yes, you will, won't you?"

He walked off one way and she the other. Once she was out of sight he hailed a taxi. He thought of asking the taxi driver to go to the house in Portland Road where her flat was, go there and thrash the whole thing out with her, maybe with William there as well. He was sure William would be there, waiting for her, listening sympathetically while she complained about lunch and him and what a bore it all was, and then giving her the benefit of his brilliant conversation.

But she wouldn't say that. She wouldn't complain about him or say he was a bore. He made a shrewd guess that she wouldn't mention to anyone that she had even seen him. Because the fact was that she really did love him. Would she meet him like that if she didn't? Who would believe all that rubbish about conscience and trying to convince him they could be friends? If a woman spoke to a man on the phone every day and met that man once a week, it was because she loved him.

Guy paid off the taxi at the entrance to Scarsdale Mews. He had bought the house ten years before when he was nineteen, an unheard-of thing to do. But he had the money. It was just before the property boom that tripled the price of the house in as many years. The second-best part of London, he called it. He had bought the house because it was a mews cottage like the one her parents, at that time, still lived in. Only his was bigger, in a far more prestigious district. A peer, a famous novelist, and a TV chat-show star were among his neighbours. The first time he asked her to marry him was when he was twenty and she was seventeen and he took her home to this house of his and showed her the walled garden with the orange trees in Roman vases, the drawing-room that had old Lisbon tiles on the walls and a Gendje carpet. The house had the first

Jacuzzi ever installed in London. He had an eighteenth-century four-poster bed and a Joshagan rug on the bedroom floor. It was better than anything her parents had. He took her to dinner at the Ecu de France where the waiters danced up to you showing you the food on big silver dishes, and then he took her home where he had Piper Heidsieck waiting on ice and wild strawberries.

"The Great Gatsby," she said.

It was the name of a book. She was always talking about books. The ring he had bought her was a large sapphire the size of the iris of her eyes. On her and for her he had spent the fortune he had amassed in his teens.

"No, I can't, I'm only seventeen," she said when he asked her to marry him.

"Okay, then later," he said. "I'll wait."

He still had the ring. It was in the safe upstairs, along with a few other, less worthy, commodities. He wouldn't despair of putting it on her finger one day. She must love him. If she didn't love him, she would simply refuse to see him ever again. That was what people did, that was what he did with the girls who chased him. He let himself into his house, went straight through to the room she said he mustn't call a lounge, but of course he did, what else, and poured himself a brandy. It reminded him, as beautiful cognac always did, of Linus Pinedo's, which they had drunk in Kensal Green. Dazed with love and liquor, they had lain in each other's arms in the long grass between the graves while butterflies floated above them on the warm summer air.

"I'll love you all my life," she said. "There can't be anyone else for us, ever, Guy. Do you feel like that too?"

"You know I do."

She loved him, she always had. Someone else had turned her against him. One of them. One or more had influenced her against him: William or Maeve or Rachel or Robin or the parents: Anthony her father and Tessa her mother. And they'd married again, the pair of them, which was why neither of them could any longer afford little mews houses in the second-

(or, in their case, third- or fourth-) best part of London. Guy smiled. Now they were Anthony and Susannah, Tessa and Magnus.

They had turned her against him deliberately. It was part of a deliberate policy to force her into their mould and separate her from undesirable elements. Anthony the architect, her father, and Tessa with the metallic fingernails and lofty know-it-all voice, her mother. Pretty gentle Susannah, the amateur psychotherapist, her stepmother, and Magnus the solicitor, her stepfather, he of the skull face and manner of a hanging judge.

And the others on the fringe: Robin and Rachel and Maeve. They were in league against him, the seven against Guy Curran.

CHAPTER TWO

When she changed schools it was to Holland Park Comprehensive she went, his school. Her mother didn't like her walking home alone on winter afternoons when it started getting dark at four, so to stop her mother coming for her in the car, Leonora said some "older friends" would go with her. The older friends were Guy himself and Linus and Danilo, just starting to be known to the local underworld as the Dream Traffic.

Her parents wouldn't just have freaked out if they'd known, they'd probably have emigrated. As time went on, anyway, it was just Guy walking her home. Linus had got himself some O Levels and gone to a sixth-form college and Danilo was in trouble breaking into flats. The Dream Traffic had become a one-man show but going from strength to strength. One autumn afternoon he and she were sitting on a doorstep in Prince's Square, not smoking or anything, just sharing a can of Coke and eating potato crisps, when her mother came by in her car. She was driving home up Hereford Road. He expected her to stop but she only waved to Leonora and went on.

"Keep your fingers crossed for me when I get home," Leonora said.

"Why? What'll happen?"

"I don't know exactly. Maybe a big scene. Maybe I'll get taken to and from school for a few weeks. God, I hope not, that'd be a real drag."

"You reckon? I bet she does what it says in my gran's woman's magazine." He spoke in a bright falsetto, " 'Don't forbid your children to see their friends. Much better encourage them to invite their friends home. Then you can get to know them. Remember, most people respond well to a happy home atmosphere.' "

That made her laugh. He remembered every word of that conversation, every detail of place and time and, of course, of her. She was wearing blue jeans with a white shirt and a dark blue sweat-shirt with a teddy bear on the front of it, a nice cuddly-looking blue denim jacket lined with sheepskin, brown leather boots, and a long stripy pink-and-blue-and-yellow scarf. Her hair was long then, really long, nearly down to her waist. She hadn't got a hat on, it wasn't yet cold enough for that, it was only October. She was thirteen.

That was when she had her ears pierced. He went with her to get it done. The things girls did to themselves that were different from what men did were what he liked, he liked the contrast. Even then he was imagining a future when he would buy her diamond earrings. Her mother had been furious, said it was "common" having it done so young. Leonora had begun wearing those fantastic earrings she still liked. The pair she had on while they were sitting on the steps were telephones with the receivers hanging on cords.

He remembered everything because that was the first time she told him she loved him. Nobody had ever told him that before, not even the eighteen-year-old (now twenty) whose sofa bed in a tiny bed-sitter he sometimes shared and whose car he drove. Why would they? Who would? Not his mother, certainly. Not even his grandmother, who had persuaded his

18

mother to name him Guy because she said Guy Fawkes was the first Catholic to try and bomb the British government.

But when he said that in a squeaky voice about being invited to her home and the happy atmosphere, Leonora started laughing. She laughed and laughed and put her head down on her knees, shook her long, dark brown hair and shook the phone earrings, looked up at him and said, "Oh, Guy, I love you. I do love you." And she put her arms round his neck and hugged him.

She liked him to say funny things or clever things, so he tried saying them as often as he could. It didn't come easily but he tried. He was still trying. And she still laughed, though there was a note in her laughter that troubled him. It was surprise.

The interesting thing was that her mother did exactly as he had predicted and got her to invite him home. That was his first meeting with any of them, any of those people that surrounded her. Robin, her brother, wasn't there. He was away at school, some toffee-nosed public school he went to.

At that time her mother must have been thirty-eight. She looked exactly like an older, harder version of Leonora: the same olive skin and page-boy face; the same dark hair, though hers was done in a sort of knot on the back of her head; the same dark blue eyes, but calculating and watchful. Guy noticed her nails. They were painted silver. They were very long and curving over at the top like claws but filed to points, and they looked like metal, like pieces of cutlery. Whenever he saw her after that, her nails were done a different kind of metal, gold, bronze, brass, or that silver again. Leonora didn't introduce her mother to him. Why should she? Each knew who the other was, it couldn't be anyone else. Just the same, the unanswerable remark was made.

"So this is Guy?"

It was raining. The little mews house was rather dark, with a few lamps lit, making pools of golden light in dim corners. Intense heat came off large gold-painted radiators. There was a polish smell of chemical lemons and lavender. Guy's home

19

was a dump, scarcely furnished. The furniture was tea chests
and mattresses on the floor, a huge television set and stereo,
Indian bedspreads pinned up to cover the windows. But he
knew what was good, what he would have one day. He looked
about him at the late-Victorian bits and pieces, the pink chaise
longue, the Parker-Knoll armchairs and reproduction Georgian dining-table.

Leonora's mother said, "Where do you live, Guy? Not far
away, I suppose."

He told her baldly, in the knowledge of her immediate
comprehension. She would know at once that Attlee House
was unlikely to be the name of a private mansion block. He
could see her brain ticking, the wheels turning and slotting
things into place, making contingency plans. Leonora was
restive, bored with it all.

"Come on, Guy, we'll go up to my room."

A hand went out to Leonora's arm and rested there, a long,
pale brown hand with, it seemed to him, preternaturally long
slender fingers, and the nails glittering like implements, like
things designed for picking bruised or damaged bits out of
food.

"No, Leonora, I don't think so."

"Why not?"

"We shall be eating the minute Daddy comes in."

They watched television, side by side on the pink chaise
longue. She would have taken his hand, he could sense she
wanted to, but he gave a tiny shake of his head, moved an inch
or two from her. Daddy came in. He looked more like a
handsome human teddy bear than any man Guy had seen
before, fair and blunt-featured and stocky without being fat.
He called Leonora's mother Tessa, so Guy did too when he
had to call her something. There wasn't anyone he called Mr.
and Mrs.; he never had and didn't mean to start, he'd had
endless trouble over it at school. "Tessa," he said and she
looked at him as if he'd called her a bitch or a whore or
something. Those eyebrows that were Leonora's—only the

20

skin round them was old and brown and freckled—went up right into her hair.

"You flatter me, Guy," she said, very sarcastic. "I didn't realize we were on such intimate terms so early in our relationship."

"Oh, shut up, Mummy, please," Leonora said.

She took no notice. Guy could have sworn the old man— well, he was maybe forty—gave him the ghost of a wink. Tessa said, "I appreciate you must have a very warm, outgoing temperament, but if you don't mind awfully, I'd prefer it to be Mrs. Chisholm for a while."

He felt like saying that in that case she could call him Mr. Curran. But of course he didn't. He said nothing, he called her nothing, he didn't want Leonora kept away from him. They talked about drugs all through the meal, that is, the parents did. It sounded as if it was all rehearsed. They couldn't know about him but they had made intelligent guesses. The father said dealing in drugs was a more despicable crime than murder or molesting children, and the mother said that, much as she hated the idea of taking life, in her opinion capital punishment should be introduced for pushers.

He was never asked back, but nor was Leonora forbidden to see him. No doubt, they knew this was something they were unable to enforce, short of moving away. Sometimes he saw Tessa doing her shopping, once coming out of the Gate Cinema. She was a very well-dressed woman, he would grant her that, and her figure was fantastic. She had those very thin long ankles that make other women's legs look like cart-horses'. But the lines were forming thick and fast on her face, there was a new, deeper one, each time he saw her. When he started taking Leonora about in a more or less official way, her accredited boy-friend, he was sometimes at the house without invitation. Then Tessa treated him with the utmost coldness or placed her little sharp barbs into his most tender places. It was as if she stuck those silver or copper or pewter daggers on the ends of her fingers into his eye sockets. He had to shut his eyes and bear it.

So he wasn't training for anything then? How was his father? *Where* was his father? Did he think his mother would ever spare the time to come and see the Chisholms? He did realize, didn't he, that once Leonora went to university he might not be able to see her for three years?

But soon after that they split up, she and Anthony Chisholm, the little mews house was sold, and Leonora for a while was aghast, devastated by a divorce she had never foreseen. Her father had found another woman, her mother another man. Leonora confided in him that she hated them all, she never wanted to see her parents again, and he rejoiced in secret. Even then, young as he was, he understood the influence they had on her. Now that she wasn't speaking to them, but longing to get away, find a place of her own, shake the dust of their thresholds off her feet, he knew she would come to him. He would have a house to take her to and they would be married. In him she should find mother and father as well as husband and lover.

She came round. The rift lasted no more than a few weeks, and suddenly they were all, so quickly, friends again, the two couples hob-nobbing, dining out in a foursome. Leonora was again talking about what Mummy said and Daddy did, and now too, incredibly, what Susannah thought and what Magnus advised. She called it civilized behaviour.

Guy accepted it, he had no choice. Besides, he had other things to think about and he told himself that, in spite of everything, he was sure of Leonora. One morning he realized he was a rich man. At eighteen he was much richer than the Chisholms would ever be.

•   •   •

He had phoned her every day for years. That kind of statement is never quite true. How could it be? He had *tried* to phone her every day. Most days he reached her. It was a kind of challenge for him or a quest, a labour of love.

When she was at university she said she didn't like his daily phone calls, they embarrassed her. He never took that very seriously. In her holidays he phoned her at Tessa's or at Anthony's, wherever she happened to be living. She went on to teacher-training college and he tried to phone her every day at the students' hall of residence. Quite often he didn't reach her but he persisted. He phoned her when she went to live with Anthony and Susannah and when she moved into that room with Rachel Lingard and when she got the flat with Rachel and Maeve Kirkland.

Usually someone else answered the phone. He didn't know why that was. When she was at her father's, Anthony or Susannah would answer, and now at the flat it was likely to be Rachel or Maeve. It was a good many years since she had lived with her mother, and he hadn't heard Tessa's voice since the Portland Road house-warming party. But he recognized it as soon as he heard it. It was Tessa who answered when he phoned Leonora's flat on the day after their lunch in the wine bar.

A languid, "Hallo?" Tessa was either languid or sharp, these moods alternating.

He said tersely, "Leonora, please."

"Who is that?" As if she didn't know.

"It's Guy Curran, Tessa." He drew a long breath. "And how are you after all this time?"

It was as if she had two taps inside her head. From one came a drawling, sluggish trickle, from the other a swift-splashing flow. She turned on the flood tap.

"I'm glad to get a chance to speak to you. Leonora is simply too kind and sweet to say what has to be said. Another girl would have got the police on to you by now. At least. Do you realize it would be quite possible for her to go to a judge in chambers and get an injunction forbidding you to pursue her?"

He didn't say anything. He held the receiver at arm's length, grubbed about for a cigarette. The voice chattered angrily out of the receiver. He held it in the hollow between chin and shoulder, lit his cigarette.

"I know you're still there," he heard her say. "I can hear you breathing. You're like one of those heavy breathers and just as sinister. That's the horrible thing, you're sinister, you're a kind of gangster. It's appalling that my daughter should be associated with someone like you—these awful phone calls, day after day, this Saturday lunch thing, like a kind of endurance test. I don't understand it, it's beyond me, unless you've hypnotized her in some way."

The only course might be to put the phone down and try later. He was thinking that when he heard Leonora say, "Come on, Mother, give it to me." She had stopped calling the woman "Mummy" at any rate. "I'm sorry about that, Guy," she said. "My mother's gone out into the kitchen with Maeve. I don't want you to think I've been complaining about you. It's all in her head really. I'm afraid she's got a very negative attitude towards you, she always has had."

"So long as you don't take any notice, my sweetheart," he said.

She didn't tell him not to call her that. "It's hard not to take any notice of one's own mother, especially if you're as close as we are."

The chill touched the back of his neck again. So the woman exerted a real influence. Leonora listened to the woman. Why did she want to be close to a person like that? Because she was her mother? He hadn't seen his mother for seven years, let alone been close to her. It was something he couldn't understand, this family unity, but he understood the results of it.

He listened to Leonora's voice, which was as pleasurable as actually taking in the content of what she said. They talked for a while. She was going out for lunch somewhere on the river with her mother, stepfather, and brother, and, for some reason, Maeve, and meeting up with the ginger dwarf later on. The last week of the primary school she taught at started next day, then the long summer holidays.

"I'll phone you tomorrow," he said.

Her tone throughout had been very sweet and affectionate. If the evil influence or influences that put her against him were removed, the love she had once felt for him would return. He corrected himself. "Felt for him," not "once felt for him." It could never die, only be submerged. Someone had told her, was probably constantly telling her, that the ginger dwarf would be a more secure bet than he, a safe life partner, more suitable. That same person was poisoning her mind against him personally, calling him a crook.

It was interesting to speculate, or would be interesting if it weren't so vital to his happiness, how things would change if Tessa Chisholm—or whatever she was called now—Mandeville?—were simply removed from the scene. He poured himself a Campari and orange juice with plenty of ice and walked out into the walled garden. A wonderful summer they were having, sunny and warm every day. His orange trees in the blue-and-white Chinese jars had fruit on them, green still but turning, a lemony bloom on their cheeks.

The garden furniture came from Florence, bronze-coloured wrought iron, and on an island in the little round pond was a bronze dolphin. Clematis climbed the walls, Nelly Moser and Ville de Lyon, pale pink and deep pink, against the dark shiny mantle of ivy. Leonora hadn't been to his house for ages. She had been coming, he now remembered, the previous summer and had phoned to say she couldn't because her mother was ill. Tessa again. He didn't for a moment believe she had really been ill. The woman was a strong as a horse. She ate like a horse too, for all that she was so thin. He imagined her now in the garden of some hotel in Richmond, eating at a table under a striped umbrella, guzzling avocado and roast duck and God knew what, those long thin gilt-tipped fingers busy with knife and fork.

It was more than possible that she had introduced Leonora to this William Newton. She was the sort of woman who would find a prospective husband for her daughter and bring them together. But he mustn't think like that. He wouldn't even put it into thought-words, the idea of Leonora marrying anyone but him. Tessa would. Tessa would be doing it all the time.

He had long ago lost touch with Linus, but Danilo he still

BEAUMONT
DISTRICT LIBRARY
125 EAST 8th ST.
BEAUMONT, CALIF. 92223

knew. Danilo wouldn't hesitate. A couple of grand was all it would take and Tessa Mandeville would be quietly removed from this life without Danilo's having sight or sound of it, his hands clean, knowing neither the time nor the place of her death. He, Guy, wasn't serious, of course. But why not be serious? Why make a joke of everything, treading so lightly with dancing steps on the surface of things? Why not confront the situation fair and square, confront the undoubted fact that Tessa Mandeville stood between him and his life's happiness, kept him from his love?

With his glass in his hand, looking at its contents, the most beautiful drink in the world, the ravishing colour of an orange-pink rose, Guy lay back in his bronze chair and remembered. Long ago, nine years ago, when he first came here. They had been here in his garden and she had said, looking into his eyes, "I *am* you, Guy. Just as much as I'm Leonora, I'm Guy."

She had meant they were so close that she was he and he was she. And then, very soon, all too soon, Tessa Mandeville had come between them. Killing Tessa would be too good for her.

· · ·

She had married a man called Magnus Mandeville. Absurd name but not one you would forget. He was a solicitor, had in fact been the solicitor she had gone to when she and Anthony Chisholm were seeking a divorce. No wonder she knew so much about going to judges in chambers and applying for injunctions.

The Mandevilles had gone to live in some suburb on the outer extremities of south London, or perhaps Magnus had lived there before. Tessa had never worked, or not since the birth of Robin, who was two years older than Leonora, and he remembered Leonora saying she had got married as soon as she left college, which was when she was twenty-one. It was art school she had been at and she was supposed to know all about art. This had been important in his relationship with

Leonora, or important in *altering* his relationship with Leonora.

When he looked back he could see that there had been a definite precise point when Leonora had changed towards him. Or, rather, when she had ceased to show him a devoted, uncritical love. Someone had put her off him, he knew that quite clearly. It had happened when he was twenty-two and she was nineteen. Then it was, when she came home from college for the long summer vacation, that she had seemed to stop wanting to touch him. In that August, which he had looked forward to desperately all summer, she kept finding excuses for not being alone with him, she had begun gently to extricate herself from his embrace.

The strongest possibility was that Tessa had found out he had been Leonora's lover and indicated her violent disapproval. He had never thought of that before. Having that set-to with Tessa on the phone had wonderfully cleared his mind. The more he thought of it, the more apparent it became that it was Tessa who had been the prime mover against him.

•   •   •

He phoned Leonora as soon as he thought she would be home from school. This time it was Rachel who answered. Leonora had met Rachel at university and they had been friends ever since. Guy didn't like the sort of girls who were overweight and hyperintellectual, who wore steel-rimmed glasses, took no interest in their appearance, and whose greatest ambition was to end up as head of Friends of the Earth.

"Off sick, are you?" he said. "You'll never make it to the top that way."

"I have a client here with me," she said. "It happened to be more convenient."

He knew what she meant by a "client." "Some child abuser, I suppose?"

"How did you guess? Leonora isn't back yet. I shan't be

27

here to tell her you rang but she'll know. Surprise day will be when you don't ring."

Leonora came in before she put the phone down. "What's she got against me?" he said. "What have I ever done to her, the bilious bitch?"

"Perhaps you're not very nice to her either, Guy."

"Have you had a good day?" he said. "Are you very tired? Will you have dinner with me?"

"Of course I won't. I never have dinner with you. I have lunch with you on Saturdays."

"Leo," he said. Sometimes he called her Leo, and in the same tone as he sometimes called her sweetheart. "Leo, your mother doesn't go out to work, does she?"

He understood that she was so surprised at getting an ordinary question from him instead of a plea to love him that she answered without thinking, she answered *gratefully*. "No, she doesn't, she never has, I thought you knew that. She does voluntary work at some hospital down there. Would it be the Mayday Hospital? Tuesdays and Thursdays, I think. Oh, and something at the CAB on Wednesday mornings."

"The *what*?"

"Citizen's Advice Bureau. I think she got it through Magnus. And they both work for the Greens." At least she was realizing the question was odd coming from him. "Why on earth do you want to know?"

"One of the people who work for me mentioned knowing her at art college. She asked if she was working and I said I'd find out."

This utter fabrication was accepted. Leonora tended to believe what she was told. Habitual truth-tellers do. He was encouraged to press on. "It's 15 Sanderstead Way they live, isn't it?"

"Seventeen, and it's Sanderstead Lane."

"Where shall we go for lunch on Saturday? Let me take you to Clarke's."

"I'm just as happy in a wine bar, Guy. Or McDonald's, come to that. I don't really enjoy food when I know that what you spend would buy meals for a whole family in Bangladesh for a month."

"Would it please you if I sent the cost of lunch at Clarke's to Bangladesh?"

"Yes, very much, but I still wouldn't want to go there."

"I'll phone you tomorrow," he said.

•   •   •

When she was fifteen and he was eighteen he had made love to her for the first time in Kensal Green Cemetery. If you told people a thing like that—not that he did tell people—they'd say, *How revolting!* or *How macabre!* But it wasn't revolting or macabre. Those who talked like that didn't know the cemetery, which was really like a vast overgrown wild garden that happened to have weathered grey stones among the long grass and wonderful tombs like little houses. There were big dark trees and wild flowers and in the height of summer wreaths dying on new graves. The cemetery was full of butterflies, small blue ones and big brown-and-orange ones, because there were no poisons or pollution in there to kill them.

Where they were was so quiet and wild and beautiful, with long seed-headed grasses swaying and creamy foxgloves growing among the grass, with tall pink flowers he didn't know the name of and moss growing over a sunken slab, moss that had its own tiny yellow flowers growing on it, that it was like a lost paradise. There were bushes with pointed silver leaves and small firs like blue Christmas trees and overhead a great spreading tree covered with green cones. The smell of London didn't come in here. It smelt like when you sniffed the jars of herbs in the health-food shop.

She was wearing a dress, very thin and soft and sort of smoky blue and mauve colours with a low neck and puff sleeves and no waist. It was one of the few hot days of a cold summer. She was wearing the dress and a pair of knickers and blue espadrilles and nothing else. When she lay on her back her breasts were soft and spread like little silk cushions. He laid her in a nest of grasses and scattered elderflower petals. He lifted the dress and drew it up to her neck. It lay there round her neck as a scarf might. She wasn't afraid, she was very excited, and when he entered her she wasn't hurt. He told her afterwards that was because she loved him and wanted him.

What Tessa said when she saw the creased dress all covered with green stains, he never knew. Perhaps Leonora contrived for her mother not to see it. It was when Tessa finally found out that things began to go wrong. If you loved someone like that when you were fifteen, if you loved him so much that though you were a virgin love-making didn't hurt you at all and you didn't bleed, that love didn't change. It didn't just go away, it was as much a part of you as your love for your parents or your brother, your love for yourself.

"I *am* you. I am Guy and he's me."

• • •

If Tessa weren't there, that love would return. Unhindered, it would become once more what it had been. If there were no one there to tell evil stories about him, call him low-class and criminal, insult his intelligence, Leonora would be him and he her. Still, the idea of harming Tessa seemed grotesque. In all his career he had never really harmed anyone. When Danilo came back after his stay in a Borstal institution they had run a very lucrative protection racket up in Kensal and once they'd had to rough up a publican a bit to show him they meant business, but the man only got a few bruises and a black eye. Of course there was the final showdown with Dream Traffic, and there was Con Mulvanney's death. But that had been no one's fault, certainly not his, it was what might be called an occupational hazard.

He refused to think about Con now. All he ever allowed himself to think of in that connection was that it had marked the end of his dealing. He had had a good run, had made a fortune, escaped from Attlee House and all its associations. His hands were clean and so was his record.

It would do no harm to ask Danilo to have dinner with him and there sound him out on the question of hit men, how to go about it and what it would cost. Not that he cared about the cost.

CHAPTER THREE

When there was a sale of his paintings in a country pub or some other suitable outlet, Guy would sometimes go and see how it went. On these occasions it wasn't his habit to let it be known who he was. He liked to see customers' reactions and was seldom willing to take his agents' word or the sales figures. It was best to see for himself whether the current favourite was *Man's Best Friend,* say, or *Carry on, Kittens* or *Lady from Thailand.*

This week one of the sales was at a pub in Coulsdon that was nearer to a country club. It was a fine day, and the traffic was never terrible in August. Everyone was away. Guy went down in the Jaguar. It was champagne-coloured, though called "beige satin," with cream leather upholstery and an air-conditioning system so good that on really stifling London days he was sometimes tempted to go into the garage and sit in the Jaguar with the engine running to get the benefit of its cool breezes. "You'll kill yourself if you do that," Celeste said when he told her and there was some sense in what she said.

The pub was called the Horseless Carriage, which was a

made-up name if ever he heard one. There were more flowers on the front of it in window-boxes than at the Chelsea show. Two large yellow posters outside advertised the sale of "original oil paintings, £7—£70, all prices, each one unique hand-work." He didn't wince for himself but only when he thought of Tessa Mandeville's reaction. He kept thinking of her. He couldn't get the bloody woman out of his mind.

The sale was in a large room at the back that had double doors opening onto a terrace and a rather shabby garden where the lawn had become a dust bowl and no one had deadheaded the roses. A lot of people were there already, in the sale-room and out on the bald grass. There was one glass of red or white wine for everybody who came. After that you bought your own. Two girls were taking the orders. He didn't know them, had never seen them before, but he could see from the growing lists on their clipboards that the orders were coming in thick and fast.

And why not? They *were* original paintings, and each one *was* painted by an artist working individually. The results were a lot more pleasing than ninety-nine per cent of what you saw along the Bayswater Road on Sunday mornings. They were harmless and pretty, their subjects innocent—children and baby animals, young girls, country cottages, or views of the sea. When he considered some of the pictures he had seen that were supposed to be so good—war and slaughter of men and horses, for instance—that he had once seen on an outing with Leonora to Blenheim Palace, or lopsided vases and deformed apples, paintings in that Guggenheim place in Venice of naked women in birds' feathers and furs. . . . He was open-minded enough, God knew, but they had disgusted him. It was madness for Tessa Mandeville to call his paintings "junk," and what was her other word? "Obscene." Those others were truly obscene.

He walked round, studying each one. Even at this late stage he liked to make sure there were minute differences between each copy of the same painting, slight variations in the curls on the weeping boy's head, for example. Tears glistened on the round pink cheeks, but in some versions there were three tears on the left cheek and in others four. *Lady from Thailand* was again proving the top seller. It was the custom of his agents to attach red stickers to paintings that had been sold—"as at a real private view," he had been told was Tessa Mandeville's comment. What was unreal about his sales no one had specified.

All four copies of *Lady from Thailand* were sold, and they were up in the seventy-pound range. He asked one of the girls if she was taking orders for that particular painting and she said she was, she had already taken twelve, it was the most popular. Guy could understand why. The girl in the painting was very young, fifteen or sixteen, and very innocent-looking. But she was sexy too, with full, gleaming lips and big, shining doe eyes, and the gold-embroidered bodice she wore parted to show, between its braiding and the gold-and-jewelled neck-laces she wore, the tops of her smooth young breasts. She seemed to gaze back into the eyes of the viewer with a look that was winsome yet pleading, shy yet provocative.

Somewhere the original of that girl must exist, for all the paintings were based on photographs. Literally and actually based on photographs which, printed in a pale over-exposed version onto plasterboard, were imported by Guy in quantity from Taiwan. They were then painted over according to a prescribed method by his workers at the factory in Isleworth.

•   •   •

When Guy, explaining his new business to members of Leonora's family, had said that many of his employees would be art-school graduates, Tessa Mandeville had actually shud-dered and said that made things worse.

"They're glad of the work, I can tell you," he had said.

"They'd do better to go on the streets," said Tessa. "Better get themselves a beat outside King's Cross Station."

What did she know about it? She had always had someone to keep her and give her a house to live in and money to save the whales and stop the acid rain and a studio where she could mess about with her paints. She didn't have a clue what it meant to need a job. He would have liked to say that but he couldn't because he had to keep on selling himself to those people, present himself as worthy to pay court to Leonora. The funny thing was—if such things were funny—that he had come along there, to some hotel it was where they were celebrating Leonora's birthday and the end of her teacher-training, with the aim in view of getting himself in good with them all by indicating his abandonment of a life of fringe-crime and explaining his new career as a respectable business-man.

·　　·　　·

As he looked at the paintings, the Thai girl and the weeping boy, *The Old Millstream* and the twin Persian kittens, he reflected that that particular evening had marked another watershed in the decline of his relationship with Leonora. It was true that by that time she had ceased altogether to sleep with him, but though that had naturally bothered him, it was not his major concern. She had once told him she thought it a bad idea for a girl to be on the pill for more than, say, four years at a stretch. While she was studying for her degree she would be afraid of becoming pregnant. He would, of course, have married her like a shot whenever she wanted it, chance would have been a wonderful thing, but nevertheless he understood she wanted to complete her studies. Then she had been away so much, and though he had phoned her every day, they hadn't met for months on end. You expected diffi-culties—awkwardnesses, coldnesses—in those circumstances.

But she had still loved him then. She had still loved him publicly and openly. Hadn't she seen to it on that July evening four years ago that he was seated next to her, he on one side and her father on the other? Robin was right down the table, stuck with the horrible Rachel. Later on Leonora had danced with him. She had said to take no notice of what Tessa said. But she, Leonora, had taken notice next day or the next. "Philistine" was one of Tessa's favourite words, but that was

35

the least of what she would have called him. Crook, thug, low-life—he could imagine. Leonora listened to Tessa, was "close" to Tessa.

Guy helped himself to his permitted glass of wine from the tray. It was Rioja, red and rough. He felt a sudden desire to see Tessa, as one sometimes does wish to see an enemy, to see her perhaps without being seen. The wish is to see the enemy in misfortune, in defeat. Has she changed? Was she grey? She was about fifty now, a solicitor's wife, living in a suburb; busy, it appeared, with good works. Living, he realized, in a suburb very close to where he now was.

He walked through to the saloon bar. A girl of about twenty-five sitting on a bar-stool alone eyed him. Guy was used to women looking at him and it gave him a certain pleasure even though he seldom responded. He asked for a dry martini and wondered what they would come up with, a glass of warm French vermouth as likely as not. When it came it was passable, at least it had gin in it and a piece of ice. He allowed himself for a moment to imagine that the girl was Leonora and she was with him. In a moment they were going to have lunch and sit long over the table afterwards with their drinks, talking about the past and the future and their love. Then they might drive down to the coast and walk on a beach in the cool evening. They would stay in the best hotel, in the bridal suite. Oddly enough, it was not the idea of making love to her that was paramount. Of course he wanted that, he was full of desire for her, but it was not the most important thing, it was only a part of the whole. What was the most important thing? Being with her, being *her* and she being him. "I *am* Guy . . ."—to hear her say that again!

He had another drink and a dried-up smoked-salmon sandwich and then he got back into the Jaguar and drove to Sanderstead Lane. Number 17 was not at all as he had imagined but half of a pair of rambling old houses, three floors high, with imposing windows framed in stone and pillared porches, which had obviously been there for a hundred years or more, long before all the rest were built. The front garden was as long as the back gardens of other houses. White-painted furniture was grouped under a spreading cedar tree.

Guy was long past the stage of hoping to impress Tessa Mandeville with his wealth and success—she never was impressed or she pretended not to be—so he was anxious not to be detected as the driver of the golden Jaguar. But there was no one to detect him, no Tessa obligingly leaning out of a window to show him the grey in her hair and her latest wrinkle, no Magnus Mandeville taking a day off from soliciting to potter about in the garden, hollow-eyed skeleton in a skin that he was.

Like a lawyer in some Dickens serial on TV. That was how Guy had thought of him when they met at that party. He had wondered what there was to attract a woman about a stooping skinny man with a little wisp of grey hair on top of a parchment-covered skull. His money perhaps. Knowing Tessa, that would be it. Magnus had a neck like the gizzard that came in a plastic bag inside a frozen chicken. His voice was high-pitched and chilly, and extravagantly, affectedly, dauntingly, Old Etonian. You could imagine him playing the part of the judge with a white wig on, sending some poor devil to be hanged by the neck until he was dead.

Guy drove half the length of Sanderstead Lane and back again. He turned down a side road and saw that a lane between high hedges ran along the backs of the houses. Their gardens had gates into it. He returned to the main road. Number 15, next door to and adjoining Tessa's, looked empty. There were no curtains at the windows and an estate agent's "For Sale" board was planted in the overgrown front garden.

In the old days, if this had been his area of Kensal and Tessa Mandeville had been running a business and had defaulted on her fees to him for keeping the place intact and not broken apart, he'd have got in there (or someone working for him would have) and either had her roughed up a bit or the fittings made to look less like they'd just come from the Ideal Home Exhibition. Midday would have been the best time, when there weren't many of her neighbours at home, but not on a

Tuesday, a Wednesday, or a Thursday. Entry by that lane at the back, the chances were the door into it was never locked, even if it could be locked, then try the back door. If it wouldn't open, knock, and when she came no games, no posing as a salesman, a market researcher or whatever, but the swift hand closing her mouth, her two hands held hard behind her. Quick march with her into the middle of the house, silence while what had to be done was done.

Fantasies—or were they? He began the drive home. Tonight he was giving Danilo dinner. There came quite suddenly into that part of his mind that made pictures, that ran videos, a sight of Magnus Mandeville eyeing him at that birthday party. Looking at him above the straight tops of his half-glasses as a judge might look at the scum in the dock, puzzled, inquiring, shrewd, astonished, unrelenting. Magnus possibly had influence with Leonora. He was a lawyer, for God's sake. Suppose he had had some inkling of his, Guy's, activities, which were then still on the edge or over the edge of what was legal; would he have warned Leonora?

Guy drew into the side of the road and parked the car. These small cameos were expanding into a picture, a panorama or group photograph, of that table on the evening of July 25. He couldn't concentrate on the road. He had to stop. Where had it been, that dinner? Not a very distinguished place, not a great restaurant or famous hotel, not the kind of place he would want to celebrate some important event in *his* daughter's life. But Guy could hardly bear to think of any possible daughter or possible son of his. It was too painful. He had had thoughts of this before and it seemed to tear open a wound somewhere inside him, it made him bleed. If he could know, actually *know,* that sometime he and Leonora would have children together, he thought he would die of happiness.

The panorama opened in his mind. At that table there had been eleven people: Leonora herself at the head of it, with Anthony Chisholm sitting on her left and he, Guy, on her right. Leonora had been wearing a dark blue dress, plain, of some silken material, austere and rather too old for her. She looked beautiful, of course, that went without saying. She was wearing the necklace her father had given her, lapis in a silver setting from Georg Jensen, pretty but not expensive by Guy's standards. Anthony was a good-looking man with a boyish face that would always have something of youth in it. Next to Anthony sat his own mother, an aged crone now dead, Leonora's grandmother.

On his own right sat a cousin of Leonora's called Janice, who had later got married and gone to Australia, and next to her Robin Chisholm, with Rachel Lingard on his right. Maeve was not in the picture in any sense at that time, Leonora hadn't met her. Old Mrs. Chisholm was sitting next to Magnus Mandeville, and next to him was Susannah, Anthony's wife. Susannah was a nice-looking woman, very slender with sleek dark hair, no more than thirty-three or four at the time, who, Leonora said, hardly ever wore skirts or dresses and was, in fact, on that evening wearing a black silk trouser suit. Janice's fiancé, whose name Guy couldn't remember, sat between Susannah and Tessa.

He let his mind's eye rove round that table from guest to guest. The men's suits had been unmemorable, vague greys, but he thought Robin had been wearing a pink tie. Robin favoured his father, was much fairer than Leonora, and, having Anthony's boyish look, seemed absurdly younger than his twenty-four years. He was a swap jockey—that is, he had later become one. He swapped sums of money between potential borrowers, thus making dollars quickly available to clients in, say, Germany, and Deutsch marks to clients in Brazil. Guy suspected he was, in a respectable sort of way, just as dishonest and on the make as he himself had once been.

"You'd think he'd like me," Guy had once said to Leonora. "I can't understand why he doesn't. We're birds of a feather, aren't we?"

"He's a snob."

"What does that mean, he doesn't fancy my accent?"

"Let's hope he grows out of it. He's still at the stage of making snide jokes about people who haven't been to public school. I'm sorry, Guy. I love Rob and I always will, but he's the only reactionary member of my family. He's a real old-fashioned Tory."

"I can believe it," he'd said, though politics didn't interest him. He was an old-fashioned Tory himself if he was anything.

Tessa hated him because he was a so-called Philistine, her husband because he was or might have been a crook—had Robin turned Leonora against him because he came from the wrong background and spoke with the wrong kind of voice? Guy closed his eyes and went on seeing those eleven people, ten without Leonora. Tessa in a greenish-gold dress of some pleated silky stuff, a thin gold chain round her neck, her new wedding ring bright and shiny and her nails to match; Susannah in her black trousers and tailored jacket, the open-necked white silk shirt and chunky jet-and-amber beads; old Mrs. Chisholm in brown lace and pearls; Rachel, that ugly four-eyes, in a flowered cotton skirt with a dipping hem and a pink blouse probably from the British Home Stores. Janice, plump as Rachel, round-hipped, wearing fancy-rimmed glasses, pink plastic. The men. Himself and Leonora.

They ate avocados stuffed with prawns. Surprise, surprise. Not to say big deal. The next course was chicken done in an uninteresting way. Guy had read somewhere that chicken, if not the best-loved, is the most widely eaten protein food in the world. When they got to the profiteroles, Anthony had said to him, across Leonora, "So what's with you career-wise these days, Guy?"

They knew he was rich. No one else had on a suit from Armani, cuff-links that were imperial jade set in 22-carat gold. And he was less than half Anthony Chisholm's age. He answered the question, told them about the paintings, not mentioning his other sidelines, of course. They were all soon to go anyway. With the death of Con Mulvanney imminent, waiting to happen, as it were, in the unknown, unguessed-at future, the remnants of Dream Traffic were to be dissolved. The last of that trading Tessa and Anthony had hinted at with such opprobrium, such violence, the first time he met them, that was almost over.

Like a vulture Tessa had been at that dinner party, watching the others kill him and then swooping to pick his bones. First that remark about going on the streets and having a beat at King's Cross, then a savage closing-in, a lecture to the assembled company about the demise of art and culture in the West (whatever that meant). And Leonora had listened, had later on no doubt been told more, and more . . .

He started the car and drove home.

•   •   •

Leonora had stopped living with her mother in the holidays and moved in with her father and stepmother. That was for the sake of being in central London. And to be near Rachel Lingard. If he was honest with himself, he had to admit that. Rachel's mother had a flat in Cromer Street and Rachel was living there because her mother was dying of cancer. He had recognized Rachel as a menace from the beginning, the kind of person he didn't want his girl-friend to know. Girls should be frivolous, they should be a bit silly sometimes, mad about shopping, passionate about clothes and perfume, always catching sight of themselves in mirrors, loving to be stared at and whistled at. They should be vain and petulant and with a tendency to be bitchy towards other women. Rachel was a feminist. She never wore make-up. She ate what she liked and grew fat. It was a principle with her to say she preferred the company of women to that of men. Her conversation was clever and to him often incomprehensible. Half the time he literally didn't know what she was on about.

Now he wondered if it was through her that Leonora had met this William Newton. He looked the kind of person she would know. And he too had that quality Leonora seemed to prize so highly, the gift of gab. He had never seen the point of it, all those discussions, arguments, all that cleverness and wit. Why bother? It might have been necessary once when there was nothing else to do, no magazines, papers, videos, music, television, no places to go to and no electric light. The art of conversation was no more necessary now than the art of writing letters. That was the way he saw it.

The rift really began when Leonora changed her mind about going on holiday with him. He had never known why. He didn't know why she seemed almost *shocked* when he suggested she move in with him. Her attitude was more what her mother's might have been, not that of a girl of twenty-two. After all, they'd been going out together steadily for years. He loved her and she loved him and both knew they would be married one day.

"You're not serious, Guy?"

"Isn't it what people like us do? I've got a house all ready for you. It's in a place you like. I presume you like *me*—well, love me. And I love you."

"Who are these people like us?"

This was one of those "clever" remarks she was making more and more often. Picking him up on old sayings he used, expressions everyone said but which she called clichés. She had never used to do it. She had caught it off Rachel. And now she was going to share a bed-sit with Rachel.

"We thought of Fulham, because of me teaching there, a big room with a kitchen while we look round for a flat."

Rachel's mother was permanently in hospital now, she would never come out again. Leonora showed Guy the bed-sit, which was as horrible as Attlee House and much smaller. Fat Rachel, her round eyes magnified by the glasses she wore, saw his expression, whispered something to Leonora, and said like someone acting on the stage, "Prithee, why so pale? Will, when looking well can't move her, looking ill prevail?"

Both girls went into gales of laughter, giggling the way he liked girls to giggle, but not when he was the butt of it. He understood the remark, bit of poetry, quotation, whatever it was, though Rachel might think he didn't. It meant she wouldn't like a miserable hangdog man, so he tried not to look offended but to laugh it off. Rachel's mother died soon after

42

that, which wiped the smile off Rachel's face for a while. No doubt she was pleased to have property to sell, though, she was as greedy as the next girl for all her airs. She and Leonora started flat-hunting.

As soon as he heard they were applying for a mortgage—a huge one—he offered to lend Leonora the money. It wouldn't, of course, really be a loan. It would be an outright gift. Secretly, in his heart, he planned this from the beginning, but of course he would let her think it was an interest-free loan.

Why did she have to bring her family and friends into everything? She was nearly twenty-three, for God's sake. Why couldn't she break away from that family? Because they wouldn't let her. They clung to her and to each other like leeches. Her parents, who weren't even married to each other any more, who were married to other people, nevertheless were always meeting, saw nearly as much of each other, it seemed to him, as when they had shared a home.

The night he made his offer she had been staying with Anthony and Susannah in Lamb's Conduit Street. *Staying* with them, if you please, though she had a home of her own no more than five miles away. Rachel had gone up north to a reunion of people she called "alumnae," which he thought sounded like bacteria, the kind of thing you picked up from eating supermarket pâté. Of course he hadn't made his offer in anyone else's presence. He and Leonora had been alone, having a quiet drink after the cinema.

"It's very generous of you, Guy," she had said, and he could tell she was moved. He thought she was going to cry.

"I won't even notice it," he said, which he shouldn't have said, he knew at once he shouldn't have.

"If only it was possible," she said, and she took his hand.

They went back to her father's. Anthony and Susannah were both there, and her uncle, Anthony's brother Michael, who was something big in television, chairman of a TV company; and her brother Robin, he of the baby face and fair curls. And black heart, thought Guy.

He was embarrassed when she came out with it. He was

also proud. After all, he had begun with nothing, less than nothing, and they had all been to universities, come from happy home backgrounds, known people with influence.

"I hope you told Guy anything like that was out of the question," said Anthony.

You couldn't get more patronizing than that. Patronizing and—what was the word Rachel was always using?—paternalistic.

Anthony had lost his nice-teddy-bear look. Guy had never seen him look the way he did then. Affronted. Shocked, really. As if Guy had insulted him instead of offering to lend his daughter forty thousand pounds.

The uncle, who was a bigger, older and somehow *furrier* version of Anthony, pursed up his lips and gave a thin little whistle. Robin said, "How to put a lady in your power in one easy lesson."

The bastard. Guy had always hated him!

"I just wanted you all to know," Leonora said, "because it was so very very kind of Guy." *Was?* What did she mean, *was?* He had been half-sure up till then that she'd take it in spite of them all. But their influence was too strong for her. "It was a magnificent offer," she said, "but of course I couldn't dream of taking it." And she looked so sad he longed to put his arms round her and kiss her better.

He hadn't given up. He had pressed her to take the money in the weeks that followed. At about the same time she started making excuses for not going out with him; she was going out with him less and less. For years he had spoken to her every day, though it wasn't easy phoning the room in Fulham where the phone was downstairs and shared by about eight people.

A kind of cold panic took hold of him when he felt she was separating herself from him, more even than when she had been away at college. Life wouldn't be possible without her. Sometimes he had moments when there opened before him a cold vision of emptiness, a grey desert from which she had walked away and he was alone.

"What's happened to us?" he said to her one day, when he

had steeled himself to it. He was so afraid of her answer. Suppose she said, "I don't love you any more?"

She didn't. "Nothing's happened. We're still friends."

"Leonora, we were more than friends. I love you. You love me. You're my life."

"I think we should see less of each other. We ought to see more of other people. This sort of monogamous situation we have isn't very healthy when you're young."

Rachel's expression. He could hear her uttering it.

"I must see you."

It was a Saturday. They were having lunch together at a French restaurant in Charlotte Street. She hadn't got into that vegetarian nonsense at that time. He could remember what she'd been wearing, a dark-blue-and-dark-green-striped cotton dress with a tan belt and tan pumps. In those days, three years ago, she still dressed quite nicely.

"I tell you what," she had said, "I'll always have lunch with you on Saturdays."

CHAPTER FOUR

It was a joke. That was how he took it at first. She could hardly have meant that. He could scarcely remember a time when he hadn't been the man she went out with and she the woman he went out with. The girl with the furnished room and the car that he'd known before he met her was a dim memory, a phantom. Leonora couldn't have meant they were only to see each other like people regularly having a business lunch.

Phoning her was very difficult; sometimes he got no answer, often another occupant of the house answered, promising to pass on a message but forgetting. Two days went by without his speaking to her and that declaration of hers, that statement of intent, became less real. He saw that she had been teasing him. How could he have been so silly as to be upset by it?

When he did manage to speak to her he asked her to come to the cinema with him the following night.

"Don't you remember our arrangement?" she said.

He grew cold. "What arrangement?"

"I said I'd have lunch with you on Saturdays."

"You can't be serious, Leonora."

She was serious. She'd see him on Saturday. Where would he like to have lunch?

That was long before he began asking himself what the reason for it could be. He hadn't even considered it could have had something to do with his offer of a loan or with his ways of making a living, still less with Con Mulvanney. By then the Con Mulvanney affair was six, seven months in the past. He told himself that she was upset about the move, the problems she and Rachel had been having in getting contracts signed, exchanged, a completion date decided on. In a month or two, when they had moved into the flat in Portland Road, things would be different. She would come back to him.

Some might say she had never gone away. He began telling himself she hadn't. He saw her regularly, there was no one else for her and no one serious for him, no one that counted. He phoned her every day, much easier now she had a home of her own and her own phone. They had lunch on Saturdays. Every day he heard her voice and once a week he saw her. There were couples he knew who didn't see each other as often as that. If you told anyone you saw your girl-friend once a week and phoned her every day, they would say you were going steady. He reassured himself in this fashion, he comforted himself.

But a man can't be expected to live celibate and there were other girls. Naturally, there were. There wouldn't have been if she hadn't withheld herself. Give him the chance and he would be the most constant lover, the most faithful of husbands. He never told her about the girls, she didn't ask, and he didn't ask her if there were other men. But he had taken it for granted that though he had to have a girl-friend, he was a man; she didn't have to have a boy-friend. She could live without sex.

"A fine example of the double standard," said Rachel, speaking of another couple they knew.

It wasn't quite like that. He made this compromise because he couldn't face a starker reality. He convinced himself there was no starker reality. This was reality: that she wasn't very highly sexed; for companionship she preferred the company of women. But she loved him—why else would she talk to him every day and have lunch with him every Saturday?

One day, he had thought, things will change. She's enjoying her freedom, she likes supporting herself, doing her job, trying to run a household on a shoestring, putting those absurd principles of hers into practice. But one day the novelty will have worn off. She'll want to get married, *all* women want to get married, and it was him she'd marry. In a way it was as if they were engaged, betrothed since childhood, the way some of those Asian people were. These days a girl wanted to prove herself, show she could be as self-reliant as a man, before doing what all women do, settling down with a man. He even said as much one Saturday when, after lunch, he went back to the new flat with Leonora.

The stairs they had to climb were incredible. He wouldn't have believed so many London flats were without lifts. Rachel was there in one of her typical designer outfits of ancient skirt from a Monsoon sale (probably the first-ever Monsoon sale) and grey Oxfam jumper. He looked at their house-plants and their posters, their Reject Shop crockery and the sofa they'd bought off a pavement in the Shepherds Bush Road, and after a while he'd made that remark about women proving themselves.

"You're a Victorian, you know, Guy," said Rachel. "The last one. You ought to be in a museum. The Natural History Museum, d'you think, Leonora? Or the V and A?"

"No, you've got me wrong," he said, trying to keep his temper, catching sight in a fly-spotted mirror of his young handsome face, his thin athletic figure—a Victorian! "You've misunderstood. I believe women are equal to men. I know women need to have careers and their own money and a job to go back to after they're married. I know what women want."

They screamed with laughter. They clutched each other. Rachel said something about Freud. He still didn't know what he'd said that was wrong or funny. After a while it didn't bother him much because it was Rachel who'd made the remark, not Leonora. And he laughed at Leonora over Saturday lunch when she reproved him for saying Rachel's trouble was sour grapes.

He was passing through a long phase of *knowing* she'd come round to marrying him one day. The possibility of her meeting someone else never really occurred to him. Or rather, with a chill like the first frost on the air of autumn, the possibility would occur and he would phone her to reassure himself. Not to explain his feelings, for they were only feelings, never as strong as suspicions, but to listen to her voice and attempt to detect in it some change. And on Saturday he would watch her and listen to the inflexions of her voice, on the watch for some subtle alteration. She was always the same, wasn't she?

She talked as she always did about the old times, about their youth, and then about her family and her girl-friends, what they'd been doing and saying. None of it interested him, but he liked to hear her talk. It was funny really what she'd said about this William Newton's conversation when she hadn't really much conversation herself. There was never a word from her about TV or music or the latest West End hit or fashion or sport. He tried to imagine the content of this fabulous conversation she had with Newton, but imagination failed him.

It was now a week since he had seen her with Newton. He was on the other side of Kensington High Street, crowded traffic-laden Kensington High Street, walking in the direction of Church Street, and they had been on the other side hand in hand. His Leonora and a skinny red-haired fellow, not much taller than she was.

Hand in hand. He had felt a rush of blood to his head, felt his face grow red as if he were embarrassed, as if he were *ashamed*. Passionately, he hadn't wanted them to see him, and they hadn't. Afterwards, having a drink at home, he had thought of it as one of the worst shocks of his life, comparable to the one he had received on the day when that woman came to his house and told him about Con Mulvanney.

• • •

"You aren't looking too good," said Danilo.

"I'm perfectly okay."

For a moment Guy felt affronted. In his new Ungaro jacket and thin Perry Ellis sweater he had been pleased with his appearance. It wasn't his habit to spend much time in front of the mirror, a quick glance was enough to convey the desired impression of deep tan, sepia brush of shadow on the hard jaw-line, white teeth, a lick of black hair. And the hard, muscular, yet thin, body shape. But that glimpse, caught as he left the house ten minutes before, had shown him something else, something tired and worn perhaps, something *haggard*.

"I've been under a bit of pressure," he said. "My migraine's been coming back."

"You want to eat feverfew."

"What the hell is feverfew?"

"God knows. I read about it in one of Tanya's papers. She's into all this alternative stuff. Seriously, though, you don't look too good."

They were in a restaurant in that expensive region round the back of Sloane Square. Danilo was a short spare leonine-faced man with a big head and yellowish-brown eyes like an animal's, a fierce small carnivore. Though he was no more than five feet four, some inches shorter than William Newton, and had longish springy sandy hair, Guy would never have called him a ginger dwarf. Danilo wore a very casual but very expensive suit of nearly black seersucker with the jacket sleeves rolled up to show the blue silk lining. He had on a blue shirt with fine dark green stripes but no tie. His two rings were of white gold, one set with a round boss of lapis, the other a square block of jade. A few years back, when it was still possible, Danilo had carried on a very profitable business importing imperial jade from China. That was where Guy's cuff-links had come from. Danilo was not Spanish or of South

50

American origin and his given name was really Daniel, but there had been no less than five Daniels in his class at primary school, so he had rechristened himself. As well as an importer of various illegal substances, Danilo was a one-remove murderer. Or so Guy believed.

The only area in which Danilo wasn't macho was drink. He had a spritzer in a tall glass. Guy drank more than he ate. He tended to do that, though he ate as well, a fine thick strip of Scottish fillet steak, brought to the table whole, charred outside, blue in, divided into two for them with one dextrous stroke of the knife.

Danilo talked about the villa in Granada he had sold and the house he had bought in the Wye Valley, a Welsh castle with thirty acres, which he intended to furnish with the contents of a Swedish baroque manor-house. There was an order prohibiting the removal of any of these tables and chairs and pictures from Sweden, but Danilo was fixing things to get around that. He wasn't a particularly self-centred man, and if he was callous, he was not hard-hearted to his friends. This invitation had not been extended for him to talk about himself.

"How's Celeste, then? That still on?"

Guy lifted his shoulders. Any mention of Celeste always embarrassed him.

"The works of art—keeping you in the style to which you're accustomed?"

"I haven't got any money worries, Dan," said Guy. "That's not a problem. You and I, that'll never be a problem with us, right?" They had once said to each other, years ago, that a man was only half a man if he couldn't make himself rich.

"Then it has to be little Miss Leo."

Guy wouldn't have allowed anyone else to call Leonora "little Miss Leo" but he minded Danilo's doing it less than he would some other people. Danilo loved her too, in a more brotherly way, of course, and he hadn't seen her for years, but he still retained for her that tender regard which is born out of a nostalgia for old wild times. She had been more skilful at nicking stuff off Boots's counters than any male companion of theirs. Once, in a single swoop, she had pocketed an electric toothbrush, a hair dryer, and a set of heated rollers. Thinking of that reminded Guy of another companion of theirs and helped him put off the moment.

"You ever hear from Linus?"

Danilo laughed. "That one, he came to a bad end. Well, I would reckon, I don't *know*. Someone told me he went to Malaysia and they hung him for having a little bit of weed on him."

"You believe that?"

"No, I don't believe most of what I'm told. What's with Leonora then? Come on, you're going to tell me, you might as well come out with it. She getting married, is that it?"

It was unpleasantly near the bone. He said stoutly. "She won't do that. Well, not unless it's to me. I want to ask you, Dan, I mean, if I want to . . ." Guy looked round. There was no one within earshot, but he lowered his voice, ". . . get someone out of the way, could you—well, fix things?"

The irises of the yellow eyes didn't change but the pupils did. They seemed to elongate, becoming black stems instead of spots. Danilo touched a red tongue to his thin lower lip.

"The boy-friend?" he said.

Guy was taken aback. "How d'you know there's a boy-friend?"

"There's always a boy-friend. You want him wasted?"

Again Guy made that impatient gesture with his shoulders. "I don't think so. I don't know." He saw that table in the hotel again, planted Maeve there instead of old Mrs. Chisholm, put William Newton in the place of Janice and her fiancé. "There's someone poisoning her mind against me, Dan, but I don't know who. I don't know which one. I thought I did. If I knew, I'd . . . I *just don't know*."

"It can be done," Danilo said calmly. "For a friend I could get a nice neat job for three grand."

"And ten nice neat jobs for thirty grand? I can't have a massacre, can I? I can't blast the lot of them off the face of the earth. Dan, I know there's just one of them that's turning her against me, one or at the most two, one or two she wants to please and be in good with. They've told her every lie they can fabricate about me."

"The fiancé it'll be."

"I don't think so. *I don't know.* Christ, if I only knew. I'm all sorts of a fool, Dan. I've brought you here for bloody nothing. I don't know who to name to you. I've brought you here for nothing."

"The steak was magic," said Danilo. "I'll break my rule and have a small Chivas Regal."

Guy said, "Dan, why did you say that? Why did you say that about Newton?"

"What did I say?"

"You called him 'the fiancé.' "

"You must have said."

"I didn't. I said she wasn't, she wouldn't. I mean, this Newton, he exists, of course he does, but he's just a chap takes her about, he's no more to her than Celeste is to me."

Danilo gave him a hard look, penetrating but not unkind. "Okay, I remember now. Tanya told me. She saw it in some paper. Yesterday or the day before. She said to have a look at this and wasn't it the Leonora Chisholm I know. It said the usual stuff about the engagement being announced and the marriage shortly to take place. Leonora Chisholm and William Newton. That's how I know the guy's name, it must be, you never told me. That's why I thought it was him you wanted disappeared."

CHAPTER FIVE

Guy's bed was a four-poster, japanned, with canopy in the Chinese style, made by the firm of William Linnell in 1753. Gilded flying dragons seemed just to have alighted on the curving scarlet horns of its pagoda-like top. Its curtains were of yellow silk. There was one very much like it in the Victoria and Albert Museum. The bedroom walls were covered with a Shiki silk paper. There was no carpet on the wood-block floor but Chinese pillar rugs with dragons and animal masks and cloud motifs.

At eight-thirty on Saturday morning Guy was in his four-poster bed with Celeste Seton. She was still asleep but he was awake, contemplating the making of coffee, eating some small light thing, as yet undecided on, and then going for an hour or two to his health club. Guy looked at Celeste's exquisite face on the pillow, like a precious delicate bronze, and thought how beautiful she was but avoided otherwise thinking about her. As soon as he thought about her he was filled with guilt. The idea that he loved one woman and used another for sexual purposes was shameful and abhorrent to him.

Of course it was not quite like that, it was *not* like that. He had never been anything but honest with Celeste. She knew he was in love with Leonora, or he had told her he was, he had been quite open. It was not his fault if she persisted in taking it in the wrong way.

"I don't mind, sweet Guy, why would I mind? I know I'm not your first, I'd be mad to expect it. You're not mine, are you?"

He let that pass. "I'm in love with Leonora, I love her. I can't imagine life without her. I'd marry her tomorrow if I could."

She had smiled at him. "Yeah, sure. You have lunch with her on Saturdays, you're with her an hour and a half. I guess I can stand that. If that's the competition, I can take it."

Her father came from Trinidad, where the people have East Indian blood. Her mother was from Gibraltar. She had a perfect Caucasian face that happened to be the colour of teak and a body like an Egyptian girl on a vase painting. She was a model. Her hair was a dark russet brown, immensely thick, and grew naturally in deep long waves, like Dorothy Lamour's in some South Seas movie of the thirties.

When Guy took her about, men turned to look at her. He could swear that once, walking behind her down the staircase at Blake's, he had heard a man growl at the sight of her. On the other hand, when he was out with Leonora—or *had* been out with her, for now it happened very seldom—no one looked at her. Of course it was true that men on scaffolds and men down road holes whistled at her, she was young and her legs were lovely and she was attractive. But the traffic wouldn't stop for her, no one would stop for her and stare. The odd thing was that this made no difference to him. The seething, positively palpitating admiration Celeste received and the indifference that greeted Leonora's appearance had not the least effect. He sometimes thought he would be rather relieved if Celeste said goodbye, it had been nice but she'd met someone else.

He reproached himself. It was horrible, it was unfair. But

what could he do? He hadn't asked Celeste to chase him, he didn't invite her to be there waiting for him when he got home. He hadn't even given her a key. She had pinched his spare one and had another cut. She was in love with him as he was in love with Leonora, and that, as he put it to himself, screwed him up. But it wasn't as bad for her as it was for him. At least he didn't refuse her, he didn't show her the door, or have the lock changed or tell her to go to hell. He didn't restrict their meetings to lunch on Saturdays. He was nice to her. He slept with her, though he often thought rather sadly that he could, if necessary, have done without that, and he told himself he should have ignored his body, obeyed his mind and heart, and, like some knight waiting for his lady, have remained chaste.

She didn't drink coffee. He made tea and put the cup on the bedtable beside her, touched her shoulder lightly, said, "Cup of tea, love."

Her eyes half-open, she said what she always said to him when she woke. "Hi, sweet Guy, love you."

She took a long time waking, especially if it happened to be a Saturday, if she happened to have come round on a Friday night and be there on Saturday morning. He wondered sometimes, feeling his own wound, if she avoided waking on those mornings because Saturday was his lunch-with-Leonora day, if she needed to postpone consciousness for as long as possible and awareness of what the day would bring. Perhaps it wasn't like that, though, perhaps he was only projecting his own feelings onto her, judging her by himself. There is something very low in trying to gauge the emotions of someone in love with oneself when one is far from being in love with that person, and Guy knew it.

He walked up to his macho health club called Gladiators in Gloucester Road. Forty-five minutes with the weights, then the steam room, cold shower, thirty lengths of the pool. He decided to miss breakfast, though he could have had a healthy one at the Juice 'n' Grains Bar. The scales showed him he had put on two pounds. So much for Danilo's comments on the state of his health.

It was still only eleven. If he had thought of it he could have gone to the rifle range in the King's Road and put in an hour's practice, but he hadn't thought of it and he only liked using his own guns. He was suddenly most unwilling to go back to Scarsdale Mews. Celeste would still be there. Celeste would very likely still be in bed and would put out her arms to him. Most things that his situation with Celeste and Leonora brought him he could take, though wincing, but not passing straight from one to the other, even though Celeste knew and Leonora wouldn't care.

Oh, but wouldn't she? It occurred to him that he had never actually, in so many words, told Leonora that Celeste was his *lover*, that she frequently slept with him the night before he came for his lunch date, that she *loved* him and often swore she would love him forever. Perhaps he should try telling her. The idea that Leonora might be jealous made him feel dizzy, he had to sit down on a seat in the park.

Today their lunch date was at Cranks, the original one in Soho. Nothing but love would have induced Guy to go there. Of course he had never been to Cranks but he was aware that it was a vegetarian restaurant and for all he knew alcohol-free. Having decided not to go home first, simply to leave Celeste (not by any means for the first time) to take herself off and perhaps phone him later, he began to walk vaguely in the direction of Hyde Park Corner. He would perhaps pick up a taxi in Park Lane or even walk all the way.

The sky was a soft, delicate blue, overspread with a fine network of tiny clouds that did nothing to hinder the passage of the sun's rays. The sun was warm, delightful, but not hot. There was no breeze or sharpness in the air. The lawns to the left of him which bordered the Serpentine were this morning the abode of waterfowl: ducks with russet-coloured heads and black-and-white ducks with long necks; barnacle geese and pink-footed geese, red-wattled Muscovies and mallards with green satin crowns. A little way ahead of him, at the point where Rotten Row comes very close to the waterside, a girl and a man were feeding the ducks from a bag of bread cubes, or the girl was feeding them while the man stood aside, watching her and polishing a pair of sun-glasses with a tissue. Guy slackened his pace. The girl screwed up the paper bag and put it in her pocket, having looked in vain for a litter basket. She and her companion began to walk away. They were on Rotten Row itself, some twenty or thirty yards ahead of him, and evidently going in the same direction. Guy had recognized them as Maeve Kirkland and Robin Chisholm.

At first he felt simple astonishment that they knew each other. But nothing, of course, could be more likely. Robin was Leonora's brother and a "close" brother, Maeve one of her flatmates for the past three years. They were not holding hands or walking particularly close together, they were not walking as Leonora and the ginger dwarf had been. There was no indication that they were lovers or even close friends.

Guy didn't want to be seen by them. He let them get farther and farther ahead of him. If one of them turned round he would simply cut across the grass onto the South Carriage Drive. He wondered where they were going and what they were talking about. Both were wearing T-shirts, Maeve's a shocking purplish-pink, Robin's white. In spite of her name, Maeve was not Irish. She was a big statuesque blonde, Valkyrie-like, a good inch taller than Robin, who was himself nearly six feet. Ten years ago women still minded being taller than their men (or the men minded), and if they could have been transported a decade back in time, Maeve would have worn flat shoes and even rounded her shoulders. Now she had high heels on that looked uncomfortable with her short denim skirt, but perhaps were not. In them she towered above Robin.

Maeve was not one of Leonora's childhood or school or college friends. She and Rachel met her when they advertised for a third girl to share the flat, which in the end was far more expensive than had at first appeared. They were aghast at what the monthly repayments on the mortgage turned out to be, but instead of accepting a further offer of help from him, they abandoned the idea of having two bedrooms and a living room, made the flat into what were virtually three bed-sits and advertised for a lodger. Maeve was the successful applicant. Mysteriously to Guy, both girls liked Maeve, who became a friend and frequent fellow-guest at those dinner parties in the flat, family lunch parties and other outings-in-a-crowd of which Leonora seemed so fond.

Guy found her bossy and noisy and far too tall. As much as Rachel, though in a different way, she took it on herself to dictate to him what his relationship with Leonora ought to be. That amounted, in her eyes, to no relationship at all. She was less subtle about it than Rachel and less obscure. And she was ruder. There was an expression his grandmother had used that he thought would apply to Maeve: fishwife.

Perhaps Robin and Maeve had been going out together for years. Leonora had said nothing but he feared there were many things in her life of which Leonora told him nothing. He watched them ahead of him, walking more slowly now towards Hyde Park Corner, and then suddenly—or it seemed sudden to Guy, who was electrified by it—Robin raised his right arm and put it around Maeve's shoulders. Almost simultaneously, as if she feared someone behind her might see and disapprove, or as if she sensed his presence, Maeve turned her head and looked in his direction.

He knew she would wave. She might not like him, he was sure she didn't like him, but they knew each other, had frequently sat at the same table, constantly spoke on the phone when he rang Leonora and she happened to answer. He began to lift his arm to make the gesture that was obligatory in response to hers. She stared hard and turned away. She didn't wave. Guy felt disproportionately shocked and angry. He felt outraged. Maeve and Robin had their heads close together now, they were talking, it seemed in whispers, though why they had need to whisper there in the open, with no one within fifty yards of them, was a mystery. They were talking about him. That was very plain. It was only natural to wonder not only what they were saying but what they had *already said* and said to Leonora.

The two heads were so close together that their hair, copious in each case, though Maeve's was longer and fairer, seemed to combine in a bright golden-brown shining sun-suffused mass like a large silky flower. And now, moved to a need for greater closeness due no doubt to Robin's agreeing with the malicious slanders she was uttering, Maeve passed her arm round his waist. They were entwined, had become Siamese twins joined at the hip. He imagined those slanders—fabrications of what he did for a living, inventions about his private life. Robin, who might well frequent the same night-spots as he did, could easily have seen him with Celeste. They would relay all this to Leonora. And Leonora was far more likely to listen to and be swayed by what her own contemporaries said than by people thirty years her senior.

He would be. He imagined the relative effect on him of Danilo's advice or caution and that of Danilo's father, a crafty old man who ran a betting shop. He would take ten times more notice of Danilo. And he would take ten times more notice of the counsel of Celeste than that of, say, his own mother if they ever again encountered each other.

The couple ahead turned off Rotten Row onto the path to Serpentine Road and the Achilles Statue. Maeve didn't turn her head again. For all he knew, they might be going to meet Leonora for a pre-lunch drink somewhere, they might be on their way to fill her up with warnings so that by the time he and she met at one, she would be well-armed against him and on her guard. He had surely been wrong to lay all the blame for Leonora's change of heart—or outward change—at Tessa's door. Others were just as much to blame, or more so. Maeve and Robin were even more powerful enemies.

It was still early. Guy retraced his steps a little way, walked through into Knightsbridge by the Albert Gate, and stood looking into Lucienne Phillips' window at the clothes that would have all looked wonderful on Celeste and at one short-skirted dark blue satin dress that might have been designed for Leonora.

•   •   •

"I suppose you had that rubbish put in the paper to please your family," Guy said.

He and Leonora were in Cranks, which was very crowded. They were not even able to get a table to themselves. As it was, they sat pressed up against the wall while four very young girls dominated the table, giggling loudly, tasting each other's food and talking about office rivalries. Guy had already reproached Leonora for suggesting they come here. It was a very long time since he had been in a self-service restaurant. He had had to queue up for his food, which was quiche and salad, the least offensively vegetarian on offer. At any rate he had managed to get a glass—in fact, three glasses—of wine.

They were both speaking in necessarily low voices. Not that their table companions took any notice of them. Leonora was also wearing the summer Saturday uniform of jeans, T-shirt, and white running shoes. Her jeans were blue denim, her T-shirt blue, white, and mauve stripes. She had a mauve headband on between her fringe and the rest of her hair. Guy thought she looked lovely in spite of what she wore, but for all that he would have liked to see her in a dress when she came out to lunch with him. The first thing he had looked for he had not found, to his great relief. The absence on her finger of an engagement ring helped give rise to his remark.

She said in a pleasant, even tone, "If it had been entirely up to William and me, no, I don't think we'd have bothered to announce it. I don't think, come to that, we'd have 'got engaged.' My parents wanted it, and so did his. It's a small thing to do to give so much pleasure, don't you think?"

"I see." He laughed a little. "I know you always do what your parents want."

She didn't deny it. "Why did you call it rubbish, Guy? I told you I was in love with William."

"I'd call that rubbish too." He finished the first of his glasses of wine. Leonora was drinking apple juice, looking at him over the top of her glass in what he interpreted as a sulky way. He changed the subject. "You never told me Maeve was going about with your brother."

"I suppose I didn't think you'd be interested."

"Everything even remotely connected with you interests me, Leo, you ought to know that. I saw them in the park. They were walking along ahead of me. Have you been with them before you met me?"

"What, just now, d'you mean? Of course I haven't, Guy. Why would I? They don't want to spend their Saturdays with me."

"Where does he live now?"

"*Now* he lives in Chelsea, he's just moved. I think he'd like Maeve to move in with him, and perhaps she will when I've gone."

He let that pass. The girls were leaving. The table was littered with their debris, but at least, for the time being, it was left to him and Leonora. He leaned a little towards her.

"You haven't really changed in your feelings towards me, have you? You feel the same as you always have, but you think, or you've been persuaded, that being involved with me wouldn't be wise, wouldn't be a good thing for you. That's it, isn't it?"

She spoke carefully, considering. "I do love you, Guy. I always have and I think I always will. It's got a lot to do with what we were to each other when we were teenagers."

His heart seemed to take a little happy leap, to dance about inside his chest. He felt the blood mount into his face. He put out his hand to touch hers, which lay on the table.

"But, Guy, we've nothing in common any more, we don't like the same things. I *hate* what you do for a living. Looking back, I hate what you've done."

That made him laugh. "Oh, come on. How about you? I was only thinking the other day how brilliant you were at nicking stuff. D'you remember how we used to get rid of it all down the Portobello?"

Her voice was very low. "You don't know how ashamed I am of the things I did. They fill me with self-disgust when I think of them. But you still think they were all right, you think anything goes so long as you make money out of it."

Her hand was flat and limp under his. He withdrew his own and looked at it as if something had stung it and he was watching for the sting to swell. "I do nothing illegal any longer," he said. "Nothing." Not since the death of Con Mulvanney, he thought, but he didn't say it aloud, she knew nothing of that, and please Christ, she never would.

"It's not just illegal things, it's—well, unethical things. Oh, Guy, you don't know what I'm talking about, do you? That's part of the trouble, we don't speak the same language. Your sole aim in life is to make lots of money and live in luxury and have power and make more and more money. And anyway, you can't wipe out the past just by saying you don't do things any longer. Someone told me you'd actually once run a protection racket. Oh, Guy!"

"Who told you?" he said, very cold.

"Does it matter?"

"Yes. I'd like to know."

"Well, then, it was Magnus."

He knew it! Hadn't he guessed as much? "And?"

"He was acting for a client, finding him a barrister, you know how they do, and this man was some sort of criminal and he mentioned your name in connection with a protection racket up in Kensal."

"And Magnus told you?"

"He said it couldn't be the same Guy Curran, but Mummy said it was and of course it was, I knew that."

"You listen to what these people say about me, don't you, Leonora? You listen to all of them?"

She said softly, "It wouldn't make any difference what anyone said. We're poles apart. We aren't *like* each other."

He didn't answer that. He said rather slowly and in a deliberate and calculated drawl, "I've got a beautiful girl-friend. Her name is Celeste. She is twenty-three and a model and she is very lovely. She stayed with me last night. She's probably still at Scarsdale Mews waiting for me to come back."

For a single horrible instant he thought Leonora was going

to smile and tell him how happy she was for him, how delighted. But a shadow had crossed her face. Her expression was fixed, the dark blue eyes steady, the lips compressed. She was jealous! He could see it, he couldn't be mistaken.

"Are you making it up?"

"Sweetheart, if it wasn't you that asked, I'd really resent that." He was aware of echoing what she had said to him when he seemed incredulous about Newton. How close they were really! They read each other's thoughts! "I'm supposed to be *attractive* to women," he said, smiling at her. "Ring her up, go on, ask her. Go and call my house."

Someone, a woman, had once told him that we always feel jealousy over the loves of our past lovers. Even if we no longer care for them, even if we have a new lover, a true love that will be everlasting, we are still jealous. The pang of rejection is still there, for we are all insecure, all terrified of desertion, all longing to be the first and only, or if not the first, the last. But he forgot that now or didn't think of it. She was jealous, his Leonora was jealous because he had another woman.

"I'm very happy for you, Guy," she said. "I hope it goes really well. I'm very pleased." A thought struck her. "But, Guy, would she mind about you meeting me like this? She does know? I mean, perhaps we ought to stop if she's likely to mind."

"Of course she doesn't mind," he said impatiently. And then, "If you've finished, shall we go? Shall we go somewhere else, even if it's only sitting on the grass in Soho Square?"

He knew she'd refuse but she didn't. "All right, just for half an hour."

He wondered what would happen if he tried to take her hand. Better not risk it. They walked along side by side. The clouds had gone and the sky become a hot, hard blue. He found himself suddenly thinking of a holiday they had planned to take together at this time four years ago. They were going to one of the less-frequented Greek islands and he had seen it, without of course discussing this with her, as the venue for resuming their sexual relationship. The sea was called wine-dark down there and the nights were warm. They were going to stay in a wonderful kind of hotel where all the rooms were little grass-roofed huts and each had its own private path down to the silver beach. She would return to him there, physically return to his arms, and soon after they came back they would be married, the job she was going to take and the bed-sit she was going to share with Rachel forgotten.

She had called it off less than two weeks beforehand. It was because he was paying, she said. It was no good, she couldn't pay her share, she couldn't afford to, and she couldn't let him pay for her, so they had to call it off. Even now, remembering it was deeply painful. In his philosophy a woman acknowl-edged a man's love and her love for him by letting him pay for things. The bargain between them consisted in a kind of loving sale, though it didn't sound pleasant put that way.

He glanced at her Egyptian profile, the firm mouth and chin, the rather severe nose, the dark curtain of hair that hung two inches across her cheek. Her head was bowed as if she was deep in thought.

"You're not going away on holiday this year, are you?" he said, thinking of being deprived of his Saturdays, of maybe missing two or three of his Saturdays.

"Not exactly on holiday," she said. "I mean, we'll be going away later."

His heart leaden, sinking. "Who's 'we'?"

"I've been putting off telling you, Guy. But things are different now you've told me about Celeste. I'm getting married on September the sixteenth, and we'll be going away after that on our honeymoon."

CHAPTER SIX

It was five weeks away.

The wedding would be at Kensington Register Office, the usual routine ceremony, with Maeve and Robin as witnesses. They weren't religious. On the evening of the wedding day Leonora's father and his wife were giving a party for them. Anthony and Susannah Chisholm lived in London, not in the Notting Hill Mews but in a flat on two floors of an early-nineteenth-century house in Lamb's Conduit Street that had belonged to Susannah and her first husband. William Newton's father and mother lived in Hong Kong and wouldn't come for the wedding because they would be in England for Christmas, but his sister and brother-in-law would be there.

She told him all about it.

"It's not him, though, is it? You wouldn't have me if he was dead, for instance, would you? It's something else."

"He won't *be* dead, Guy. Why should he? He's a healthy man of thirty."

"If I thought it was him, I'd like to kill him. I'd like to fight him, challenge him to a duel and kill him."

"Don't be ridiculous."

"Can he handle a gun? No, don't tell me. I don't want to know about him. He's just an excuse, anyway. Any man but me. I'd like to know why, Leonora. I'd like to know what happened to turn you against me."

This conversation took place not in Soho Square but on the following Saturday in a restaurant which, for once, she had allowed him to choose. It was in that part of Notting Hill called Hillgate Village, on the southern side of the Bayswater Road. Leonora was wearing a dress. It was a hot day and the dress was short and made of some clinging diaphanous fabric, white with misty pink and mauve flowers and a plain mauve belt or sash. She had white stockings on and flat pink shoes. On the coat rack at the entrance to the restaurant she had hung up her hat of fine white straw with lilac ribbons. After lunch she was going to the wedding of a friend of William Newton's, mention of which had given rise to talk of her own.

Guy wished she would always dress like that. He ached with desire for her. He heard his own voice cross-examining her and he hated himself for the bullying tone, the reiterated questions, but he had to know. She gave him an injured, sullen look. She wouldn't have a dessert, cheese, or coffee, in case she was late. Pressed, she said nothing had happened to turn her against him. No, it wasn't his offering to buy her a flat that had done it, nothing had "done it," it had been a gradual process that began in her late teens. She had grown out of him and wished he would grow out of her.

"You were jealous when I told you about Celeste," he said. "I could see it in your eyes. That means you really love me still."

"That's nonsense, Guy."

"If you marry him while you love me you'll be committing a crime against yourself and me."

She laughed at him. He thought her very cruel but understood it was a defence. If she hadn't laughed she would have burst out crying. It was a hard, unwomanly sound, that laughter, more pain in it than amusement.

She went away to William Newton's relative's wedding after that and left him sitting at the table drinking brandy.

Maeve and Robin, Anthony and Susannah, Tessa and Magnus, Rachel Lingard—one of them or one set of them had done this. But done what? Convinced her that he was entirely unsuitable so that, bowing to their coercion, she had thrown herself into the arms of the first man who came along. They had probably brought the man along themselves, found him and vetted him and introduced him to Leonora.

He phoned her as usual on Sunday, on Monday and Tuesday. He refused to admit the possibility that she would actually get married on September 16, but if anything so impossible and *wicked* did happen, just if, he intended to go on phoning her every day. Sometimes he imagined still doing it when they were old and she was a grey grandmother and he an aged millionaire, single but with many beautiful unloved mistresses. But it wouldn't happen because one day, if not this year or next year, the year after or the year after that, she would marry *him*. Out of his path he would clear those who stood between them. Rachel answered the phone on Sunday, Maeve on Monday and Tuesday.

Rachel said, "I'll fetch her," followed by a heavy theatrical sigh and a remark that made him grind his teeth: "She guessed who it would be. She had the sort of premonition psychic people have just before a road accident."

Maeve said when he asked to speak to Leonora, "Must you?"

He was furious. "What the fuck d'you mean, 'must I'? What affair is it of yours?"

"Don't speak to me like that, please. You won't get to talk to Leonora by using obscene language."

"Oh, won't I? I'll keep ringing this fucking number till I do. And by the way, thanks very much for ignoring me in the park last week. Charming manners you and your boy-friend have."

"I never saw you in the park, last week or any other time."

She went away and Leonora came on the line. Next day Rachel answered the phone again and said there was such a thing as having Telecom change the number, did he know that? He didn't reply.

"Alexander Graham Bell's got a lot to answer for," said Rachel.

She really hated him, there was venom in her voice. It was extraordinary the way these women, Tessa, Rachel, Maeve, thought they were *being loyal to Leonora* by putting her against him, when in fact the best possible thing they could do for Leonora was encourage her to marry him and thus ensure for herself, apart from the love and romance aspect, a future free from financial worry and a life of happiness and luxury.

Guy never stayed at home in the evenings. What would he do there? He hadn't made a fortune in order to sit in his house eating take-away and watching videos. Susannah Chisholm, who had always been nicer to him than any of the rest of that lot, had once told a story of someone she had met in New York who said that since he came to live in Manhattan he had never once eaten his dinner at home. The other people there had laughed and wondered at this and been amazed, but Guy, though he didn't say so, had wondered what all the fuss was about as he, since he came to Scarsdale Mews, had never eaten dinner at home either. Going out in the evening meant drinking out, eating out, and then going on to a club for more drinking out.

He seldom went to a theatre but occasionally to the cinema, to please Celeste. Having flatly refused to consider *Woman on the Verge of a Nervous Breakdown* at the Lumiere, he had consented to go to *Paris by Night* at the Curzon West End.

They had been to the six fifty-five showing because both preferred to eat afterwards and it was only nine o'clock when they came out. Guy had booked a table at a restaurant he particularly liked in Stratton Street, where Leonora would never have allowed him to take her for lunch. It was a warm, airless evening after another hot day. Celeste was wearing a dress of white cotton broderie anglaise, short and tight but not obviously so because she was so slender. She had white sandals on with straps of alternating white and gilded leather, white and green bracelets on both arms, and each separate tiny plait of her hair, at least fifty of these, ended in a gold-pointed tip. Guy wore a linen suit in a very light greyish-beige with a bitter-chocolate-coloured open-necked shirt, a belt of plaited grey leather, and white running shoes with a grey leather trim. He had thought, some hours before, that they made a handsome couple, but this was simply an opinion, it gave him no particular pleasure.

As they were coming out of the cinema he saw Leonora and William Newton leaving ahead of them. Although he had spoken to Leonora that afternoon, he still felt at the sight of her those extraordinary and characteristic sensations, which were even stronger when on very rare occasions he came upon her by chance. His heart seemed to stand still, then to beat not faster but somehow more *loudly*. Those people who surrounded him and her, a considerable crowd of people, mostly young or youngish, who until he saw her had seemed attractive and colourful, some of them very well worth looking at, now faded to faceless shadows, the dead perhaps, or extras in an old monochrome film. Only he and she existed in the world.

This sensation lasted a few moments. By the time the crowd had faces again, he and Celeste, she and Newton were all out on the pavement. Leonora turned her head and looked straight at him. She was pleased to see him, he could tell she was. She was smiling her lovely, carefully governed smile and, taking hold of Newton's sleeve, drawing him over in their direction.

"Guy," she said, "you didn't say you were going to the cinema."

"Nor did you. This is Celeste. Celeste, Leonora." He wasn't going to utter Newton's name.

"This is William."

Loving her so much, he could admit to himself that she looked awful. A couple of hippies left over from the sixties they might have been, Newton in a pair of khaki cotton loons from Dirty Dick's and a T-shirt that must have been pale blue before it was put through the cold wash with a lot of navy and red garments about a hundred times. Her dress was one of Laura Ashley's less successful lines, bought no doubt in a sale three or four years ago, a now-faded or washed-out navy-and-white viscose print with elasticated waist and too-long short sleeves, a hem that came halfway down her awful scuffed red leather boots. Guy was pleased. A woman who would dress like that to go out with a man couldn't care much about him.

He told them about the restaurant in Stratton Street and suggested they join him and Celeste. Newton said he didn't think so, thanks. Guy's eyebrows went up. Well, had they eaten or hadn't they? They had to eat.

Guy thought a ghost of a smile crossed Newton's face at that remark, he couldn't think why. Newton was a bit taller than he remembered, by no means a particularly short man, though the horsy face and ginger hair were just as he recalled them. *And* he was wearing glasses. Guy thought that any young person with a scrap of self-esteem who had trouble with his eyes would have gone into contact lenses.

"We eat at home, Guy," Leonora said. "We had something earlier."

"That must be hours ago."

"We'll come with you and have something cheap," she said. "We'll have pasta, just one course."

She wanted to be with him! Now they'd met she couldn't bear to go straight home! She could see him in contrast to Newton. She could see him *with Celeste*. He felt a great warmth and affection for Celeste quite suddenly and he took her hand. The gesture was not lost on Leonora, who looked at their joined hands but did not take Newton's. When they got to the restaurant the two women went straight to the ladies' cloakroom. He was left alone with Newton and girded himself for a fight or a silence.

But Newton, who Leonora had said at lunch on Saturday was something at the BBC, a producer of documentaries on social questions or something equally boring, began to talk about the film they had just seen. He asked if Guy had liked it and why. Guy hadn't much liked it but he found it hard to say why not, so he changed the subject by asking Newton if he liked Paris, if he had been there recently and would he have liked to have been there for the 200-year anniversary of the Revolution. He lit a cigarette because that helped him concentrate.

Newton didn't wave the smoke away or anything like that, but he moved his chair a little. To Guy's surprise he had a drink, the same gin and tonic as Guy himself, instead of alcohol-free beer, which might have been expected. He'd been to Paris in the spring, he said, to see the Gauguin exhibition, which he began to describe and praise. Guy wondered if this was designed to get at him, a snide attack on his hand-done original-oil-paintings enterprise. Newton seemed to see that he was bored, stopped talking about Gauguin and said Paris would be too crowded, and anyway he usually went to Scotland for a couple of weeks in August, though he wouldn't be doing that this year.

Guy knew why he wouldn't be doing it this year. Why he *thought* he wouldn't be. Where had the women got to? They had been away ten minutes. Perhaps they were scratching each other's eyes out somewhere over him. Scotland in August meant only one thing, as far as he knew. He had to find something to talk to the man about.

"Shoot, do you?"

"Only in self-defence," said Newton, "and no grouse has attacked me yet."

Whoever said that sarcasm was the lowest form of wit was right, thought Guy. "It's surprisingly easier to become a good shot than you might think. There's something very satisfying when you bring down your first bird."

"If that's the way you look at things, yes, I expect it is. Considering the stalwart band of thickies who do it so excellently, it must be. I shouldn't care to shoot birds or animals. The fact that they've been bred for the purpose of being shot rather makes things worse."

"What would you like to shoot then? People?" Guy laughed rather loudly at his own joke.

"I've managed to live for thirty years in reasonable contentment without shooting anything, Guy, and I expect I can go on in the same way for another thirty. A death-dealing banging about doesn't appeal to me."

"A man should be able to handle a gun," Guy said. "I belong to a rifle club. Of course we shoot at targets."

Newton slightly inclined his head, the way a bored person does who doesn't really want to be rude but doesn't care much either. Guy said, "The girls have been a long time." Another nod from Newton. Guy didn't know what made him think of it, but having thought of it, he felt an unexplainable surge of excitement. "Ever done any fencing?" he said.

Now Newton turned to look him fully in the face. He looked right into Guy's eyes. The smile was there again, very slight, somehow in the eyes and inside his head rather than in any movement of the lips. Guy saw that his eyes, which he would have remembered as greyish or fawnish out of Newton's presence, were in fact a deep blue-grey, of that shade which is less like an animal's than any other.

He took a long time replying. Then he said, "At school."

"At *school?*"

"And a bit later on. You belong to a fencing club, do you?"

"Me? No, why should I?"

Guy knew Newton must be getting at him, something he wasn't going to put up with, and he was about to repeat his question when Leonora and Celeste came back. They both looked pleased with themselves, Guy thought. Leonora asked what they had been talking about and Newton said, grinning, that it had been about martial arts.

They gave their orders, Leonora and Newton sticking to their decision to eat pasta, though Guy did his best to make Leonora change her mind. He didn't care what Newton ate. That wasn't quite true, as he would really have liked to see him eat something poisonous, something laced with cyanide perhaps, or infected with one of those fashionable germs, listeria or salmonella, and roll about the floor in front of the women, groaning and frothing at the mouth. He hated Newton

73

and his grin and his cool clever eyes. He was talking more about fencing now, or rather about early prize-fighting, in the sixteenth and seventeenth centuries, when—before the days of bare-knuckle fighting—men attacked each other on public stages with blunted blades and often with "sharps." Guy thought it an unsuitable subject at table and with women present.

This then was an example of Newton's vaunted "conversation." Apparently he possessed a pair of sabres which, crossed, ornamented a wall in his flat in Camden Town. He was thinking of selling them; Leonora didn't want them in their new home. Guy would have liked to know where they had in mind but wasn't going to ask. Celeste asked.

"I'm selling my flat. Leonora's selling her share of their place to her friend, who owns half of it already."

"Rachel's grandmother died and left her some money, so she'll buy my half," Leonora said. "We're not in a hurry, anyway. I shall live at William's place in the meantime."

Why did no one ever tell him these things? Why was he kept in the dark? It was a wonder that Rachel bothered to work at all, the way her rich relatives kept dying and leaving her slabs of wealth. His steak arrived, an enormous bloody wedge of it, which he fancied Newton was looking at in a mocking way, though when he raised his eyes he saw that the other man had his back to him and was saying something to Celeste. Guy was drinking rather a lot. No one wanted any more out of the second bottle of wine, so he finished it and began drinking shorts, dry martinis without ice, though it was so warm.

Before the bill came Newton leaned towards him and said they would split it.

"Absolutely not," Guy said. "I invited you."

"Please, Guy," Leonora said, "we'd much rather."

"I wouldn't dream of it, I wouldn't entertain it for a moment."

"Well, thanks for entertaining us then," Newton said and he immediately got up and went off to the men's.

Had that been a dig at him for using a phrase which a clever bastard like Newton might think was incorrect or out of date or silly or whatever people like him did think? He was instantly sure that Newton was double-crossing him and meant to sneak up to the waiter and pay his share before the bill came to Guy. That this had not happened, that the bill when it came was for the four of them, surprised him very much. What was the man up to? What was his game?

A taxi now had to be secured. Leonora looked tired, she looked as if she hadn't enjoyed the evening, had found it for some reason a strain and was now worn out. She had seen Newton and him together of course for the first time. Was she, after what she had seen, having—glorious idea!—second thoughts about Newton? Had she compared them and Newton, as he must, had come out wanting?

"If you're going north," he said to Newton, "why don't you take the first taxi? Leonora can come with us and we'll drop her on our way."

"I can't do that, Guy, I'm staying at William's till Friday. And we won't take a taxi, we'll go by tube."

"Green Park to Warren Street and then up the Northern Line," said Newton, smug and cool. "Nothing easier. Good night. Good night, Celeste, it's been nice meeting you."

In the taxi Guy said, "I should have asked her for his phone number. If she's at his place, I won't be able to talk to her tomorrow."

"Try the phone book," said Celeste.

"Yes, he'll be in the book. What did she say to you all that long time you were in the Ladies'?"

"This and that. She talked about us and about William."

"He's a bit of a shit," he said.

"I liked him, I thought he was very nice."

"But you can't imagine a woman falling in love with him, can you? The idea's grotesque."

"I'll tell you what she said if you like. She said she was really happy to see you so happy with me. She said I was beautiful and you were lucky to have me and she was sure you

75

knew your luck and she hoped we'd be very very happy. D'you want to know what else she said?"

"Not really," said Guy. "It doesn't sound very inspired. I don't suppose you want to come back with me, do you? Not if you have to get up early for that l'Oréal job. I'll tell the driver to go along the Old Brompton Road, shall I? Celeste, you're not crying, are you? For God's sake, what is there to cry about?"

• • •

Guy fell asleep very quickly and dreamt he was fighting William Newton with swords. They were in Kensington Gardens, on the lawn by the Albert Memorial below the Flower Walk. It was very early in the morning, dawn, the sun not yet risen, and there was no one about but they themselves and their seconds. His second was Linus Pinedo and Newton's was a man whose face Guy couldn't see because it was covered by a fencer's mask. Guy had done a certain amount of fencing some four or five years before, had taken lessons and belonged to a club, but had given it up in favour of squash, which was so fast and better exercise. But in the dream he was very good, he was like some thirties' film star in *The Prisoner of Zenda*.

His aim was only to wound Newton, though perhaps severely, but the man was clearly terrified and scarcely able to put up a defence. Guy, intending a thrust to his left arm— Newton, at any rate in the dream, was left-handed—jumped forward, executing the move called the balestra, followed it by a flèche at great speed, which passed in a single swift lunge through Newton's heart.

Newton made no sound but sank on to his knees, his foil dropped, his hands clasped together on the forte of Guy's sword. He fell over onto his side onto the green, now blood-splashed, grass. The death rattle issued from his pale lips and he gave up the ghost in the masked man's arms. Guy withdrew his sword, which came out clean and shining.

Linus looked into Guy's eyes and said, "That'll give you breathing space, man. That'll give you time."

Guy felt happy, he felt an enormous relief. Newton was dead, so Leonora couldn't marry him. Now he could discover *at his leisure* the slanderer who had poisoned her mind against him. He bent over the dead man, feeling grateful to him, almost caring for him. The masked man, in a single swift gesture, took off his mask and revealed to Guy, who was now trembling and horrified, his identity. It was Con Mulvanney.

●　　　●　　　●

In the morning, still quite shaken from the dream, Guy looked up Newton's number in the phone book, found his address in Georgiana Street, which he then looked up in the ABC London Street Atlas. Linus's opinion in the dream, that getting Newton out of the way would give him time, now returned to him. Newton might not, as a man, be a serious threat, but he was *there* and Leonora would marry him on September 16, no doubt soon regretting the step she had taken, though by then it would be too late. One thing to be glad about was that divorce was relatively easy.

Why had Con Mulvanney come to him in the dream? If Guy had inherited little from that hopeless feckless mother of his, and derived less, he had at any rate brought with him, through the years and changes, some of her superstitions. To this day he would not walk under ladders. His broken-down push-chair had been made to take avoiding detours, often to the very real danger from passing cars to its dirty-faced infant occupant. He touched wood in times of anxiety, and threw salt over his left shoulder when some was spilt. Omens he trusted, while saying he didn't believe in them. Premonitions he recognized in sudden vague apprehensions. The totally unexpected appearance of Con Mulvanney in his dream, something that had never happened before—he had never before dreamt of Mulvanney—was a clear omen. What else could it be?

He began to wonder if it was possible anyone had told Leonora about Con Mulvanney. On the face of it it seemed unlikely. Very few people knew. Of course hundreds, thousands knew who he was and what had happened to him, though no doubt most of them had now forgotten; but surely only he himself and that woman knew his own connection with Mulvanney's death.

The police knew. Correction—the police had been *told*. It wasn't the same thing. They had found nothing, they had probably in the end not believed her or knew it would be hopeless to prove it.

The woman had a name he would never forget, no one could forget; she was called Poppy Vasari. She had threatened to tell everyone she knew. But what would be the point in naming him to people as the supplier of LSD to Mulvanney when his name would mean nothing? To the police . . . now, that was another story.

But suppose she had carried out her threat and talked of it to friends and acquaintances, given some sort of description of him? "A handsome dark man, very young." He had been only twenty-five at the time. Or, "Very well-off, the way these people are, living in one of those pretty houses in a mews in South Ken." Those details would be enough to arouse the suspicions of anyone who knew him only slightly. Robin Chisholm, say, or Rachel Lingard. Suppose they had then asked his name? Poppy Vasari would tell them, of course she would. She had nothing to lose.

And they would have told Leonora.

No surer way could have been found to put her off him. Four years ago. That was about the time she began radically to change towards him, to change her mind about that holiday, to turn down his invitations, to *wean* herself gradually away from him, to refuse his offer of money to buy that flat. And once she was in the flat, to cease altogether to go out with him in the evenings, to cease kissing him (except in the way she kissed Maeve, on both cheeks), sending others to answer the phone when he rang, gradually achieving the present situation of daily phone calls and lunch on Saturdays.

At ten he dialled Newton's number. Leonora answered.

There was a pause, a silence, when she heard who it was, then she spoke cheerfully as if she was really pleased, asking him how he was, saying how much they had enjoyed the previous evening and meeting Celeste.

"Where would you like to have lunch on Saturday?" he said.

"Anywhere you like, Guy. Clarke's if that's what you'd like. After all, we've only got four more."

CHAPTER SEVEN

Some of the people who worked there called it a factory, Guy had been told, but to him it was always the studio. It was at Northolt, in Yeading Lane. Guy usually drove out there every couple of weeks to see how things progressed. His other enterprises, the travel agency and the club in Noel Street, got on perfectly well without his presence, and if he went to the club sometimes that was because he enjoyed it.

Tessa, the fine arts graduate, had called the studio a sweat-shop, though of course she had never seen it. This was in any case a manifest lie, as the people Guy called his work-force painted in clean, light, airy surroundings, with plenty of space, did not work particularly long hours, and were reasonably well paid. He could have paid them more because the paintings were selling better than he had ever imagined they would, but as it was they earned more than they would have by teaching, more, for instance, than Leonora did. Instead he was seriously thinking of starting a second studio to cope with the demand.

No one seemed to mind him looking over their shoulders while they worked. No doubt that was because, as he frankly told them, he knew nothing about art but admired what they did. He paused and watched a very talented young Indian girl who had been at St. Martin's School of Art painting in the tears on the cheeks of the weeping boy. It was wonderful to see the skill with which she did this. How wet the tears looked! Like real drops of water, as if someone had lightly splashed the painted face. And surely she had managed to make the child look sweeter than usual and sadder. Guy could almost identify with him, recalling distant days of deprivation in Attlee House.

What Tessa, and to a lesser extent Leonora, meant by saying that what was done here was morally and—there was some other word, yes, "aesthetically"—wrong, remained a perpetual mystery to him. It was true that his artists had a basic pattern or guide to follow, that there were affinities here, though remote ones, with painting by numbers. But was that very different, *any* different, from what had gone in the studios of those Old Masters? Guy remembered his feeling of triumph when, on holiday in Florence, he had found out from a guide how people such as Michelangelo had workshops like his, with young painters in them learning their craft, copying the master's pictures, filling in backgrounds, working regular hours and working to order. Leonora had laughed when he told her this and said it wasn't the same thing, though she had not explained how it differed.

And it wasn't as if these people's original work were any good. The girl he watched putting the finishing touches to *King and Queen of the Beasts* had actually once shown him one of her own paintings. He had said, "Very nice," but it was terrible, just lines of sludge with something that might have been eyes peering out. In the house in Scarsdale Mews he had a Kandinski that was the nearest thing to it he had ever seen, but at least the Kandinski was in bright colours and very big and complex, which accounted, no doubt, for the very high price he had had to pay for it.

81

He had coffee with his artists and one of them asked him if he had any paintings from the studio on walls of his house. He said he had, though this wasn't true and made him wonder obscurely why he hadn't. There was another sale that day in South London, in Clapham this time, and he had thoughts of dropping in and buying a painting like an ordinary member of the public.

Guy drove south and crossed the river by Kew Bridge. This was a mistake as he didn't know this part of London at all well and got lost. By now he had given up all ideas of buying a painting, he could much more easily have one sent to his home, and was even wondering if he would get to Clapham Common before the sale was over. Somehow he had managed to get himself and the Jaguar south of Wimbledon Park and he must make his way northwards.

If asked, he would have said he had never been in this neighbourhood before. The commons of South London were confusing, there were so many of them, but this certainly wasn't Clapham Common, perhaps Tooting or Tooting Bec. A sign here pointed to Clapham, Battersea, Central London, and he found himself in a big thoroughfare that seemed vaguely familiar. It was Balham, that was where it was, this was Bedford Hill and in that pub, that great Victorian mansion of a pub, he had on that fateful night been accosted by Con Mulvanney.

"Have you got any shit?"

The question, ugly, ridiculous, meaningless but having a special meaning to those in the know, remained in his memory, the words reverberating there like so many plucked strings, while much of the rest of what had happened that evening had faded. He hadn't replied, of course, he had pretended ignorance, disgust even, had turned his back, but the man had been insistent, had returned to the attack, now rephrasing his question, now simply saying.

"Have you got *anything*?"

Guy drove on up to Clapham Common, where the sale was being held at the Broxash Hotel. One last space remained in the hotel car-park. He walked about looking at the paintings with a glass of Rioja in his hand. He had sometimes asked himself what he should have done to escape Con Mulvanney on that night, to give him the slip, but he hadn't then known that giving him the slip was important. He had understood only that Mulvanney did not know his name, and that seemed to him all that mattered. Come to that, although he thought of him *in the context of that time* as Con Mulvanney, he had not then known his name either, had not known it until the man was dead, or even, in a curious way, until sometime after that.

The woman who was presiding over the sale, an untidy dark woman in a black dress, reminded him faintly of Poppy Vasari. She wasn't really like Poppy Vasari, who had been thinner and wilder-looking and dirtier. Guy was no longer used to dirty people, to men and women who seldom washed their clothes and hardly ever bathed, and they disgusted him. Perhaps it had something to do with there having been rather a lot of such people around in his childhood. The woman selling his pictures and taking orders was probably quite clean, the ingrained dirt in her fingers the result of gardening, the dandruff on her black shawl collar due to mischance. He noted that, unlike in Coulsdon, the painting of the noble lion standing on the rocks with his couching mate beside him was the best seller here, and then he left.

This must have been the way the taxi took him home that night from the pub in Bedford Hill—over Battersea Bridge, up Gunter Grove, Finborough Road, or perhaps up Beaufort Street and into the Boltons. Could you go that way? Would the traffic system permit it? It had been late and very dark. Too dark to see or at any rate to notice the little dark red 2CV following the cab.

•   •   •

Guy never went to pubs. He only went to this one because it was a party, and anyway he didn't know it was a pub till he got there. Robert Joseph, the man he was going into partner-

ship with in the travel agency, was celebrating his fortieth
birthday. He had described the pub to Guy as an hotel.

Sensibly, he had come late. The pub had an extension till
half past midnight and Guy didn't get there till nearly eleven.
A female impersonator, very old and hideous, in black sequins
and yellow feathers, was capering about on the stage and
singing a song of such incredible obscenity that Guy could
hardly believe he was hearing those words in that sequence. A
youngish man standing at the bar ventured a mild protest and
was immediately, almost before finishing his sentence, frog-
marched by two heavies to one of the doors and put outside.
The doors were closed and locked. Guy decided to drink a lot
in order to make things bearable.

Bob Joseph, by this time, was drunk but not too drunk to
notice Guy was there, to throw an arm round his shoulders and
call him his best pal. A group arrived on the stage and began
singing old Beatles songs. Guy had another vodka martini and
another. It was then that Con Mulvanney, whose name he
didn't know, came up to him and asked his question.

"Have you got any shit?"

He meant hashish. Guy had seldom dealt in hashish. He had
at one time been involved in an enterprise supplying Black
Nepal, but later was interested only in cocaine and the best
marijuana, usually Santa Marta Gold. In any case, not since he
was a young boy had he actually purveyed the stuff himself,
handled it. He was altogether loftier than that. At the time Con
Mulvanney came up to him with his question it was almost
exclusively cocaine in which he was dealing, though giving
some thought to the possibility of this new thing called crack,
which was smoked.

This time, in reply to the question, "Have you got
anything?" he said, "I don't know what you mean. Go away,
please."

"I know you have. I was told about you and that you'd be
in here tonight. You were described to me."

That made Guy feel very odd and very vulnerable. Afterwards he wondered why he hadn't asked who had said he

84

would be in there, who had described him. But he didn't ask. He said, "You're mistaking me for someone else."

The man who was Con Mulvanney didn't persist. At least, not then. He was a thin, slight man, neither short nor tall, with narrow shoulders and a slight stoop, who looked unwell, who looked a generally rather unhealthy person. His face was long and pale, and the lips and chin were like a woman's, as if they could never grow hair. The hair of his head was longish, wispy, no-colour or the colour of dust. His eyes were a light greyish-brown and they shifted away from Guy's when he tried to meet them.

Guy walked away from him and started a conversation with Bob Joseph, and then, after Joseph had moved away into another group, with some neighbours of his, a man and a woman who lived near him in Chingford or Chigwell or wherever. The encounter with Con Mulvanney, whose name he didn't then know, sent him in quest of another drink. When he had had two more vodka martinis he thought he had had enough—of drink and these people and the awful place— and anyway it was gone midnight. He didn't call a taxi but walked out into the street and one came obediently along. As it moved off, a dark red 2CV moved off behind it.

Guy didn't see the 2CV again all the way. He didn't look out of the back of the taxi. When they got to Scarsdale Mews and he was paying the cab driver, he saw a small car moving away from the end of the street. That is, he thought afterwards that he remembered seeing a small car at that point. He remembered that on the following evening, when, just as he was leaving to go out to dinner somewhere, Con Mulvanney appeared on his doorstep.

The doorbell rang and Guy thought it was the taxi he had ordered. At the sight of him, Con Mulvanney said facetiously, "Mr. X, I presume?"

"Yes, you do presume," Guy said. "I've nothing for you. Would you go, please?"

"Look, can I explain what it is I want?"

"You have. Now go."

"I haven't actually," said Con Mulvanney, and then he said, "You can call me Mr. Y."

"Don't be ridiculous," Guy said. "Please go away. I've nothing for you. I am just going out." The doorstep and the hall floor were on the same level, without further steps, and Con Mulvanney, or "Mr. Y," the absurd name but the only one Guy then knew to call him by, had got himself onto the doormat and one foot on the hall carpet. "I didn't invite you in. I don't want you in my house. If you force me to, I'll put you out."

"I want a hallucinogen," Mr. Y said, lowering his voice. "Whatever sort there's available. I know nothing of these things. You must know. I'll pay the market price. Don't they call it the street value? I'll pay that."

Guy said, "I haven't got anything like that."

He was beginning to think Mr. Y was a policeman. The man didn't look like any policeman Guy had ever seen, but of course they wouldn't use a man who looked like a policeman, they would use someone who looked like Mr. Y. The front door was still open and now Guy's taxi arrived. The driver got out and Guy called to him to wait a minute. He shut the front door. He said to Mr. Y that he would meet him later, he would meet him at ten—but where? Nowhere was safe. There were just some places safer than others. Mr. Y said that when he hadn't got his car he used the Northern Line and how about Embankment Station? Guy said the middle of Hungerford Bridge at ten o'clock.

He didn't go. Of course he didn't. He had no intention of going. But he thought about it all through dinner and after-wards. He saw himself standing in the middle of Hungerford Bridge, that cold, exposed, dark foot-bridge, where someone had told him murders frequently took place, meeting Mr. Y, and then, as he returned to the Embankment end, two men stepping up to him out of the shadows. Returning home an hour or so after the time he had set for the meeting, he wouldn't have been surprised to find Mr. Y waiting for him, but there was no one. It was not until the following day that Mr. Y came back, this time in the dark red 2CV.

Guy pretended not to see him. He put the Jaguar in the garage, entered the house from the inside. The doorbell rang. Guy let it ring. He had a small quantity of marijuana in the house, some capsules of Durophet, and a little LSD. He could open the door to Mr. Y, *give* him the grass, close the door on him and forget him. That might be the best way. The doorbell rang again, insistently, in a prolonged way. Guy went upstairs and looked out of his bedroom windows. There were no cars in the street at this end except the 2CV, no one who could conceivably be watching the house unless they were planted in the houses opposite, which Guy realized was extremely unlikely. He opened the safe in which Leonora's sapphire engagement ring was in its box alongside the various drugs. He took the marijuana out, locked the safe and went down to the front door as the bell began ringing again.

Mr. Y said, "I don't want what you've got there. It's a hallucinogen I want."

"You what?"

"Mescaline maybe or psilocybin. That magic-mushroom stuff. I didn't really want cannabis resin. It was just that someone told me if I asked for it and called it shit you'd know I was serious."

A policeman who could be that naïve, in that way, could sound like that, would have to be a genius. To the Drugs Squad he would be worth his weight in gold—worth more than his weight in the best Colombian gold. He had to be genuine. Guy said, "All right. you'd better come in. I don't want to know your namc."

"I don't want to know yours."

Why had he done that? Why had he invited Mr. Y in? Because, if Mr. Y didn't know his name, he plainly knew him as a dealer, knew where he lived, could avenge himself for rejection by giving this information to the Drugs Squad. Of course, by that time, Guy would see to it that the house in Scarsdale Mews was totally clean, but that was not the point.

He didn't want the police there. If the police came once, he knew he would have to give up dealing, he would have seen the writing on the wall.

Up until then he had been spotless, a citizen of the same irreproachable respectability as any of his neighbours, and he must keep clean. A single blot and it would all be over. He reminded himself of something that he kept ever before him, that always hovered a little below the thin top skin of his consciousness: The maximum penalty under the Misuse of Drugs Act for possession of Class A drugs with intent to supply is fourteen years imprisonment.

Mr. Y came into the house but showed no desire to go farther than the hall. He sat down in one of the Georges Jacob side chairs. He said, "You didn't come last night. I waited a long time. I went in the end because I was afraid of missing my last train."

"What exactly is it you want?"

Guy had not, until that point, thought of Mr. Y as mad. Odd, naïve, eccentric, peculiar, up to something, perhaps, but not mad. What the man said next radically altered this opinion.

"I must tell you that I am a reincarnation of Saint Francis of Assisi."

Guy just stared. He said nothing.

"You know who I mean? You've heard of Saint Francis?"

Guy made an impatient gesture. He said, "I asked you what you wanted."

"The proof is in my hands." Mr. Y held out his hands, palms uppermost. They were not very clean. "You can see the stigmata very well today."

"The what?"

"Saint Francis—and therefore I—was the first man to exhibit on his own body the wounds inflicted on Christ at his crucifixion. There is no real dispute about this. The claims of Saint Paul the Apostle and Saint Angelo del Paz can in no way be allowed. In the case of Saint Francis and therefore myself, all the marks are present: the nails on hands and feet, the spear wound in the side, and the marks of the crown of thorns."

His tone had become pedantic, professorial, and rather shrill. Guy could see no marks on his hands except those of ingrained dirt, and when Mr. Y lifted his hands and smoothed back his wispy dust-coloured fringe, saw nothing on his forehead either.

"All right, but what has all that to do with me?"

Mr. Y began to talk in a very rambling way about all nature being the mirror of God and about the new Franciscan rule of life that he would formulate. It had something to do with the only hope for mankind being in a return to communion with God through a new reverence for nature.

"But I can't do this unless I can get into my own inner space."

That was something Guy understood. Years ago, when he was a young teenager, he had heard someone who had used a psychedelic drug say he had "got lost in my own inner space," a phrase which at the time he had found disquieting.

"I haven't got any mescaline," he said. "I've no peyote or anything like that."

But up in the safe he had some lysergic acid diethylamide, LSD-25, which he would quite like to be rid of, out of his house and his life. It was in tablet form.

•   •   •

In those days he had been seeing a lot of Leonora. She was coming to the end of her teacher-training course at a college in South London. She had no other boy-friend, he was sure of that, but they did not make love, they had not made love for years. He told her that he wanted her, that he longed for them to be lovers again. She didn't exactly say they would be but she didn't say no. Once even, he thought he remembered, she had smiled and said "one day." That, of course, meant "one night." Their earliest experiences notwithstanding, those cemetery idylls, she wouldn't go to bed in the afternoons, or at any time but night-time, come to that. It was her excuse. She was

89

at college, her room was not private, there would be difficulties; staying overnight at his house wasn't possible.

That was the time when she was saying she had no real home any more. Though a bedroom was religiously kept as hers at Tessa's house in Sanderstead Lane and another at Anthony's flat in Lamb's Conduit Street, it was not "the same." In any case she couldn't possibly take him there. Not for the night. It would be awkward, it would be embarrassing. But they went out together. They went to the cinema, they went out for meals, for walks, they spoke often on the phone. Though there was no love-making, he was her boy-friend and she was his girl-friend. They had arranged to go on holiday together and then, he told himself, the long period of chastity imposed by Leonora would be ended.

While she had been at university, there had been long separations. Sometimes he hadn't seen her for a whole term. She hadn't asked him what he did for a living but he knew that the time would come when she would and he must be prepared. It was in a large part due to the presence of Leonora in his life that he had acquired a share in the club, then become sole owner, embarked on the travel-agency business, started the paintings enterprise. He couldn't have told her he lived by dealing. He had to tell her lies and make them into truths. Eventually, when they were lovers again, when marriage was coming, the dealing would have to be altogether given up.

Four years ago, all of it had happened almost exactly four years ago. Mr. Y, who was Con Mulvanney, had sat in his hall on the Georges Jacob chair, on one of the last days of July, perhaps the very last day—after that party, anyway—talking about Saint Francis of Assisi and how to get into one's inner space. And he, Guy, to shut him up and get rid of him, had given him the acid he had in the safe. *Given* him, not sold him, though he couldn't remember now why he had shown this unusual generosity. Panic, probably, an overwhelming wish to get Mr. Y out of his house.

Guy himself had never used LSD. He had never used anything but marijuana very occasionally and cocaine twice.

Because he was afraid of snakes, the commonest of phobias, he had never dared experiment with LSD in case he had a "bad trip" and "saw" snakes. Besides, acid, so popular during the late sixties and early seventies, the hippie phenomenon, had gone out of fashion in his own teen-age years and was only recently coming back. But he knew enough about it to give Mr. Y a routine warning. "Have you ever used it?"

Mr. Y said no. "I know the risk is you can get confronted with too much reality too quickly."

"Never mind that. Just have someone there when you do it. Don't be left alone. You want to come back from that inner space, not get left in there."

No money passed. Guy told himself that this was good, though he really knew it made no difference. When Mr. Y departed in the dark red 2CV he experienced an enormous relief, a great sense of lightness. He went back upstairs to put the marijuana back in the safe with the amphetamines and then to lock the safe. For some reason, simple caution perhaps or one of those superstitious feelings, one of those premonitions, he didn't do this. It went against the grain, he might regret it, but just the same, he took the drugs into the guest bathroom and flushed them down the lavatory. In the light of what happened, it was just as well.

Two nights later he was taking Leonora out. She was living with her father and stepmother in Bloomsbury.

Anthony Chisholm was nicer to him than any of the other people who were close to Leonora. Anthony and Susannah. She was nice to him as well. Of course she was only eight years older than he was, there was no feeling that here was another parent. Like an old-fashioned suitor, Guy called for Leonora in Lamb's Conduit Street and took her home.

He got there early. He always got there early when he went to fetch Leonora. She was in the bath. Anthony, who was an architect, a partner in a city firm called Purdey Chisholm Hall, was not yet home from work. Susannah did PR for a cosmetics company and some toymakers and handled her accounts from home. She gave him a drink, said they had people coming and she was cooking something tricky—would he excuse her? The evening paper that Leonora had brought in with her was lying on the arm of the settee.

Guy drank his drink and read the front page. There was a bizarre story about a man in South London being stung to death by bees.

The man's name was Cornelius "Con" Mulvanney, which meant nothing to Guy, who read the story, and then another about a tennis player's divorce, and had started on one about a fire in Fulham, when Anthony came in.

CHAPTER EIGHT

When Guy phoned Leonora's flat on the day after their lunch at Clarke's, Rachel Lingard took the call.

"I'm afraid Leonora isn't here."

"Where is she then?"

"I'm not my sister's keeper."

"*What?*"

"We may not know what God said to Cain after he made the statement I paraphrased but I emphatically dissociate myself from that kind of involvement."

She talked like that. She often did. He had long ago ceased to ask her what she was on about.

"She's round at the ginger dwarf's, I suppose. Okay, you needn't answer that. I've got his number."

There was no reply from Georgiana Street. He tried again an hour later and an hour after that and then every half-hour. He took Celeste out to dinner and then to a drinking club in Green Street called Greens. From there, at eleven, he again dialed William Newton's number and again there was no

RUTH RENDELL

answer. It wasn't very late for him but he knew it was late for most people. There were either not in or Newton had a plug-in phone that made a ringing tone to the caller even if unplugged. Newton had unplugged his phone to make it impossible for Leonora to speak to him. Most likely, almost certainly, Leonora did not know this.

Next day he tried her at home. There was no reply. The phone was not answered throughout the evening and the phone in Georgiana Street was not answered. Just before ten he asked directory inquiries for the number of an M. Mandeville in Sanderstead Lane, South Croydon, obtained it and phoned Tessa.

When she heard who it was she said first of all that she had no idea where Leonora was. Leonora—she called her "my daughter"—was twenty-six and "her own woman." Then she said, "You know it's only right to tell you I think you must be a very seriously disturbed person. You ought to be having therapy. Though it may be too late for anything like that to do any good. Permanent damage was done long long ago."

"What's that supposed to mean?"

"I used to think of you as a criminal, but it's more pity I feel now. I pity you, I really do. All that filth you took into your system over the years is bearing fruit now. You're reaping the whirlwind."

Guy put the phone down, badly shaken. It was the first hint he had ever received that she, or anyone connected with Leonora, knew what he had once done for a living. Was there anything the Mandevilles didn't know about him? Leonora herself had said Magnus knew about his protection network in Kensal. Tessa, however, had got it wrong. He had never been an addict. Had Leonora told her he was? The notion of Leonora talking derogatorily to her mother about him was deeply painful.

But there was another way she might know, or think she knew. Tessa lived in South London. So did Poppy Vasari, so *had* Con Mulvanney. Of course there must be about five

94

million people living in the vast metropolitan area south of the river, but Poppy Vasari was a sort of social worker. And so in another way was Tessa Mandeville. Hadn't Leonora told him about her mother's doing voluntary work in a hospital and having some sort of job at the Citizen's Advice Bureau? What more likely than that she and Poppy had encountered each other?

Suppose Tessa and Poppy had met regularly, at the CAB or chauffeuring geriatrics about. Guy was vague in his ideas about this but it could be something like that. Poppy, talking about the death of Con Mulvanney, might so easily have described him, Guy, to Tessa, and told Tessa in her indignation what he had done. She knew his name, she had found that out. She could have told Tessa his name.

There had been no mention of Poppy in that original story, the account of Con Mulvanney's death he had read while in Anthony Chisholm's flat. But Poppy was not Con's lover, didn't live with him, perhaps wasn't even all that close a friend. Some of those do-gooders could get very steamed up about what they called "social injustice" or "outrageous" breaches of something or other. As for him, he had read it and been interested, mildly appalled at Con Mulvanney's fate, an awful fate however you looked at it. This Mulvanney, who-ever he was, seemed to have taken the roof or lid off a beehive and been stung all over his head and face and neck by bees. Could you *die* of that? Apparently. There would be an inquest. Con Mulvanney was described as being thirty-six and unem-ployed, living in the "garden flat," or ground floor, of a house in Upper Tooting.

·   ·   ·

Anthony Chisholm arrived home. Since his second marriage he had more than ever that look of a handsome teddy bear, his smile more boyish, his eyes less tired. No wonder. Any man would feel himself in a seventh heaven of bliss to have escaped the clutches of that bitch Tessa. It was a mystery to Guy how he had stuck her so long. At that time, that summer four years past, Anthony was being very nice to Guy, very pleasant.

"Have you got a drink, Guy? Oh, good, Susannah's been looking after you. Where's that girl of mine? No, don't tell me, I can guess. I thought two bathrooms were more than anyone could want in a mere duplex, that's what the Americans call them, you know, duplexes, but I now see three are needed."

Guy asked if he minded his smoking. He wouldn't have asked Tessa, just got one out and lighted it.

"D'you know, I think I'll have one too. Officially, let's say *matrimonially*, I've given it up, but having one of yours doesn't count."

What could be more comfortable? More matey? The easygoing, cultivated, urbane and affectionate parent with his prospective son-in-law. His wealthy, jet-setting, successful prospective son-in-law. Guy was sure Anthony saw him in that light. He did *then*. Anthony wasn't any more worldly or greedy than the rest of them, but he was a sensible realist, he had an eye to the main chance. Whatever Leonora herself might have thought of this attitude, she with her feminist ideas, Anthony saw a rich, successful husband as a snip for his daughter. Guy had had a Porsche at that time. Anthony would have seen the Porsche outside (on a double-yellow line before the days of clamping—who cared about the fine?), would have heard from Leonora about Guy's house, knew from that none-too-happy birthday party of Guy's business interests. He might in his heart have preferred some intellectual for Leonora, but intellectuals aren't often rich and a bird in the hand is worth two in the bush.

So Guy reasoned in those days and was pleasant to Anthony, accepted another drink, gave him another cigarette, said what an awful case that was in the evening paper. Who would have thought a man could die from bee-stings?

Guy, who remembered everything that had happened during those days, recalled that on the following morning he went to his rifle club for the first time. He was taking lessons, it was his first lesson. The instructor said he had a good eye and his control was good. After that he took a taxi into the West End to pick up his air tickets for the holiday on Samos. The travel agency he and Bob Joseph were setting up was still at the planning stage. Guy had booked the hotel's "honeymoon hut," which was actually on the private beach. They were flying first-class and he was wondering if he could possibly trick Leonora into believing that this luxurious mode of travel was in fact economy class. She insisted on paying for herself from the proceeds of some holiday job she had taken. Perhaps he could make her think the airline had "upped" their seats because there were vacancies in first class.

He foresaw trouble with Leonora over payment. She would realize that the hotel was astronomically beyond her means. They might even have the price of the honeymoon hut up on a notice somewhere, inside the clothes cupboard or behind a door. By that time, however, it would be too late for her to do anything about it, she would have to put a good face on it and let him pay as he wanted and indeed longed to do.

Guy had a lunch date with Bob Joseph and a lawyer who was fixing up the lease of their new premises in Milner Street in the most advantageous-possible way. He intended to go to Gladiators for a workout later, so he thought he was justified in drinking rather a lot. When he got home it was nearly four.

There was a woman in a car outside, having an argument with a traffic warden. Scarsdale Mews had residents' parking throughout most of its length and five meters at the Marloes Road end. Guy pointed out to her that someone had just pulled away from one of the meters. If he had known this was Poppy Vasari and what she had come about, he wouldn't have given her any help, he'd have liked to see her car towed away. She didn't say who she was or that she wanted him. He let himself into the house.

Two or three minutes later the doorbell rang. There she was.

She said her name and that she was a friend of Con Mulvanney's. Guy, who had forgotten the name of the man in the bee-sting story though not the story itself, said he had never heard of Con Mulvanney.

"Oh yes, you have, Mr. X," she said.

"Am I supposed to know what you're talking about?" He did, though, or he had an inkling.

"You gave him a hallucinogenic drug," she said.

She said it out loud, in her normal voice or louder. Guy thought he was going to faint, fall on the floor. He said, "For God's sake," and then, because anything was better than having her go on like that out here, "you'd better come in."

She was a big, gypsyish woman, wearing large gold hoop ear-rings and gold chains and strings of coloured beads round her neck. She had a lopsided, raddled, much-lined but vivid face, a hooky nose, black burning eyes. She was dark and her long wild hair was black. Her clothes were draperies, perhaps worn to conceal bulk or just for their loose, floppy comfort: a red tunic, a black layered skirt, a long loose grey cotton jacket, a red-and-blue shawl. Bare legs, bare feet, sandals.

He must have taken all that in later, he certainly wasn't capable of it at the time. In those first moments she was Nemesis, come to make him mad and then destroy him. Her wild look, her clothes were even appropriate. But he smelt her smell as she pushed past him. Instead of perfume and toilet water and bath oil and body shampoo, which the women he knew smelt of, there emanated from her a powerful reek of sweat. She smelt like a cheap hamburger restaurant. Ever since, he had associated the smell of cooking hamburger with her.

"You'll have read about it," she said when they were in his drawing-room. "You'll know all about it or what the papers know."

"I didn't know it was him," Guy said.

She looked at him. She laughed. It was the most unpleasant laugh he had ever heard. "So this has been a shock?"

"You could put it that way, yes."

"Good. I like to think your punishment is beginning."

She wasn't the least bit afraid of him. She was a woman, a

good fifteen years older than he was and out of condition, she was in a strange house with someone she no doubt thought of as a criminal, at his mercy, but she wasn't afraid. She held her head high and looked fiercely into his eyes. And she was right not to be afraid. The strength had gone out of him. The drink had too. None of its magic remained to give him false nerve.

"He begged me to give him something. He pestered me, he gave me no peace." Guy knew he was being indiscreet, worse than that, but there were no witnesses. "I didn't take any money," he said, as if this were a defence. "I warned him to take it under supervision."

"He did. My supervision."

"Yours?"

"I was there. I'd been working in a drugs rehabilitation centre, I ought to have known better."

"Yes, you ought." Guy clutched at this straw. "Fine bloody supervisor you were."

"Shut up," she said. "Shut up. Don't you dare speak to me like that. D'you want to know happened? I'm going to tell you anyway. It'll all come out at the inquest. D'you want to know?"

"Of course I want to know."

"Well, then. He didn't know your name, only where you live. *I* know it, I asked the people next door before you came back. He told me he was going to take the tablets you gave him in order to get into his inner consciousness. Some tripe like that. I told him not to. I said he didn't know enough about it, didn't know how long you'd had it, for instance, or where it came from. I said its use had to be properly controlled. He talked a lot more rubbish. If I wouldn't be with him he'd take it on his own, he said. He was as daft as a brush anyway, all that reincarnation tripe. I used to be a nurse on a psychiatric ward and I can tell you that's one of the first signs of a psychosis, people claiming they're reincarnated.

"He was the last person should have been allowed near a substance like that. But you can't tell people what to do, not without putting them under restraint. That bloody acid filth—

God, and I thought that was the end of it when it went out in the seventies. Okay, well, the upshot was he took it and he—I was going to say he had a bad trip, but he didn't, he had a *good* trip. He kept saying he could see lovely things, lovely colours. There's a garden where he lives—lived. The flowers in it weren't marvellous, well, they wouldn't be, but he started describing the flowers, daisies they were that you get in lawns, he said they were sunflowers, as big as dinner plates and with the scent of roses. The sparrows were kingfishers and para-keets and God knows what. He started talking to the butter-flies. They were cabbage-white ones but he said their wings were blue and purple and scarlet."

"What about the bees?" said Guy, dry-mouthed.

She looked grim. She stretched her mouth into a nasty smile. "The bees, yes. The bees were in a hive in the garden at the end of his garden. Some of the neighbours had complained to the council—I work for the council—but there were just as many liked the bees on account of they were good for flowers and fertilized their fruit trees. This'll be the end of them now, that's for sure." Her eyes came back to meet his. "He climbed over the fence."

"But *why?*"

"To talk to the bloody bees. He was Saint Francis—remember? Brother Bee and Sister Butterfly. There was a lot of that, and then he got over the fence. It wasn't very high and there was a wooden box he stood on on his side. I couldn't stop him—how could I? He did what he wanted, people do. The couple who lived in the house, the bee-keepers, they were out at work. Everyone was at work or somewhere.

"He went up to the beehive, talking to the bees. He liked bees, though I don't think he talked to them when he was—well, normal. It's a wooden hive with a top that comes off. He leaned very close and said to me it would be all right, the bees would recognize him, they would know their friend. I got hold of him and he pushed me away. He said I'd upset the bees and maybe I would have, maybe I *did*. Anyway, he took the top off the hive.

100

"The bees came out. I mean, hundreds, it seemed like hundreds. A great swarm of them, all angry. I knew they were stinging him because he was shouting and slapping at them. He ran and fell and the bees came after him. Bees aren't like wasps, they do come after you. They sting you and they leave the sting inside you and half of themselves with it. That's why they die. Christ, it's amazing, people actually believe in a God that'd make a creature whose way of defending itself is its own death."

The tears were running down her face. She made no attempt to wipe them away. Guy felt he was gaping at her and he turned aside.

"They stung me," she said. "They got in my hair. They stung my hands and my neck. I was full of stings and bits of bee."

"You didn't die, though," he said stupidly.

"I'm not allergic."

"He was *allergic?* You'd have thought that'd have stopped him. Why did he go near the bees if he was allergic?"

"He didn't know he was," she said. "He can't have known. You don't if you've only been stung once before. The first time nothing much happens, it's a question of getting sensitized. It causes a strong adverse reaction to later contacts with the substance, whatever it is. Bee-stings or shellfish or poison ivy, it's all the same."

"And that's what he had?"

"I didn't know," she said. "I tried to drag him back. Those bloody bees . . . I started screaming, you can scream a hell of a lot in London before people take notice. A man did come. I said to get help, a doctor, ambulance, the police, anything. The bees were there, everywhere and angry, it was hell."

"The police," he said. "Did the police come?"

She jeered at him, "Is that what worries you? Is that all that worries you? No, they didn't. They're never there when you want them. Another thing, it's bloody hard to convince people in a situation like that; they don't believe you, they don't believe someone's going to die of bee-stings. I could *tell* he

101

had an allergic reaction, they would have been able to tell in a hospital if we could have got him there in time. He was dead before that, he was dead in less than an hour. He choked to death. He swelled up and choked to death."

Guy said nothing. He just sat there and he looked away. He looked out of the windows onto his own pretty town garden with its round pond and the island in the middle. No bronze dolphin then, no Florentine furniture, the orange trees tiny in their Chinese vases, up against the wall blue and dark green junipers he had later had cut down to make way for the clematis. It was raining a little, the raindrops puncturing the surface of the pond. A single pink water-lily had been in bloom. He remembered everything.

"He wasn't able to speak," she said, in a cool, neutral sort of voice.

Did that mean he had told no one about the LSD?

"I know what you're thinking. He didn't tell anyone."

"He'd told you."

She laughed. "Oh, yes. That filth you gave him may show at post-mortem, I ought to know that but I don't. Anyway, it doesn't matter." She looked slowly round the room. He knew, as if she had said it aloud, what was going through her mind. He's got all this, ill-gotten gains, but not for long, on, no, not for long, all to be swept away, all lost. Fourteen years, thought Guy. "I told the police," she said. "I told them everything I knew. I imagine they'll come here. They said I shouldn't try to see you, but I had to. I had to *confront* you. I'll go now."

"How was I supposed to know he was allergic to bees?" Guy said.

He would have liked to kill her but of course he didn't touch her. She was crying when she left. Crying seemed to make her body smell worse. He wasn't too keen on his neighbours' seeing a weeping woman in flapping robes and with dirty bare feet leaving his house, but there was nothing he could do about it.

Less than an hour later the Drugs Squad arrived.

CHAPTER NINE

What makes you love someone? Why can't you choose, when you can choose almost everything else in life? If you're rich, that is. You can choose what to do for a living, where to live, what kind of a house and car and clothes and entertainment to have. Why isn't the person you love a matter of choice too?

Guy often asked that about himself and Leonora. Why was he in love with Leonora when he didn't want to be, when it was so inconvenient, when it was so destructive and time-wasting? She looked beautiful to him but he knew she wasn't all that good-looking, she didn't dress well, she didn't like any of the things he liked, and he disliked most of the things she liked. They hadn't anything in common. She wasn't interested in eating and drinking and expensive clothes, staying up all night, exotic places, fast cars, sunny beaches and going to the races. Sport meant nothing to her. She had never been skiing or on a yacht. Diamonds might be a girl's best friend but not her sort of girl, and she campaigned against the fur trade.

She liked books and serious films, preferably made in Japan

or Chile and with subtitles. She liked camping or hostel holidays with a backpack, health foods, fruit juice, Badoit and Ramlosa, cycling, fringe theatre, classical music, and "green" documentaries on BBC 2. He would make himself get to like all that if they were together again, but at the moment he hated it. He hated her clothes and the fact that she hardly ever wore make-up, wore it even less often since she had taken up with the ginger dwarf, never put varnish on her nails. Hairy legs would be the next thing, he sometimes thought.

But when he saw her coming towards him, coming into their Saturday restaurant, his heart moved. His heart turned a little sideways and beat hard as in shock. Every time that happened. Something inside his head, the skull itself perhaps, expanded with a kind of warmth, with a faint pain. But his body grew cold; if he did not exactly shiver, he felt the cold stroke him, running down his arms and sides, touching his heart. Every time.

And why? It was something about her, that was all he could say. Perhaps that was what it always was with love. Something about someone. A glance, a smile, a way of opening the eyes wide, a gurgle in the laugh, a movement of the shoulders, some little thing. That of course didn't explain why the little thing could do so much. With him and Leonora it was her smile, the way she smiled, a curious tightness of her lips, which never stretched quite as far as you imagined they could, a kind of control in her smile. The teeth, of course, were perfect, small, white, and even. The only smile like hers he had ever seen had been Vivien Leigh's in *Gone With the Wind*.

Did her smile mean so much to him, madden him and pain and delight him, cause him to long for something he couldn't define, not because it was controlled but because he knew it could break the bounds of control and be full and complete, but never would be for him?

Three days had passed without his speaking to her. On the fourth day, in Georgiana Street, she had answered the phone. They had been out a lot, she said, they hadn't been at home much. William had been working. William had been working on a film about men who had to care for their disabled wives at home. What a thrilling subject! The viewing figures would really be something else! As if he cared where bloody William had been. He would have liked to kill William several times over.

"Where shall we have lunch?" he asked, and she said what about going back to that place in Kensington Park Road. So there he was, the first to arrive this time, sitting at the bar being served a vodka martini by the French boy who was the barman there. He had taken off his sunglasses, not wanting to be accused of looking like a mafioso.

Passing the mews where once she had lived had made him think of love and of her smile. It was August 19, exactly four weeks to go to her wedding day—well, to the date she called her wedding day. He wasn't giving in as meekly as that. He wasn't giving in at all. He had made himself not look at the spiral staircase, and he was just thinking he would have to look, he would have to turn round, when she touched him on the shoulder.

"Guy, you're dreaming."

The shiver went through him and his heart moved. He looked at her. She smiled at him and he told her what he had been thinking about her smile.

"It's why I love you. It's sort of the essence of why."

"Suppose I had plastic surgery and the shape of my mouth was altered, would you stop loving me?"

"I don't know. Maybe. I always have this feeling that you don't smile properly for me, you don't smile as much as you could. You *govern* your smile when you smile at me."

"Don't be ridiculous, Guy," she said.

"What does Newton think about you having lunch with me on Saturdays? Does he hate it?"

"He understands," she said.

They sat at their table. Leonora had an orange juice, he had a Campari and soda. She ordered a grapefruit-and-avocado cocktail and stuffed courgettes and he ordered escargots and then calves' liver in a raspberry coulis. He thought about

Newton's "understanding." Big of him to "understand," the patronizing bastard.

"Someone started turning you against me when you were nineteen," he said.

"Oh, nonsense. What nonsense."

"Didn't you like my house?"

"I loved it, it's a beautiful house."

"It's better than your parents' house was, isn't it?"

"Much better, but I don't see where all this is leading."

"I want you to tell me something. I want you to tell me if there was anyone else between me and Newton." A little humility would be in order, he thought. "I suppose I've no right to ask, but I hope you'll tell me."

"There was no one very serious," she said.

He didn't care for that, it caught him by the throat. "But there were other men between me and Newton?"

"Of course there were."

"Who were they?"

Her eyes sparkled. He couldn't tell if she was pleased or angry. She said crisply, "All right, if you insist. There was Robin's friend that he was in partnership with, and two men at university, and, yes, now I come to think of it, there was someone I met at Robin's twenty-fifth birthday party. Is that what you want to know?"

"Did you sleep with them?"

"That's nothing to do with you, Guy, it's not your business. You said you'd no right to ask and you haven't."

"You did then." Having a heart attack must be like this, it would be the same kind of pain, clutching at his chest, bringing a kind of paralysis. "I just wonder what your father would say," he burst out.

"You *what?*"

"I said I wondered what your father would say to that. He'd be horrified. Any man would be about his daughter. Your father would very much have liked you to marry me. He would have liked me to be the one and only, I know he would, he'd die if he thought you'd been promiscuous."

"I wasn't promiscuous. Don't be silly."

"One man after another, what else is it? Why, anyway? What was wrong with me? Were they better-looking, richer? What had they got that I haven't got? I was the one your father would have liked to give his daughter to."

She started laughing. Then she shook her head.

"What's so funny."

"You are. You're so old-fashioned. You think of yourself as a sort of trendy yuppie—well, you've yupped—young and trendy but in fact you're really old-fashioned, and a sexist too. 'I just wonder what your father would say.' Really, Guy, you sound like someone of sixty. My father himself wouldn't say a thing like that. And men don't give their daughters in marriage any more, hadn't you noticed?"

"Don't deny your father has a lot of influence over you, Leonora."

"That has nothing to do with it. I'm not denying it. I'm only saying we've come a long way since men chose husbands for their daughters."

Hating the look on her face, her smile, he said morosely, "He changed towards me, your father."

From that night forward, he thought. That evening when he came to take Leonora out and read the story about Con Mulvanney in the paper, that was the last time Anthony Chisholm pressed him to have another drink, smoked his cigarettes, treated him like an old friend. It was a few weeks before he saw him again and the change was marked. At the time he had thought Anthony preoccupied with business cares, worried about something, and after that evening months went by before they saw each other again. When they did he, Guy, was making his offer to "lend" Leonora the money for the flat, and Anthony, who had somehow been brought in on it, was stern and dismissive. The loan was not to be considered, he understood Leonora had already refused; just as long as Guy understood his offer was appreciated but must be utterly out of the question.

Guy ordered himself another Campari. He lit a cigarette

while they waited for the food to come. "You never told me how you met Newton," he said.

"Why would I? You never asked."

"Well, how did you? Where did you?"

She gave him an odd sideways look, as well she might, considering what was coming. "In Lamb's Conduit Street."

"At your father's? Come on, say what you mean, Leonora."

"And you can come on, Guy. Who else do I know in Lamb's Conduit Street? As a matter of fact, my father introduced us."

"What? He what? You see! I am right. I'm not all those things you said, old-fashioned and sexist and whatever. *Your father introduced you to the man he wants you to marry.*"

"*I* want to marry him, Guy. I am going to marry him. Anyway, it wasn't like that."

"What was it like then?"

"William was making this programme about architecture. It was sparked off by something Prince Charles said. He came to see Dad for a preliminary interview at home and I happened to be there."

"When was this?"

"Don't interrogate me, please, Guy. It was about two years ago. Well, it was July."

"You weren't living with them then. You'd been in your flat for over a year by then."

"I didn't say I was living with them. I said I met William at their place. It was Dad's birthday. I called in with Dad's birthday present and William was there."

"That doesn't explain how you started going out with him. Or did your father arrange it? Maybe he told Newton you'd got an undesirable boy-friend and he'd welcome someone more suitable. Maybe he gave him your phone number."

"I gave him my phone number," she said. "He asked me for it."

How was it possible to be so angry with someone and still love her? How could you dislike almost everything about the way a person dressed and behaved and still love her? Love her better than anyone else in the world. Better than yourself.

"If you're so—I think the word's progressive. If you're so progressive, why do you think of marrying him? Why don't you go and live with him?"

"I am living with him now—more or less."

Their food came. Leonora asked for some water, he for a bottle of red Graves. "Why marriage?" he said when the waitress had gone.

"To make a public commitment is the usual reason, isn't it? Yes, I suppose that's what we want to do. Commit ourselves to each other for life."

"For *life*. You're counting on this lasting for *life?*"

"Why not? People used to take it as a matter of course that marriage would last for life. I hope ours will. I don't know, I can't tell, how can anyone tell? All we can do is try."

She had taken a roll from the basket but wasn't eating it. Her left hand lay on the table. He took hold of the wrist, held it loosely like someone feeling for a pulse, then tightened his grip.

"Do something for me."

He thought she sighed. "What would that be, Guy?"

"Don't get married. Wait. Wait a year. You're young, he's young—what's a year? Live with him. I don't mind that—well, I do but I can bear it. Live with him and see."

She looked at him, shaking her head very slightly from side to side. "Let me go. You're hurting me." She pulled her hand away.

"Do that for me. It's a small thing."

"A small thing! To postpone my marriage because a friend, an ex-boy-friend, tells me to!"

"I'm more than that to you, Leo. I am the love of your life and you know it. If you refuse me I'll stop you. I won't let you get married. I have a right to forbid your marriage and I will."

"Guy," she said, "sometimes you say things to me which make me very seriously question your sanity. *I mean that.*

And it's getting worse. I honestly think you need to do something about it."

"You've been listening to your mother."

"Why not? Yes, maybe I have. I do listen to my mother sometimes. I think she's got a lot of sense. But I haven't been listening to her on the question of your sanity, I've never discussed it with her. I think you're losing your mind, Guy, and all because you've got this crazy idea in your head that you and I would be happy together. We wouldn't. You'll do much better with Celeste, if only you'd look at it rationally. Actually, it'll be better when I'm married and out of your way, when you can't see me. You'll get over it then."

They were neither of them able to eat their lunch. He drank the wine, though, he could always drink. She drank her water and made the bread roll into a heap of crumbs. She said that these days meeting him only made her miserable and him too, but she promised to have lunch with him again on the following Saturday.

She had given him a lot to think about. When had he made the offer to pay for her flat? It must have been in the December and January three and a half years ago. Between then and the previous August someone had told Anthony Chisholm about the Con Mulvanney affair. Perhaps Leonora had told him. But who had told her? Who was it had said, "Do you know the sort of person you've been going about with?"

But it had happened long before he offered the "loan," it was just that he hadn't seen Anthony for six months. No doubt Anthony had deliberately avoided him. He must have known a few days after Poppy Vasari put the police on to him. Poppy had immediately started telling people, as she had threatened to do, and one of the people she had told was—why hadn't he thought of that at once?—Rachel Lingard.

The chances of Poppy coming across Tessa were not very great. Tessa was only a voluntary worker in a hospital and the CAB. But Rachel was a social worker for some London borough, he couldn't remember which one, if he had ever known. If she worked for the Social Services in some South London borough while Poppy worked with addicts, what more likely than that they knew each other? They might even be friends.

"His name's Guy Curran, he's got a luxury mews house in just about the best part of Kensington."

"Guy Curran?"

"Don't say you know him!"

"Oh, I know him. My best friend's thinking of marrying him."

She *had* been thinking of marrying him once. The first time he took her to see his house, on the way there in his car—he'd had a Mercedes in those days—"It'll be your house too," he'd said, and she had given him that smile, only he remembered it as freer and more open then, less contained. "When we get married," she'd said.

She *had* said that? He hadn't imagined it? Of course he hadn't. He wasn't losing his mind. She had loved him entirely, but the separations imposed by university and training college had driven them apart. It was natural, it would have happened to anyone. The point was that she was coming closer to him again, she had agreed to go on holiday with him, they were going out together two or three times a week. And then Con Mulvanney died.

•   •   •

Poppy Vasari had been gone no more than ten minutes when the Drugs Squad arrived. They searched the house and found nothing. There was nothing to find. Thank God he had put that grass and those amphetamines down the john three days before. They had been known to take the drains apart. Not that they did that in Scarsdale Mews. He could tell they were impressed by the house, they couldn't help being, and it had to affect them, the elegance of it, the quietness, the beautiful things.

They questioned him at home and at the police station. The interrogation went on for hours. He denied everything. The club was doing well at that time, the travel agency was well past the planning stage, the original-oil-paintings business had started bringing in the money. They could see where the money came from.

His two new rifles came to light, each in its case. He had his gun license, as member of an accredited rifle club. He said he had never heard of Cornelius Mulvanney, the man had never come to his house. One thing he would like to tell them, he said, was that while he was at a party in a pub in Balham at the weekend, someone had come up to him and asked if he had any hashish. In those words? Well, no, not in those words, he didn't want to repeat the words, but if they insisted, what he had asked had been, "Have you got any shit?" How did he know what that meant? He had been curious, he had asked a man in the pub, who had told him.

Describe the man. Which man? The one who asked him for the hashish. Guy had said he couldn't, he couldn't remember. Eventually he came up with a vague outline of a thin man, pale, with longish, fairish hair. The name of the pub? The time? Whose party was it? What time did he leave? On and on it went. At midnight they let him go home. He never heard from them again.

Poppy Vasari, however, returned a few days later. She said she wouldn't come in, thanks. (He hadn't asked her.) She'd stay on the doorstep because he might do her a mischief if she was alone with him in there. That made him laugh. As if he would even touch someone so repulsive! The smell was still there, ingrained in her clothes probably. He stood holding the door and laughing at her, it was all so ridiculous.

"You murdered Con," she said, "so why not me? It wouldn't make any difference to you. You're evil."

He was forcing himself to keep on laughing, it didn't come naturally. If he shut the door she would only keep banging on it until he opened it again.

"You're safe from the law," she said, "but you're not safe from your peers."

"What d'you mean, peers?" he'd said, getting a sort of picture of the House of Lords.

"I'm telling everyone I know about you, everyone. And I'm telling everyone Con knew. I'm telling them the truth, that Con may have died from bee-stings but he only got stung because of the drug you gave him. You murdered him by giving him a lethal drug and that's what I'm determined everyone's going to know. I've started at home. Now I'm going to start here. I'm going to find your friends and tell them. I'm going to knock on every door in this street and tell people what you did."

The trouble with doing that sort of thing, at least in Britain, is that the recipients of statements of this kind, delivered like that, think the messenger is mad. He or she is a "poor soul" who ought to be put away, ought never to have been let out, needs looking after, is best ignored, forgotten, and, as for the information thus relayed, no one gives it credence. No doubt the neighbours in Scarsdale Mews did think Poppy Vasari mad if she carried out her threat—Guy didn't look to see—and perhaps she was temporarily a little mad. I mean (thought Guy), imagine it, the TV chat-show chap coming to his door and getting an earful of "I think you ought to know that the man who lives at number seven killed my friend with drugs."

It didn't even worry him much. If she thought these people were his friends, she was making a big mistake. He had never been matey with the neighbours. An invitation from one set of them to drop in for a Christmas drink he had refused. In the ensuing days he was a bit wary with them, but everyone went on just as they had been before, either saying "Good morning" or "Hi" or not saying anything. As he thought, they hadn't listened. But that was a far cry from Poppy Vasari telling someone she knew personally, someone she worked with, especially when she had calmed down a bit. It was a far cry from her telling someone *who knew him, who recognized his name*.

Rachel Lingard.

It was within a fortnight of the Con Mulvanney inquest that he and Leonora were going away on holiday together. Nothing of importance came out at the inquest. His name, thank God, wasn't mentioned. Poppy Vasari got a reprimand from the coroner for sitting by and doing nothing while Con Mulvanney took a prohibited substance, a dangerous hallucinogen. She was specially to blame in the light of her training and the job she had been doing, from which, the coroner was pleased to inform the court, she had resigned. The verdict was accidental death. But Rachel must have been busy because in the middle of the following week, when he and Leonora met in Cambridge Circus—he was taking her to the theatre to *Les Miserables*—she told him she wasn't coming to Greece.

She wasn't abashed about it, she wasn't awkward. There was no question of saying to him that she hated telling him, that she felt awful. She came straight out with it.

"I can't come, I'm sorry."

He was appalled, he protested. Was it the cost that was worrying her? Was it because he would have to pay for both of them?

The shock of it made him careless and he uttered the phrase she hated and he had promised himself not to use. "I won't even notice an amount like that."

It always made her wince. "It's that, and other things. I can't. Don't ask me to explain, it would be painful to explain. Let's just forget it—can we?"

Once he thought it was the money and perhaps—unpleasant notion—she might feel she'd *have* to sleep with him if he'd paid, so it was better not to go. Now he knew differently. Rachel had told her about Con Mulvanney.

She lived with Rachel, Rachel was always there, poisoning her mind, influencing her against him. He would like to kill Rachel.

CHAPTER TEN

The barbecue at Danilo's was operated by cooks in striped aprons and high white hats and the food served by waitresses dressed like eighteenth-century dairymaids. The barmen and barmaids were dressed like Hawaiian dancers. Fortunately, it was a warm evening. The garden of Danilo's neo-Georgian house in Weybridge was enormous, planted here and there with imported, nearly mature, palm trees, which were doing all right this summer but might be less happy by next spring. His latest novelty was the fountain, installed in an ornamental pool on the lawn below the terrace. The fountain was floodlit this evening, pink rose-trees in pink pots stood round the marble coping and pink dye had been put into the water. Danilo explained to people admiring the effect that the natural-looking rocks were real rose quartz.

About a hundred people had come. Guy knew some of them slightly. Bob Joseph was there with his girl-friend and Bob's ex-wife was there with her new husband, Danilo's wicked old father with his third wife and Danilo's brother, who had taken over the turf accountant's business and now had a chain of betting shops. There were a lot of friends of Tanya's in the rag trade and a lot of girls who looked like models but probably weren't. Danilo and Tanya, though always talking about getting married "one day," had not yet done so, in spite of having four children.

These four, intolerably spoilt in Guy's opinion, instead of being in bed or supervised in some distant suitable place by their two nannies, ran about among the guests screaming, throwing food about, and splashing anyone who came within the line of fire with pink water from the fountain. They were dressed up to the nines, the two boys in striped trousers and monkey jackets with bow-ties, the girls in white organza with layers of petticoats, as if their parents were Italian peasants made good instead of cockney parvenus. The elder boy, Charles, but always known as Carlo, had got himself a Bellini, which, because this was Tanya's party, had brandy in it as well as champagne and peach juice, and, surrounded by shrieking girls in hip-high miniskirts, was swigging it down and smacking his lips.

Fairy lights were strung among the palm trees, along with ultraviolet mosquito-repellent rings. A tape was playing music of the down-below-the-Rio-Grande type, thus fostering the illusion Danilo and Tanya liked to create that they really were of Latin origin. The garden smelt of burning oil and charred steak in spite of the patchouli-scented candles. Guy understood that he could never have brought Leonora here. She would call it vulgar, or worse, would laugh. Her idea of a party was fifteen people in a flat in Camden Town, drinking white wine and Perrier and talking about the environment. But giving up Danilo and Tanya for Leonora would be an endurable sacrifice.

The night sky was purple, starless, with a lemon-coloured sickle moon that must be real but looked as if Danilo had hung it up there when he dyed the fountain. A slight breeze moved the palm fronds. Guy had drunk one Bellini for form's sake, then moved on to vodka. He could see Celeste enjoying herself dancing with Danilo's next-door neighbour, a million-aire and former member of a highly successful sixties rock group. She had a bright red ankle-length skirt on and a black-and-gold tank top that left bare two inches of golden midriff. Her hair in those scores of gilt-tipped plaits was like the crest of some glorious tropic bird. The smallest of Danilo's children, a little girl in bouncing white tutu, came running up to her and Celeste drew her into the dance, the three of them holding hands. Celeste loved children, he had seen signs before.

He was walking towards the bar for a vodka refill when a more than usually loud splash and shriek from the direction of the fountain made him look to his left. There, among a knot of guests brushing water-drops off their clothes—Carlo had been active at the fountain edge—was Robin Chisholm.

Guy fetched his drink, moved to a shadowy point of vantage where only scented candle-light penetrated. Robin was talking to Tanya, a man Guy didn't know, and two string-thin bizarrely dressed women with hair like huge cumuli of candy-floss, lemon and strawberry, respectively. Tanya's hair was not dissimilar, except that candy-floss does not come in ink flavour. Tanya was wearing a kind of camisole in gold lamé with black-and-gold-striped pleated trousers and high-heeled green shoes that she had probably put on by mistake and then forgotten to change. There was no sign of Maeve.

Robin looked as if he had stepped straight out of a musical set in Edwardian times. All that was lacking was the straw boater. He had taken to wearing his fair wavy hair parted in the middle. It looked very strange. His face was as youthful as ever, not simply youthful as that of a man of twenty-seven is, but like a boy's ten years younger. His cheeks were rosy, his lips red as a girl's. He had white flannels on and a striped blazer, seemed prosperous and immensely pleased with him-self.

Guy said to Danilo, "I didn't know you knew him."

"I used to know him just like you did. Not so well, maybe, till lately. He swapped some pesetas for me. I sold my villa

117

and it was a question of getting the funds out. I should have asked little Miss Leo, eh? Is that what's going through your mind? Little Miss Leo and the fiancé?"

"Not at all," Guy said stiffly. "How did you run across him again?"

"I wonder why you ask. Still, my life is an open book between friends. It was a chance meeting. Tanya's sister had a flat in the same block as him by Clapham Common. That's her talking to him, the strawberry blond one."

"In *Clapham?* He lives in Chelsea."

"This was three or four years ago," said Danilo. "Why are you so interested all of a sudden? Oh, I begin to see. You aren't putting a contract out on him, I hope. He's valuable to me. Where shall I find another swap jockey with a baby face and no scruples? Look at him, he looks about twelve."

Guy fetched himself another drink. What he would have liked to do was walk up to Robin Chisholm and throw the drink in his face, see what happened. He had never thrown a drink in anyone's face, but the idea of doing this was suddenly very attractive. It was as if this was something he had to do before he died. The evening was no longer very warm. For the first time in his life Guy thought that nights are never warm in this country—well, maybe one a year might be warm. Then he walked up to Robin, who was still with Danilo's strawberry-blond sister-in-law, and, by now, an elderly man someone had said was a dress designer.

"Hallo, how are *you?*" He said it in that transatlantic manner that places all the stress on the "you" and runs the words together in a meaningless way. It was deliberate, unaccompanied by a smile.

Robin chose to answer this rhetorical question literally, which made the strawberry blond laugh. "Oh, I'm marvellous, never been better." He gave Guy a purposely vacuous grin, looking like one of the "big boys" in *Just William*.

"Maeve not here?"

This occasioned an offensive pantomine search. Robin looked to either side of him, stretching out his neck and peering round the back of the dress designer. His eyebrows rose, he immediately became short-sighted, baffled, looked at the ground, pursed his lips in a silent whistle. "She doesn't seem to be," he said at last. "No, I'd say not." He had assumed, for the evening only perhaps, for Guy only perhaps, a hearty, ingenuous manner. "I say, is that awfully pretty girl with you?"

It was a mistake to ask which one but Guy asked it.

"The coloured one with the Rastafarian hair."

Guy threw his drink in Robin's face.

Danilo's sister-in-law screamed. The dress designer shouted, "For heaven's sake!" Robin shook himself, spat, tossed back his hair, and leaped for Guy with arms extended, like a cat fighting. The whole party was silenced, was staring, movement suspended, adrenaline rising. Guy's fist shot out and caught Robin not where it was meant to, on his jaw, but against his right collarbone. Almost immediately Robin's flailing hands made contact with Guy's face, the longish nails extended, tigerlike. Guy struck again as people began to intervene. Someone seized him from behind as someone else grabbed Robin by the shoulders, but not before he had slammed his fist into Robin's left eye.

They were both gasping, snorting really.

"Stop it, cut it out," someone was saying.

"Are you crazy?"

"This is *my* party."

"What in God's name is going on here?"

"I couldn't believe my eyes."

"Yes, he threw his drink at him, right in his face."

"He's a shit," Guy said. "He's the biggest shit in London."

"And you're a criminal psychopath and murderer," said Robin, holding one hand over his eyes. "Why don't you fuck off back to the slum you came from?"

●　　●　　●

Celeste drove them home. Guy sat beside her, nursing his bleeding face. He had been scratched on his right cheek, the right side of his upper lip, the left side of his chin, and on his neck.

"I shall probably get blood-poisoning. God knows what filthy bacteria a shit like that carries; listeria, hepatitis B, it could be anything."

"Silly Guy," said Celeste. "You're so silly. You can go to the doctor tomorrow. He'll never believe it was a fellow did it—you can say I did it, right?"

He didn't love her but he loved the way she talked, that accent. Rastafarian, that shit would call it. Tomorrow was "tomorr-*oh*" and doctor "d'ctah."

"Celeste, I want to tell you something."

It was dark inside the Jaguar. Darkness helped. He lit a cigarette. He would rather have died than tell Leonora about Con Mulvanney, but he was going to tell Celeste and tell her without many qualms, with hardly any inhibition. Was that because he didn't really care what she thought of him, whereas what Leonora thought of him was all-important? Was it because if she said as a result of what he told her that she no longer wanted to know him, he would be indifferent? Or something else altogether—that Celeste knew him for what he was and loved the man she knew, the real man; he had no need to pretend with her. Leonora, on the other hand, for all their long and close association, didn't really know him and he didn't want her to know him, he wanted her to keep her illusions about him.

"Go ahead, then," said Celeste.

He told her, he didn't conceal anything. It all came out—his doubt, his trepidation, his cowardice, his later awareness that someone had passed it on to Leonora. Rachel Lingard, he had thought it must be, but at the party he understood it wasn't. It was Robin Chisholm. At the time Robin had been living in Clapham, only half a mile away from Poppy Vasari.

"And that's why you threw your drink at him?"

The real reason had been because of Robin's racist remark directed at Celeste, but he wasn't going to say this. It might hurt her, besides showing him in a ridiculous chivalrous light. "More or less, yes."

"Guy, sweetheart, you are a bit crazy, do you know that? You are a bit obsessed with this thing about Leonora. Do you even know if someone told her? Have you asked her? No, because that would tell her the truth if she doesn't know it already. Don't you see this is all in your head, and your head is very strange these days, Guy, let me tell you."

"She changed towards me. Within two weeks of what happened to Con Mulvanney, she changed. She wouldn't go on holiday with me."

"She didn't want you to pay. She wouldn't go because of the strings attached, right? That was the only way she changed. Okay, so I'm not like that. A man want to pay for me, he can, he's welcome, I'm happy. If he want me to do things he want and I don't want and he come on strong, then I throw him out the window. I have not been going to T'ai Chi classes for five years for nothing, I can tell you."

Guy laughed in spite of himself. He glanced out of the car window but he knew where they were without looking. This was Balham Hill, and over there to the left was Clapham Common. Con Mulvanney country. He had a sensation as of it crossed with a million invisible wires, a network of transmission, each carrying whispers of his crimes and his culpability. Robin Chisholm's voice spoke to him again: *Psychopathic criminal and murderer.* How could Leonora's brother have known that those were the words to use unless he had been told the facts?

Celeste was driving them across the river by Battersea Bridge. "Sweet Guy," she said, "I don't want to hurt you." He smiled to himself. That made two of them, each not wanting to hurt the other. "But, Guy, isn't it most likely she changed because she was realizing you'd nothing to share any more? You're not the same kind of people. Even I can tell and I've only seen her once. Okay, so I'm biased, I'm jealous; it's true, I am. But that doesn't mean it's not the truth. She woke up, she got to understand."

"At that precise moment? That would make it the biggest coincidence of all time."

"Well, maybe it would, if you were lovers right up till then, if you were living together or sort of living together, like us, I mean, if you'd promised things and were going to make it permanent. Then it would be really strange. If it was *me* it would be really strange. But was it like that, Guy?"

He said nothing. He shrugged. It was she who didn't understand. The streets were dark but shiny with yellow light, the brassy light from lamps, a cold summer night, the cold small hours of a summer morning. The scratches on his face felt sore. He told her to leave the car in the street, not to put it away. A cat crouching on the opposite wall gave him a long inscrutable look from its light-filled, almost pupil-less yellow eyes. Perhaps it was a connoisseur of scratches. If people asked he would tell them he had been clawed by his neighbour's cat.

This was a night when he would have preferred not to have Celeste with him. It would be unthinkable to send her home. Poor thing, he thought, poor fellow-sufferer. And then anger filled him, anger against Rachel Lingard and those Chisholms, all the Chisholms. His fists clenched. Celeste went ahead of him upstairs, but not jauntily, not with any air of part-possession of the house, more as if she expected him to call her back, even send her away.

She sat on the Linnell bed, picking the gold tips off her plaits. "Guy," she said, "sweet Guy, was it just marijuana you dealt in, and maybe a bit of acid?"

How he would have seized this lifeline if Leonora had asked him! There was no point in prevaricating with Celeste. He didn't have to impress her. It wouldn't be true to say he didn't care what she thought of him, rather that he believed in her unqualified forgiveness. "The hard stuff too," he said. "Everything."

"Opium?"

"Heroin, yes. Heroin's opium, isn't it?"

How absurd that, after all these years and the fortune he had made, he still didn't quite know. Perhaps he hadn't wanted to know. She nodded, watching him.

"People don't come to any harm from the stuff itself," he said. "It's the related things—dirty needles, infection, unrestricted use. And it's no worse than being addicted to drink, only alcohol's socially acceptable. And as for dealers, you might as well condemn a wine merchant."

"I've a friend whose grandfather was Kurdish," she said. "He was an *aga*." She must have seen his incredulous smile starting. "No, that's not only a Swedish stove, it's a kind of feudal lord in parts of Turkey. They all grow poppies there, they make base morphine. It's what you do in that place, that part of Asia. It's funny what you say about the man and the bees because that's what they once did, kept bees, but now the smugglers pack the hives full of the drug.

"Her mother's family is very big. They have four laboratories processing morphine in the villages near Van. Her grandfather sent the young men away to learn the chemistry and two of her uncles got caught in Iran and executed. Thousands of smugglers and chemists get executed in Iran all the time."

"Why do they do it then?" he said hollowly.

"Poverty."

The word fell with a hollow sound. Poverty was a condition he had once known well, but the word itself was seldom heard in this house.

"You could say it's not all bad then, not if it creates employment."

She went on as if he hadn't spoken. "They don't use it themselves. No way. And there's no other work, not even in the fields. They don't have a choice about what they do. You can earn six thousand pounds taking a kilo of heroin to Istanbul, and much more per kilo if you're a chemist."

He had never heard her talk like this before, that serious tone, that articulate, almost authoritative manner replacing her usual lazy simple speech. It was more the way Leonora and her friends might talk.

"I expect it's much the same in South America," she said. "You may not die through using it, though you do, thousands do, but you sure do die getting it to the users." She said in a voice he'd never heard from her before, hard and clear and aimed straight at his guilt, his soft sensitivities: "Shame on you, Guy, shame on you."

He wasn't angry, he felt rather sick. It came to him that he had drunk a great deal, but the effects were only now becoming apparent. Not able to see very clearly, suffering a slight duplication of vision, he looked at the cuts on his face in the bathroom mirror—the deep scratch across his upper lip that would probably scar, the scorings on his throat. What kind of a man would scratch another man? Now that Guy thought of it, he remembered Robin had always worn his nails rather long, another unpleasant habit.

Celeste had got into bed and was lying with her arms over her head and her face in the pillow. He lay beside her, reached for the switch and turned out the light. The sudden darkness moved his memory. The last time they had had lunch together, he and Leonora, last Saturday, she had confessed to him she had been out with a friend of Robin's. Someone Robin had been in partnership with was one of the men between him, Guy, and William Newton. And there had been another man she had met at a party given by Robin. It wouldn't be going too far to say Robin had hated him so much that he had thrown one man after another in his sister's way. He had practically pimped for her. Guy heard himself make a sound, a kind of groan.

Celeste heard him too. She put her arms round him and held him close.

CHAPTER ELEVEN

Something Guy hadn't thought of on that night was that Leonora might be angry with him because he had given her brother a black eye. That he had done so he was certain. Robin Chisholm would have more explaining-away to do than he had. Guy's doctor had looked at the scratches and not believed the story of the cat. He had scarcely believed the true story of a fight with another man but he gave Guy an anti-tetanus injection.

Leonora was in Georgiana Street. He reached her there in the afternoon. Yes, she knew all about the fight; Robin had told Maeve on the phone that morning and Maeve had told her and then Robin himself had told her. Guy wasn't surprised. It just confirmed what he already knew of the closeness of that family and the influence each one of them exerted over the others. Robin was telling everyone how Guy had sprung upon him "like a madman" for no apparent reason, only he privately knew that the reason was his absurd obsession with Robin's sister.

"Not at all," Guy said coldly. "He insulted Celeste."

That interested her. "Did he? What did he say?"

Guy told her, not minding in the least that she knew he could be heroic and chivalrous. "Are you angry with me?"

"Not more than usual. I expect it was six of one and half a dozen of the other."

"Has Robin told you awful things about me?"

There was a hesitation. "When? D'you mean recently?"

He could hardly have asked for clearer confirmation. "Never mind," he said. "Where shall we have lunch on Saturday?"

Suppose she wouldn't because he had given her brother a black eye? The silence lasted about fifteen seconds but it was an hour to him. "You choose," she said. "I'm always choosing, it's time you did, especially as there won't be many more."

He winced at that. "We've got three more from now," he said. Hundreds more, he told himself stoutly, that wedding's a dream, it'll never happen. He said, making his voice light and teasing, "Come off it, sweetheart, you know you're not really getting married."

There was more silence. This time it really did last for nearly a minute. A click on the line made him think for an awful instant that she had rung off.

"Leo, are you still there?"

"I'm wondering," she said in a remote voice, "what to say. I don't know what to say to you when you talk like that. I suppose that if you want to live in a world of illusion, I just have to let you."

He let it pass, he even laughed, a knowing, sophisticated laugh. "Where shall we have lunch?"

"Come and have it with me in Portland Road."

"We wouldn't be alone."

"We aren't exactly alone in restaurants. Rachel's hardly ever there on Saturdays, and Maeve will go out with Robin. They always do."

"I'd love to," he said.

• • •

After the Drugs Squad had searched his house he had given up dealing. Well, he had phased it out. And it hadn't been altogether easy. He had been in actual danger. One of his suppliers had threatened him, if not with death, with some kind of attack, with spoiling his "handsome face." It was rubbish saying only women cared about their looks, he no more wanted to be scarred than a girl would. He had gone about in fear for a few weeks, had carried a gun. Nothing had in fact happened, and within six months he had given up all dealing. He never heard from the police again or from Poppy Vasari. No direct evidence came from Poppy or anyone else that she had carried out her threat and whispered everywhere his part in Con Mulvanney's death.

But in the ensuing months the Chisholms changed towards him. Leonora changed. He didn't care about the others, but Leonora was his life. First, she wouldn't go to Samos with him, then the other refusals began. Less and less would she go out with him in the evenings. Anthony became cold and distant. Now, when he looked back, he could remember Anthony's almost violent repudiation of the money he wanted to "lend" Leonora for that flat.

"You must see it's out of the question."

"It would be a loan," he had said. "She has to get a loan from somewhere. Why not me?"

"Are you seriously asking that?"

"Yes, of course I am. Why shouldn't I offer her an interest-free loan?"

"Because you're a man and she's a woman," Anthony had said roughly. "Good God, man, you're not a relation, you're not her brother or her cousin even. What kind of an obligation would that put her under?"

And Robin, at that time, in those months? The trouble was that Guy couldn't remember Robin at all that autumn and winter, apart from that remark about getting a lady in your power in one easy lesson. But he could imagine all too well the conversations between him and Poppy Vasari, the woman who was his neighbour in the block of flats by Clapham Common.

"Your sister's thinking of *marrying* him?"

Robin cocking his head on one side, his fair curls bobbing, his face winsome as a ten-year-old's. "That wouldn't be a good idea?"

"You won't ask that question when I've told you how he makes his living. I'd like to start by telling you what he did to my friend."

But if he gave Danilo three thousand pounds to dispose of Robin Chisholm—and he could imagine doing that, he could imagine not being too worried if the "disposal" was that far removed—it wouldn't undo the past. It wouldn't, at any rate, undo what Robin had told Leonora in that fateful August four years ago. Perhaps not, but it would prevent Robin's poisoning her mind against him now, and he had no doubt that was going on at present, all the time. How many more vile slanders had been repeated, for instance, during that phone conversation about Robin's black eye? And there was another aspect. If all else failed, there was no way Leonora was going to go through with her wedding on September 16 if her brother was killed two weeks before that date.

He was unpleasantly aware that he was no longer talking to Leonora every day. It was no longer possible to get hold of her every day. Living as she did for three or four days a week in Georgiana Street, she never answered the phone during the day. When he asked her why not she said it hadn't rung or she was out.

He could hear Robin saying, "Don't answer it, there's your remedy. Nothing will happen to you if you don't answer the phone, you know. There are no *penalties* attaching. There's no inquisitor going to get hold of you and have you up before the bench and make you say why you didn't answer the phone. Let me give you three little words on magnets to stick on the fridge: LET IT RING."

She could so easily. No one important would phone Newton

in the day. They knew he was at work. Few people knew she was there. If it rang it would be him, and however much she might want to speak to him, she could be made to believe it was wiser not to. Her family had her under their thumbs, under their five thumbs, six if you counted Rachel Lingard, and you almost had to, she and Leonora were so close, like sisters.

It was Friday when he phoned Danilo.

"No need to apologize," said Danilo. "These things happen in love and war."

Guy hadn't been going to apologize. He knew very well that the fight had considerably enlivened a flagging party and given guests a subject of conversation that would last for months.

"Tanya was upset, but she'll forgive you." Danilo laughed so loudly that the phone made a noise that hurt Guy's ear. "So what's with you then?"

"Dan," Guy said, "it's him, he's the one."

He felt a reluctance to speak an actual name. It had physical symptoms, a constriction of the throat, a whisper of nausea. Danilo was silent but his breathing was just audible, the faint small gasps a man makes before he sneezes. The sneeze didn't come but a snigger instead, very soft and breathy.

"How about my financial transactions?"

"There are other swap jockeys."

Danilo seemed not to be listening. He said, "It was a good party, wasn't it? We were lucky with the weather."

"Fuck the weather. Do you want the money now?"

"Of course I do. I trust you, but there are limits."

•　　•　　•

He had only twice been to Portland Road. The first time was soon after they moved in and he was invited and Rachel called him a Victorian. The next occasion was a house-warming party Leonora and Rachel and Maeve had given. They had been in the flat two or three months. By then he had lost his special place in Leonora's life. No one, least of all she herself, would have described him as her boy-friend. Nobody would have spoken of him to the Chisholms as the man "your sister" or "your daughter" was going to marry. She still sometimes went out with him. She had told him they ought to meet less often, they ought to "see."

A year and more was to pass before the coming of William Newton. Perhaps that was why, although he hated him, he didn't blame Newton for her defection. She had already, long since, allowed her family to persuade her he and she were unsuited. There was no man at the party for her but Guy himself, though Maeve had someone, Robin Chisholm's predecessor, and even Rachel had an owlish fellow in glasses. He tried to remember if Robin, on that occasion, had been particularly antagonistic or if Rachel had, but he could only recall the malicious false sweetness of Tessa who, encountering him for the first time since those loan-and-mortgage discussions, commented that she was surprised he wasn't married yet.

"I was sure you'd arrive with some glamorous creature in tow. I said so to Magnus, didn't I, Magnus? 'Guy Curran will turn up with some beauty from a TV commercial, I said.'"

The street was unchanged, the Prince of Wales still looking like a nice pub to take your girl for a pre-dinner drink. He could live here—give him half a chance! He hated the fantasies that came to him unbidden but he was often unable to control them. Now he imagined in spite of himself that he was buying one of these houses, the whole house, of course, because a miracle had happened, because Leonora said she had really loved him all along. She liked the area, she would want to stay. Dinner at Leith's, he thought, drinks first in the Prince of Wales, just he and she, dining out in the first week after they came back from their honeymoon. He'd have taken her to India, to Kashmir, Jaipur, Agra, and a week in the Maldives. Hand in hand, by moonlight, they would approach in awe that gleaming palace that was the Taj Mahal, turn to each other and kiss in the shadow of its shimmering walls.

The top bell had all three names on a card above it. Her

voice came out of the entry-phone, polite, hostessy, expressing pleasure that he was so early. The stair carpet was already
worn, the walls already marked. It was a long way up, too,
forty-two stairs. He counted. And when he considered what he
could give her . . . ! She need never climb stairs again so
long as she lived.

She was wearing a track suit. Gear for a day at home, no
doubt. It was dark blue and probably had looked all right until
the first time it was washed. Since then it had been washed
about five hundred times. He reminded himself that she didn't
dress up for Newton. It was a good sign, those dark blue pants
and top, bare feet and Dr. Scholl sandals. She could be relaxed
with him, she didn't have to bother.

"Fantastic earrings," he said.

She smiled, and about as widely as she ever did for him.
The earrings were cheap Indian things, he could tell that at
once, but pretty: white enamel daisies with yellow centres.
They nestled against the peach-pink lobes, the golden-brown
neck, like real flowers tucked through her ears.

He didn't know what he had expected of the flat, perhaps
that they might have done great things with it. But what could
be done with three bed-sits, a kitchen, and a tiny bathroom?
Posters and house-plants, things from the Reject shop and
things from the Indian shop. Fastidiously, he noted that it
wasn't even very clean, not the way his house was with Fatima
coming in four days a week. He stood about in the kitchen
while she opened packets from Marks and Spencers and cut up
a loaf from her favourite Cranks. After a while he lit a
cigarette.

"Do you mind, Guy? This flat is a smokeless zone."

"I don't believe it," he said.

"None of us smokes and we don't like the smell, so we
decided it was only sensible to have a total ban."

"Can I have a drink?"

"Oh, God, I'm sorry. I forgot. You should have asked
before. There's sherry up on the shelf there and white wine in
the fridge. It's in one of those box things, you turn the tap on."

They inhabited different worlds. It wasn't that she preferred her world, he thought, no one could. The point was that it was all she could afford and she was proud. The "box thing" had a printed pattern of vine leaves and grapes all over it. He turned the plastic tap and the pale yellow wine dribbled out. He hated sherry, so there wasn't much choice.

"If you have to have a cigarette, you can always go out on the balcony while I'm seeing to this."

It opened out of her bedroom. The bed was made but in the sort of way people do who only use a duvet and two pillows. He couldn't help asking himself how many times William Newton had shared it with her, perhaps even the previous night. The room had an air of having been hastily tidied. A drawer in a chest was stuffed too full to shut properly. One leg of a pair of green stockings hung out. There were books on the floor on one side of the bed, one of them lying open and face-downwards. The glass doors to the balcony were open. He went out, leaned on the iron rail and lit a fresh cigarette.

The roofs and spires of Notting Hill lay below him, the looped crescents and the great bow of Ladbroke Grove. Dusty trees made nests of dark green among the custard-coloured Victorian terraces, the new red blocks, the dove grey of stucco and the dark grey of stone. Yes, it would be right for them to live somewhere near here, in the place where they had been born, where they had first met, where their lives had been interlinked.

He felt a yearning nostalgia for it, as if he couldn't bear to be away another instant. To return to South Kensington would be like going into exile. Why hadn't he come to live on her doorstep, sold his house and bought another here, so that he would see her every day and she him?

He would find a pretty house. There were plenty on the market, estate agents' windows were full of them. With prices falling, a million would buy a little dream at the "best end" of the Grove. Lansdowne Crescent perhaps or some other street among those concentric circles of faintly shabby elegance. He imagined her furnishing it. He would come home for lunch and find her sitting on the floor among carpet samples and books of fabric and books of wallpaper, some poofy interior designer nodding and smiling, suggesting this and that while she concentrated, her face wearing that grave frown . . .

"Lunch is ready, Guy," she said behind him.

He surfaced. It was like emerging from a warm scented bath in which one has fallen half-asleep. Awakening from these dreams brought him a sharp unhappiness, but still he couldn't stop them or even control them. He followed her through the room, carrying his empty glass and his pinched-out cigarette end.

She had laid the tiny table in the kitchen. He sat squashed up against the side of the fridge. The wine box was on the table next to a carton of orange juice and, between two plates, pastrami and salad for him, cheese and salad for her. He longed for a cigarette, and in spite of being there alone with her, having achieved, if temporarily, what was the summation of all his wishes, he felt his temper rising. It was her pride he was fighting, he thought, the arrogance that made her stoutly endure this poky dirty kitchen, eschew decent food, deny herself good clothes.

"Do you remember saying you'd share my house with me when we got married?" he said.

"No, I don't remember."

"It was a long time ago. Nine years. It was when you first came to the house."

"Yes, I remember, but I don't think I said that."

"All right. Do you remember saying 'I *am* Guy and you are Leonora'?"

"Oh, Guy, probably. I was a child. I did *Wuthering Heights* for O Levels."

"What's that got to do with it?"

She was eating bread and cheese, putting up a pretence of enjoying it more than all the delicate food he offered her. "It's a book," she said kindly. "The girl in it talks like that—well, she says, 'I am Heathcliff.'"

He shook his head impatiently. "I don't understand why

133

people want to be always saying things out of books. Surely life's more important."

"Sometimes things in books apply to life."

He didn't understand and her laughter irritated him, making him angrier. He said in an abrupt change of subject, "Do you think what your brother does for a living is exactly what you'd call pure and ethical?"

"What?"

"Swapping sums of money. He must be contravening currency regulations all the time."

She got up to take away their plates, took Greek yoghurt and a dish of stewed dried fruit out of the fridge. "I'm not responsible for what Robin does for a living or what anyone else does, come to that. It's nothing to do with me. I'm only responsible for what I do—oh, and maybe what William does."

Greatly daring, "Does that apply to me too?" he said.

"I'm not responsible for you, Guy, or what you do. I've told you before, I know how you make a living and I don't care for it, but it's not my business. Except, well . . ." He saw her face change. She laid down her spoon. "I suppose I really ought not to let you buy meals for me if I don't approve of the source of your income."

"Oh, for Christ's sake!" He pushed the yoghurt away from him. "I can't eat this muck, Leonora. It's like being at the fucking Festival of Mind, Body and Spirit. I can't eat fermented sheep milk." He took out a cigarette without thinking, saw her eyes on it, crushed it in his palm, his anger boiling. "Who does bloody Robin think he is, telling tales of me? It's not as if his own hands are clean. He's lucky not to be in jail."

She said, "Guy, I really don't know what you're on about and I don't think you do." She was filling the kettle, bent on making filthy instant coffee, he thought. "Do you know anything about nervous breakdowns?" she said.

"What?"

"Nervous—mental—breakdowns. People do have them,

you know. It's when everything gets too much for them and they lose their hold on reality and can't cope—all that sort of thing. Only, Guy, I think you're having one. Well, I think you're going to have one if you aren't careful."

That made the second woman this week to tell him he was going mad. He hoped the look he was levelling at her, patient, controlled, bored, though with seething undercurrents, would silence her, maybe make her say she was sorry.

With near disbelief he heard her say, "Guy, William's got a friend he was at university with who does Jungian therapy, he's very good." Mercifully, she was interrupted before she had said more than, "If you'd just think of seeing . . ."

The kitchen door opened and a tall, thin, almost unrecognizable blond girl came in. Her face was white, her eyes glazed. Pausing in the doorway, holding the handle, swaying a little, she started past them. Guy thought she was drunk and silently cursed this unexpected interruption.

Leonora jumped up in consternation.

"Maeve, what is it?"

"Robin . . . It's Robin, he's been in an accident."

CHAPTER TWELVE

Robin Chisholm wasn't dead or even badly injured. Guy felt angry with Maeve for causing Leonora unnecessary anxiety. The woman made a drama out of everything. No doubt going in the ambulance to hospital with him and seeing him taken off for a brain scan had made her hysterical. But as far as Guy could tell, Robin had simply got a mild concussion and a few cuts and bruises. To add to that black eye, he thought.

She had told her tale after Leonora had ministered to her with an aspirin and a glass of the stuff he wouldn't dignify with the name of wine that came out of that cardboard box.

"We were coming out of the park, you know that bit where the roads sort of meet and come out into the Bayswater Road and there are lights and everything, where the Royal Lancaster is. I don't know what you call it."

"The Victoria Gate," said Guy.

She took no notice of him. She hadn't since she came in. He might as well not have been there, except that it wasn't natural, when talking, to avoid ever looking to the right side of the room. She kept her head turned away the way she might if there were vomit on the floor.

"Well, we were coming from the Kensington Gardens side, we were going to go in the Swan for a drink. You know it's always dicey crossing the road there because the traffic tears round the—is it called the Ring? So we were very very careful but naturally looking to the right, if you see what I mean, we didn't think the left mattered on account of the lights being red and nothing being there anyway. And then it happened. This car came tearing out of whatever that road's called by the side of Hyde Park Gardens . . ."

"Brook Street," said Guy, expecting no acknowledgement and getting none.

"Robin had gone over ahead of me. My shoe-lace was undone. I was bending down doing up my shoe-lace, only he didn't realize and he'd gone on over. This car came tearing out of nowhere—well, out of"—she looked at him at last—"Brook Street, I suppose, right through the red light; the lights might not have been there for all the notice he took. Thank God Robin's pretty quick on his feet and I saw and I yelled. I screamed out, 'Robin! Look out!' The car hit him, but only a glancing blow. It didn't hit his head, he hit his head on a lamp-post.

"There are never any police about when you want them, are there? A great crowd gathered, though, you can always depend on that. I wasn't in shock then, the shock didn't hit me for about an hour—well, it doesn't, does it? Most of the people came there just to gawp and get the maximum thrill—you know the type—but there was one man with a bit of sense who phoned for an ambulance. The ambulance man asked me if I got the number of the car but of course I hadn't, you have other things to think about at a time like that."

Guy felt a certain relief, though Danilo's hit man would certainly have used fake registration plates. A failure but a brave attempt. Better luck next time. Maeve at any rate had no suspicion, as far as he could tell, that the incident in the park had been any more than the result of a piece of reckless driving. What Guy would have liked to say was that it served Robin right for having the bad manners to go across a fairly dangerous street on his own, leaving his girl-friend on the pavement tying up her shoe-lace, but he thought better of it. Leonora seemed both upset and relieved, Maeve much restored by having told her tale and got it off her chest.

"Is there anything to eat?" she said. "We never got around to lunch, as you can imagine."

If only Leonora had chosen that moment to go to the bathroom or something, he could have said what he wanted to, something on the lines of, "Oh, really, how amazing, I'd have expected them to be serving caviar and blinis in the ambulance," or, "You mean you never went to the dear old Swan after all?" But Leonora stayed, dispensing extravagant sympathy and a pastrami sandwich.

Fortified, Maeve gave a deep sigh, helped herself to more from the vine-patterned box. Her face had grown pinker; she was really a very pretty girl, if you could use that word about someone so statuesque, with such flashing blue eyes and so much lion's-mane hair. Guy was just thinking that her legs were the same sort of length as another girl's height, when she turned to him and said with the utmost venom,

"It's all thanks to you. If you hadn't *bludgeoned* him he'd have had a better idea of what he was doing. He was half-blinded, do you know that? He's been having the most crushing headaches. If anything shows up on the brain scan it's just as likely to be through you."

Guy's reply was to extend his neck and turn his face from side to side so that she could see the deep scratch marks, which, though healing, looked rather worse than they had immediately after Robin had inflicted them.

She said with a light scathing laugh, "Oh, I've no doubt he had to defend himself."

"Yes, like a fucking tom-cat," said Guy, he couldn't help himself. "They do tend to get run over in the Bayswater Road."

Both girls were on him for that. How could he? How could

he talk like that? When poor Robin was lying in a hospital bed, when he might have some serious injury. Hadn't he any ordinary human feelings?

"Haven't you any affect?" said Maeve incomprehensibly.

He apologized to Leonora, who said that that was all right, but perhaps he had better go now. She would have to phone her parents. Perhaps she would go to the hospital to see Robin, she and her mother would go together. It pleased Guy that there had been no mention of the ginger dwarf in all this. He, it appeared, was quickly forgotten. If only Maeve had taken herself off after the announcement had been made, he was sure Leonora would have come running into his arms for comfort. When the story was being told, at one point she had actually rested her hand on his shoulder, as on the natural place to steady herself. He must, ideally, try to be with her when the news ultimately came of Robin's death, as in a day or too it must.

Next day, as usual, he phoned her. She was at home. That in itself was good, was reassuring. You would expect her to run to the man she talked of marrying but she hadn't done that, she had stayed at home. He had no qualms about ingratiating himself with her.

"How is Robin?"

"Do you care?"

"Leo, of course I care. Just because we had a bit of a disagreement when we were both pissed—I mean, for God's sake. Men do fight, it's the way they are, you have to accept that." Did they? Not in her world perhaps. "It doesn't mean I'd bear a grudge, no way."

"I suppose I don't really understand. It's not just me as a woman. William wouldn't either." His heart dropped. His heart was a small cold stone dropping through him. "Robin's okay," she said. "They're keeping him in till tomorrow. It isn't just the accident. They're harking back a bit to that trouble he had four years ago—you know, when he was in hospital all those weeks?"

It had been around the time she had changed her mind about

139

going to Samos with him. Weeks had gone by and she had been cold to him and he angry with her. But he seemed to remember some trouble of Robin Chisholm's—headaches, dizziness, suspected epilepsy. Of course, it ultimately turned out there was nothing wrong with him.

"It so happens it was exactly four years ago," Leonora said. "Well, he must have gone into hospital the first week of August and he stayed there till nearly the end of September. I don't see how that could affect him now, do you, Guy?"

Guy said no, he didn't think so, and especially (trying to keep the sarcasm out of his voice) since all the tests that first time had been negative. Was Maeve feeling better?

"She's in a really bad nervous state, Guy." He loved the way she kept calling him by his Christian name in that confiding way. "It must have been an awful shock. I think she's very much in love with Robin."

Too bad, thought Guy. She'll just have to bear it when her love comes to nothing. I'm very much in love and who gives a shit about me? Something was bothering him, something about Robin Chisholm, though he couldn't think what it was. Often these days he experienced this fuzziness, a cutting off, almost. To call it confusion was too strong, it wasn't as bad as that.

"Will you have dinner with me tonight?" he said.

"No, Guy, dear, I never do. You know that."

"No one need know, Leo. I'll be very discreet about it. They needn't know."

"Who's 'they'?"

He expressed it carefully. "Your family. The people who're close to you."

She was silent. When she spoke she sounded distressed. How is it that you can love someone and yet be *glad* when they're distressed? "Oh, Guy, how I wish . . . It's no use. Phone me tomorrow," she said.

His heart, which seemed to have shrivelled to the size of a pea, was suddenly huge, was swollen and soft and palpitating.

She had sounded as if she was going to cry. And over him. *She had been moved to tears by him.*

"Darling Leonora, have dinner with me tomorrow, any day, you name the day. Or I'll come over. Shall I come now?"

"No, Guy, of course not."

"Then let's meet tomorrow."

"We'll have lunch on Saturday," she said. "Goodbye." The phone went down before he could protest.

When he dialled her number next morning he still hadn't been able to identify what was haunting him, what unease lay just below the surface of his consciousness. He had had a curious dream. He was an observer, watching but invisible, at a meeting of the residents' association of a block of flats in Battersea Park. This mansion block was in fact where no buildings could be, in the centre of the Pleasure Gardens, overlooking the pier. The residents included Rachel Lingard, Robin Chisholm, and Poppy Vasari. They were discussing applications from people who wanted to come and live in the flats. One was from himself. Rachel read his letter and read out his name.

"Guy Patrick Curran, 8 Scarsdale Mews, W.8."

Dreams were strange because that wasn't quite his address. His address was 7 Scarsdale Mews. Robin Chisholm said nothing. He spat. He spat the way he had after Guy had hit him at Danilo's party.

Poppy Vasari, who was even dirtier and more unkempt than in reality, said, "We don't want him. He's a murderer. He murdered my lover with a substance classified Class A under the Misuse of Drugs Act, 1971."

After that Guy wanted to leave. Even though they couldn't see him he wanted to escape. Knowing he was dreaming, that this was dream substance and dream time, he began willing himself to wake up. Before he did, a man he didn't know and had never seen before got to his feet and began to sing a song about opium. He sang that opium poppies first grew on the spot where Buddha's eyelids fell when he cut them off to stop

141

himself from falling asleep. Guy woke up shouting and groaning.

He tried to phone Leonora at ten in the morning. There was no answer. He made a second attempt at just before eleven and got Rachel Lingard.

"You get a lot of holidays in the Social Services."

She had an accent like the head of a women's college at Oxford making a television appearance. "I'm not on holiday. I'm at home in bed with a bug. You got me up."

Guy restrained an impulse to say that was the only thing she was ever likely to be in bed with. It wouldn't be true anyway. Even the plainest, most repulsive girls got men these days. He didn't know why, but it was so. Rachel had never been without a man all the time he had known her, she always had some bearded or spotty-faced intellectual in tow.

"Where's Leonora?"

"I don't know. I was told to say if you rang that Robin is better and coming out today."

"Well, fuck him. When you were 'told' that, where were you 'told' she'd be?"

"Please don't take that hectoring tone with me. And you can leave out the 'fuck,' it's offensive. I get quite enough of that from the low-life I encounter at work. Perhaps you'd like to get this clear: I don't know where Leonora is because, knowing you'd ask, I was careful not to ask her. I'm not lying to you, I don't tell lies. Do I make myself plain?"

"You don't need to, my love," said Guy, knowing he would regret it. "Nature did that for you." He slammed down the phone.

He dialled William Newton's number. The line was engaged. That would be Rachel ringing Leonora to repeat to her what he had said. Anger began to rise inside him in that uncontrollable way it had. It was happening all the time these days. It would start in the way nausea started, a stifling feeling that worked its way up to his throat where it settled and needed not to be vomited but screamed out. Only he had never yet screamed it out. He walked across the room to the open double doors. It was sunny again, it was like being in Spain or Italy. The flowers on the water-lilies in the pool were all open to the sun. He turned back, picked up the Chinese vase that stood on the red lacquer cabinet just inside the doors, and smashed it down onto the stone flags.

The shattering of the vase had an effect on him, if not quite the one he had aimed at. Certainly his anger was temporarily appeased, it had done that. It awed him, too, and brought him a kind of fear of himself. Why had he done it and without thought? He had simply done it, on an impulse.

It was August Bank Holiday Monday, so not one of Fatima's days. He kicked the fragments, pushing them into a heap with his toe. The vase was *famille noire,* cherry blossom and linnets on a black glaze, worth about fifteen hundred pounds. Thinking of that made him shudder. He lifted the phone, dialed William Newton's number and got no reply. If he stayed there any longer he might break the place up, that was the way he felt, so he took a taxi to the rifle club and practised target shooting. Gladiators after that, the weights and some acrobatics on the parallel bars. He weighed himself and found he had lost those two pounds plus three more. In the steam room a gay Norwegian eyed him lustfully. What wouldn't he give for Leonora to look at him like that?

He tried her again in the afternoon. There was still no answer. Suppose he couldn't get through to her all the week? They hadn't yet named a restaurant for their Saturday lunch date. Suppose he couldn't get in touch with her, what would happen to their Saturday lunch? Most likely she had gone to Robin's. She and Maeve would have gone to Robin's to be there when he came back from the hospital. Guy started looking up Robin's number in the phone book.

It wasn't there. No Robin Chisholm was listed anywhere in Battersea. Then he realized that of course Robin didn't live in Battersea any more, he lived in Chelsea. He realized a few more things with startling suddenness. Why was he so confused these days? Why had he been telling himself for days now that Poppy Vasari had lived in the same block of flats as

Robin when it was not she but *Danilo's sister-in-law* who had lived there? And wasn't there something else he hadn't thought of which was now staring him in the face?

Robin *couldn't* have been told about Con Mulvanney by Poppy or anyone else in August four years ago because he was in hospital undergoing those brain tests. He couldn't have been told, and he couldn't have passed that information on to Leonora. He wasn't there. Leonora must have known about Con Mulvanney two weeks before they were due to go to Samos because that was when she had changed towards him, but it wasn't Robin who had told her. Robin was shut up in Barts or St. Thomas's or somewhere, interested no doubt in nothing but the fate of his own head.

Guy had a quick image of a white-coated surgeon bending over Robin's bed and applying a scalpel to his throat instead of a stethoscope, or of an armoured truck ramming the taxi that was taking him home to Chelsea, of two hooded men with sub-machine-guns jumping out of the back of it. He reminded himself he wasn't living in a TV thriller and went back to the phone book. Chelsea. There it was: St. Leonard's Terrace, a very nice address. He must be doing well. Guy dialled the number. He wouldn't have been surprised not to get a reply, but Maeve answered.

"Yes? Who is it?"

What a way to answer the phone! For the first time he noticed her rather "common" voice, more akin to his own than to Robin's patrician accent.

"It's Guy, Maeve. I just wanted to ask how Robin is."

She was stunned into silence, as well she might be. Then she said in a tone in which suspicion seemed to war with a willingness to live and let live, "He's really quite okay." Evidently thinking furiously, she paused. "Thanks, Guy. I mean, well, thanks."

"I'm glad to hear he's doing all right."

For a moment he thought she was going to ask if he was kidding. She didn't. "They're very pleased with him. There won't be any, you know, ill effects or whatever from the concussion."

"You tell him to take care."

This was the true purpose of his call. "I shouldn't let him go out again today. Keep him quiet." He nearly said, *Don't answer the door*. She would think him crazy. "Say hello to him for me, will you?"

"Sure, I will, yes, Guy, thanks."

He hesitated. "Is Leonora there?"

"No, she's not." The former tone, surprised, gratified, touched, had changed to Maeve's aggressive voice. "Why ever would she be? Of course she's not. Is that the real reason you rang?"

He said goodbye. He tried to phone Danilo. This was never easy, as it was always possible for Danilo to be in any of about ten different places—clubs, two Soho offices, his old dad's place, one of the establishments of his brother the turf accountant, or at a race meeting. Five attempts having failed, he got Tanya at her Richmond boutique. Danilo was in Brussels, she didn't say why; he would be back tomorrow very late in the evening.

Guy was by now almost certain it was Rachel Lingard and not Robin who had told Leonora about Con Mulvanney. That is, he was certain it wasn't Robin and not quite sure about Rachel—nearly sure but not absolutely. Removing Rachel from Leonora's immediate circle would in any case be a good thing. He wished he could, with a word or by the pressure of a switch, divert Danilo's hit squad from Robin to Rachel. He really didn't wish for Robin's death any longer, it would be inconvenient, it would be *unnecessary*.

He poured himself a drink, the first of the day, a very strong Campari orange, three quarters Campari and about a spoonful of orange juice. As he was dialling Newton's number the doorbell rang.

Guy's doorbell hardly ever rang unless someone was expected. Celeste had a modelling job out at Totteridge, it couldn't be her. Anyway, she had a key. Listening to the phone ringing on and on, in an empty place unanswered, he thought: it's Leonora. He put the phone down. Of course it was Leonora—what could be more likely? On the phone the day before he had felt her changing, returning to him, her better instincts taking over, all that perverse stubbornness of the past years faded, gone.

"Oh, Guy, how I wish . . ." she had said. Wished what? That she could bring herself to swallow her pride, of course, to come back to him and be as they once were.

The bell rang again. He set his drink down. A second thought made him thrust it behind a vase. He must not die of happiness when she came into his arms . . . It was all he could do not to run to the door. He strode there, threw it open, already smiling a delighted welcome.

On the doorstep stood Tessa Mandeville.

CHAPTER THIRTEEN

"Can I come in?"

His disappointment was so terrible—worse, he thought, than on that day four years before when Leonora had said she wasn't coming to Samos with him—that he couldn't have spoken to her. He was quite dumb, staring like a fool, yet seeing her only through a haze. Unable even to answer her, he stood there while she pushed past him into the hall.

At any other time, he would have been gleefully proud of showing off his house to one of the members of Leonora's family. None of them had ever been there. Well aware of the suburban Victoriana in which Tessa herself lived, he would have taken great pleasure in watching her note the evidences of his wealth—the carpets, the antiques, the Kandinski. She, of all people, would very likely know it *was* a Kandinski. But as it was, he cared not at all. He followed her silently into the drawing-room.

She was dressed, as usual, very smartly. She had on a tobacco-brown linen dress which, though waistless and quite straight, could only have been worn by a very thin woman. To the hot weather she made few concessions, wore shoes the colour of polished acorns and stockings patterned with sprays of leaves. More lines had appeared on her face since last he saw her. She had a young woman's shape and legs and hair and a wizened face with lines as deep as scars. Her fingernails were painted the colour of a copper kettle in an antique shop.

"It's quite brave of me to come here alone, isn't it?" she said.

He found his voice. It came out like a sigh. "Brave?"

"Though I'm warning you, at least half a dozen people know where I am. In case you want to try anything, you won't get away with it."

"Don't be ridiculous," he said.

"You persecute my daughter, you beat up my son, you attempt to run my son over in a car . . ."

He was indignant at the unfairness of that. "I was having lunch with Leonora when that accident happened, I was in her flat." Then he realized there was in fact nothing unjust in her accusation. "Tessa, I went to Leonora's in a taxi. Anyway, I wasn't anywhere near Lancaster Gate. You can't believe I'd . . ."

"Can't I? It's funny you knew all about it. Maeve said you corrected her, you told her exactly where it had happened. You kept on saying things like 'Brook Street' and 'Victoria Gate' as if you'd been there. I think you're mad. All you want is to wipe out the people who're close to my daughter, kill them or disable them. I should never have let her have anything to do with you, I blame myself for that. I should have put my foot down all those years ago. You'll do some harm to William next. I know what you're up to, I know everything. I saw you parked outside my house that time in that flashy car of yours."

There was an uncanny accuracy in what she said. She was quite close to the truth. He moved away from her, opened the French windows. He no more fancied being closeted in here with her than she did with him. The heat came in, the scent of his climbing rose. He saw the pile of broken china still on the paving stones and she saw it too.

"Been smashing the place up, have you?"

"What did you come here for, Tessa?"

He hadn't asked her to sit down but she did. Probably his calmness, his air of indifference, had reassured her he meant to do her no harm. She stared at him without speaking. He picked up his drink and, aware of the absurdity of it, asked her if she would like one.

"Of course I don't want a drink!" She almost spat the words.

"What *do* you want then?"

"To tell you this. First of all, my husband will get a court order to stop you molesting Leonora if you don't leave her alone from this moment. Is that clear? Secondly, Leonora is getting married on September the sixteenth. At twelve noon at Kensington Register Office. I'm here to give you a very serious warning, very serious indeed, not to start anything on that occasion. Right?"

"What would I start?" he said, very nearly amused by her. She was a figure of fun, glaring at him like that, long bony fingers with those copper-kettle nails clasping exposed polished knees. The intensity of her frown contorted her face grotesquely.

"Anything, I don't know, a—a ruckus! You're quite capable of turning up there and shouting things—well, forbidding the banns or something."

"They don't have banns," he said, though uncertain what banns were.

"You're capable of attacking William, grabbing my daughter—oh, anything! Shouting that you've got some insane prior claim on her."

"So I have."

"So you have not, Guy Curran! How dare you speak like that! She loves William and he loves her and they're going to be tremendously happy. I will not have a clod like you, a common piece of rubbish from a council house, from the worst part of London, interfering with my daughter!"

Anger began to well up inside him. Her snobbery had cut

149

into him where her threats never could. He would have liked to tell her this was his house and to get out of it, not to speak like that to him in his house, but he thought of Leonora, of all this getting back to Leonora. It was bad enough, the way he had insulted Rachel, or she would think so. He must stay calm. With extreme controlled calmness he said, "She isn't going to marry him. She'll never marry him."

Tessa Mandeville went quite white. "You filthy drug-trafficker," she said. "Oh, yes, you can look like that. I tell you, I know everything about you. A very good friend of Leonora's told me all about your drug peddling, ruining young people's lives, giving their parents a hell on earth."

"What friend?" he said.

"Oh, yes, I'm likely to tell you, aren't I? So that you can go and beat them up, I suppose. A good friend, that's all I'm saying. Someone who's been a better friend to Leonora than you ever could be."

He said, "I don't want to put you out of here, Tessa. You're Leonora's mother and I can't forget that. I'm going upstairs and while I'm away perhaps you'll go."

It was to be alone really, not just to get away from her. So he had been right about Rachel. It was Rachel who had done and who was doing all the damage, Rachel who was probably with Leonora even at this moment, feeding her poison. Leonora had been more gentle with him, more loving, that day than at any time he could remember since she moved into the flat. True, it had been on the phone. But Saturday it hadn't been on the phone. "Oh, Guy, how I wish . . ." What had she been going to say? *How I wish we could be as we once were? How I wish I'd never met William?*

Now, though, she would be back home with Rachel, sick, bed-bound Rachel. He could imagine her sitting on the side of Rachel's bed and Rachel repeating what he had said to her, adding, "What can you expect from low-life like that?"

Downstairs he heard Tessa's footsteps. They stopped. She had paused. Of course. She had stopped in front of the Kandinski, was taking it in, valuing it. The footsteps started again, the front door closed hard if not quite with a bang. He went into his bedroom and watched her from the window. She was going in the Marloes Road direction, looking for a taxi. He hoped she wouldn't get one, she probably wouldn't, not at this hour.

So it was Rachel. The connection must have been the one he first thought of, through the social work she and Poppy Vasari had in common. He went downstairs and was starting to dial one of the numbers he had for Danilo when he remembered what Tanya had told him, that Danilo was in Brussels. It slightly troubled him that he was as yet unable to call off the dogs that menaced Robin Chisholm, but there seemed nothing to be done about this.

Something was puzzling him and continued to do so on and off throughout the night. Dining with Celeste at the Pomme d'Amour, meeting Bob Joseph afterwards for a drink at the club in Noel Street, his mind kept reverting to Tessa Mandeville and the things she had said. What had she really come for?

That was all rubbish about getting a court order preventing him from "molesting" Leonora. How could you molest someone when she wanted your company? It was Leonora herself who, three and a half years before, had made that arrangement to lunch with him on Saturdays. When Rachel and the rest of them no doubt had persuaded her to stop going out with him in any real sense, to stop being his girl-friend, she had proposed the regular Saturday meetings. Leonora wanted those lunch dates as much as he did, that was certain. She wanted him to phone her. Hadn't she said when he left her on Saturday, "Phone me tomorrow"?

So Tessa hadn't really meant that at all. That was just a cover for something else. What she had come for was ostensibly to stop him from making some sort of scene at Leonora's wedding but really to *tell him where Leonora's wedding would be,* a venue he knew quite well already. He was suspicious of them all and now he was even more suspicious of Tessa. What was she up to? Why come all that

151

way, visit him at home as she had never done before, just to tell him that?

Then he understood. He nearly laughed out loud, there in front of Celeste. The woman had told him Kensington Register Office because it wasn't going to be there at all. It was going to be at the Camden Register Office, which was at King's Cross, and in Newton's borough. You could get married in your own borough or that of the person you were marrying, it was matter of choice. She had told him Kensington in case he decided to go along. The woman was so transparent it was really quite funny.

Not that it mattered. Leonora wouldn't get married. She wouldn't *want* to get married. He heard her voice again and the tone seemed infinitely soft and yearning as she expressed her wish for what might have been. "Guy, dear," she had called him when she had explained she couldn't dine with him. They probably threatened her with all kinds of things when she told them she was thinking of going back to him. Rachel, for instance, who was buying Leonora's share of the flat from her—Rachel had very likely told her the deal would be off if she persisted in having any further to do with him. Anthony Chisholm was capable of cutting her out of his will or at least of stopping any money he might be making over to her.

"Guy, sweet," said Celeste, "a penny for your thoughts."

He told her about Tessa's visit. Her face clouded over. She said nothing. "I've got a headache," he said. "I usually have these days. D'you think it's being angry most of the time?"

She went home with him. "You have to accept it," she said gently. "Sooner or later you have to accept she's going to marry William."

"You'd like that, wouldn't you?"

She knelt on the paving, picking up the pieces of broken vase. He wished he hadn't said what he had said, but she didn't reply. Danilo would be back tomorrow night, he'd keep on trying to phone him from ten onwards. Probably, to compensate for all the trouble he was causing, he'd have to give Danilo another fifteen hundred, but who cared?

Celeste said, "Buy her a really nice wedding present, why don't you?"

She was never bitchy, but this time . . . ? Surely she didn't mean it seriously? He poured himself a last drink, vodka on the rocks, realizing as he did so that he had been drinking non-stop since the Campari orange he had when Tessa came at five.

In the morning, while Celeste was still asleep, he phoned the flat in Portland Road. Maeve answered. She was about to leave for work. He didn't ask for Leonora, not immediately.

"How's Robin?" He really wanted to know. Worrying about Danilo's hitman getting at Robin had kept him awake most of the night.

"He's fine," she said. But did she know? Had he just been fine when she left him the night before?

"You've spoken to him this morning?"

"Just now, Guy."

Oh, the relief! It wasn't that he cared about Robin Chisholm's fate but he realized, after that black eye and what Tessa had said, that Leonora might so easily blame him for any harm that came to her brother.

"He rang me. He'd had such a super sleep, he was feeling really refreshed, you know, he sounded on top of the world. Isn't that great?"

Guy said it was and could he speak to Leonora?

"She isn't here, Guy. She's at William's."

He phoned the Georgiana Street number. It was early, of course, it wasn't yet nine, but he was still surprised to hear Newton's voice—no, more than that, astounded, thrown. He nearly put the receiver down. Instead he said, "It's Guy Curran."

"Oh, hallo." It wasn't said in a friendly way. But Guy would have despised the man even more than he already did if he had spoken in a hearty or ingratiating manner.

"How're *you?*" he said in his best transatlantic style, but coldly.

"I'm extremely well and I hope you are. Now, what can I do for you?"

"I'd like to speak to Leonora."

Most people, before imparting unwelcome information, say that they are afraid. "I'm afraid I've something rather unpleasant to tell you . . ." Newton didn't do that and Guy noticed.

"She's not here."

"Now come on," said Guy, the ready anger rising. "I've just been told less than five minutes ago that's she's with you."

The man sounded bored, still within the limits of patience. "Less than five minutes ago she was. Two minutes ago she went out. Would you like me to tell you where?"

"Of course I would. Where is she?"

"At her father's. Susannah's mother has died and Leonora has gone with her to see to things, register the death and see undertakers. I've now told you all I know, so if you'll excuse me, I'll ring off as I'm already late. Goodbye."

He had no idea where Susannah's mother had lived, had barely known Susannah had a mother. Hopeless to try and find them, hopeless to pursue that inviting image of himself sitting in a waiting room with Leonora, talking to her softly, then taking the two of them out to a wonderful lunch somewhere. A comfort for Susannah, whom he had never disliked, take her mind off her mother, whom she had probably been fond of. He would have to catch Leonora later in Lamb's Conduit Street.

He took a cup of tea up to Celeste. "Thank you, sweet Guy," she said.

She opened her eyes and then she put out her arms to him. It was weeks since he had made love to her. Sexual desire seemed to have been drained out of him by all that had happened, by fear and anger. But he bent down and let her hug him. She was warm and sweet and she felt silky to touch. He lay down beside her and held her, not realizing how very hard he must have clutched her until she struggled and freed her nose and mouth from the pressure of his face, until she gasped, "No, Guy, you're hurting!"

While she was in the bath he called Anthony Chisholm's number. The line was engaged. Five minutes later it was still engaged. He got the operator to check it, was told the number was indeed engaged speaking, and decided to give up until the afternoon. Fatima arrived as he was leaving the house. She made a noise like a distressed hen-bird with a lost chick when she saw the black-and-pink shards. Guy got his car out. He was going to Northolt to the studio, then to make a check on a picture sale at a motorway hotel at the start of the M.1. Backing the car across the cobbled mews, driving slowly down towards the Earl's Court Road, he wondered if perhaps he had outgrown his house. In his position he was past the little mews-house stage. After all, he would be thirty in January. A house in Lansdowne Crescent or maybe even something in the neighbourhood of Campden Hill, Duchess of Bedford Walk . . . . Would Leonora mind being that side, the *good* side, of Holland Park Avenue?

Carry On, Kittens did better in Barnet than even *Lady from Thailand*. The woman who was running the sale and with whom he had a nasty lunch in the motel dining room (oval plates piled with gristle-bound blackened steak, tinned peas, tomato halves, chips, mushrooms as slimy as slugs, and broccoli spears like toy farmyard trees) told him she could sell twice, three times, as many. Guy undertook to provide that number. On the motel phone he tried to call Lamb's Conduit Street and failed but succeeded in getting Tanya at her boutique. Danilo was expected home in the late evening, certainly by eleven.

Guy had a ferociously unpleasant image of Robin Chisholm pressing the button on his entry-phone, opening the door in his towelling robe to the man who had come to mend something or read some meter. The silenced gun or cosh, or, if Danilo's "help" was being really vicious these days, the thin swift stiletto.

He drove to the travel agent's. Business was booming there too. In the office at the back he phoned the flat in St. Leonard's Terrace. There wasn't going to be an answer, the bell rang and rang, ten times, fifteen. He put the receiver back and redialled. This time Robin's voice answered after four rings. Probably he'd misdialled that first time. It was a great relief to hear Robin saying, "Hallo, hallo?" with increasing irritability.

They buoyed him up wonderfully, the considerable and varied successes of the day. Things hadn't gone so well for a long time. Going home, even going to the West End, it would have been usual to take a route north of Regent's Park, but he found himself approaching the Euston Road. Across Tavistock Place, into Guilford Street, and Lamb's Conduit was just down there . . . He wasn't supposed to see her except on Saturdays, except for Saturday lunch, but—well, come *on*. She wanted to see him. Hadn't she said how much she wished they could be together again?

It was hot, the still, yellow heat of London in sunshine. Any place he had been in with her and been happy brought him pain. It was as if he had two levels of feeling about her, the upper, in which he was optimistic, cheerful, confident, and the lower where fear was, and doubt. The places they had been together evoked images in that lower world. He remembered rejections, he remembered, with something that was more like panic than pain, that it was now six years since they had made love.

The houses in this part of London are old, early rather than late nineteenth century. Their brickwork is a dark greyish-brown, their doorways and windows are long and narrow, their roofs invisible. Very little green was to be seen except distant tree-tops showing like vegetation in a walled garden. Susannah had window-boxes that contained, instead of the usual geraniums, small-leaved ivies and plants with yellow-grey fluffy foliage. Guy rang the bell, preparing himself, as he always had to, for his first sight of Leonora.

The door was answered by a woman he recognized but couldn't immediately place. She seemed to be having the same difficulties identifying him.

"Guy Curran," he said.

"Oh, *yes*. I'm Janice. We met at Nora's birthday party."

He hated the diminutive that was allowed to her family but not to him. The woman who had used it he now remembered as the cousin who had been going to Australia to get married. She was rather plump with a pale moon face, prominent eyes, and a great deal of long mousy hair worn in a French plait. Guy particularly disapproved of Indian cotton dresses (cheap, badly cut, and shapeless), and she of course had one on, tan-coloured with black hieroglyphs and white bits. Her hips were round and the effect in his opinion was of someone going to a fancy dress party as a granary loaf.

"I thought you were an undertaker, actually," she now said. "Susannah's expecting an undertaker. You know her mother died?"

"Yes. Someone told me. Can I come in?"

Janice admitted him grudgingly. He felt she was looking him up and down as if he was committing some awful social faux pas. "She's just lost her *mother*. I mean, mostly people write or phone."

"It's Leonora I've come to see," he said impatiently.

But at that moment Susannah herself put her head over the banisters. The living room was on the upper floor of the flat, the bedrooms on the lower. Susannah didn't react towards him as did all the other women close to Leonora—including this indignant Australian—in an aggressive or judgemental way. She called out to him and said how nice of him it was to have come. Obviously she hadn't heard his remark to Janice. When he got to the top of the stairs she came up to him and, putting her arms round him, kissed him in an almost motherly way, though she wasn't anywhere near old enough to be his mother.

It was quite a shock to be kissed *nicely* by a woman, though of course Celeste did it all the time. But this was different. Susannah very evidently took the purpose of his visit to be of condolence. Well, that was all right with him. He felt warm towards her and approving. Susannah might be sad and in mourning but it didn't show. She was carefully and quite heavily made-up, which Guy thought proper for women, her thick wiry dark hair was teased into a fashionable sea-urchin shape, she wore black silk trousers with a chocolate-and-black-striped top and a lot of rather elegant silver jewellery of the chain-mail kind, including a wide glittering belt. What a pity Leonora couldn't or wouldn't learn from her example!

As he followed her into the living room, where he hadn't been for nearly four years, he thought of the time when Leonora had lived here after leaving teacher-training college, and of calling to take her out and being given drinks by Anthony Chisholm. Well, it wasn't so long ago . . . The first thing he saw, even before he saw Leonora, was a white card on the mantelpiece with a silver edge. A wedding invitation, it had to be, but he couldn't read the print at this distance.

Leonora got up when he came in. His heart had already done its turning-over stuff, sending a beat up into his head. She looked horrible but what did he care?

She kissed him. There was no hugging and not much warmth, but then she hadn't just lost her mother. (More's the pity, thought Guy.) Janice, behind him, was going into some long tale about recognizing him and not recognizing him, then thinking he was an undertaker or a florist. Leonora wore black-and-white plastic earrings. Not a scrap of make-up, of course, and her hair looked greasy. She had green track-suit pants on and a black sweat-shirt, rusting with age and bad washing. Since knowing Newton, Guy thought, whatever dress sense she had once possessed had gone to pot. The fool probably told her he loved her for herself, not her appearance.

At any rate she didn't ask him what he was doing there. He remembered in time to say something appropriate about Susannah's mother.

"It was really thoughtful of you to come, Guy," Leonora said, beaming. He thought her smile was surely fuller and freer than he had seen it for months. "We've had such a day. Some of those people are so insensitive. D'you know what the registrar said to poor Susannah? It was a woman, apparently they mostly are. Men won't take the jobs, they're too badly paid; it's the old old story. She said, 'Is this the first death you've ever registered?' And when Susannah said it was, she said, 'I don't suppose it'll be the last. Good morning.' Can you imagine?"

Janice had departed to make a cup of tea, having had some whispered communication with Susannah. Leonora began explaining how her cousin was staying with Anthony and Susannah, her cousin's husband would be coming over next week, and it was very sad for poor Janice, who had been particularly fond of Susannah's mother and arrived too late to see her alive. No other family Guy had ever come across had been so closely interlocked as these Chisholms. Even those on the outer fringes of the root system, people not even related, were mad about each other. Leonora was giving the impression this Janice had come twelve thousand miles to be at the deathbed of an old woman, the mother of her aunt by marriage, whom she had probably only met once or twice in her whole life. How right he was not to underestimate the influences that worked on Leonora!

From where he sat he kept trying to see the mantelpiece and the card on it but Susannah insisted on remaining standing, and in front of the carefully preserved Georgian fireplace, leaning on the mantelshelf. He didn't like to dodge his head about too obviously. Susannah had begun talking about the funeral.

"We find ourselves in a dilemma, Guy. We really don't know what to do. Shall we ask his advice, Leonora? Perhaps a fresh mind, do you think?"

Leonora gave him another lovely smile. "We'll see what he says."

"Now my poor dear mother didn't leave any instructions about—well, I mustn't mind saying it bluntly—about whether she wanted to be buried or cremated. Of course most people are cremated these days, but cremation seems so . . . I nearly said 'so final,' as if death itself wasn't final, but perhaps you know what I mean."

"Oh, I know what you mean," said Guy, craning his neck.

"And then it's a question of where? All the nice London cemeteries are full and it means going right out into the sticks.

159

My mother lived in Earlsfield, but the churchyard there of course is out of the question and has been for about a century, I should think . . ."

Janice came in with the tea, which she placed on a table in such a way as to oblige Guy to turn his chair around, with its back to the fireplace. It was near enough to real drinking time for him not to want tea but he drank it, refusing a slice of the peaches and cream torte that fat little Janice should have known better than to tuck into. A plan was forming in his mind of managing to drive Leonora home—well, of getting her in his car, starting to drive her home and then persuading her not to go back but to have dinner with him.

Janice was telling an elaborate story—in the worst of taste, Guy thought—about the adventures of someone she knew scattering a loved one's ashes from the Cobb in Lyme Regis. Susannah said that was a coincidence because she and Anthony were going for a short holiday in Lyme in a couple of weeks' time. The doorbell called Janice away from further anecdote. Though repeatedly told by the others to sit down and do nothing, she seemed to have appointed herself a temporary au pair. To Guy's great pleasure he and Leonora found themselves for a moment or two alone. The undertaker had arrived and Susannah was summoned downstairs.

"I do hope she's made up her mind," said Leonora. "She'll have to tell him one way or another."

"Have dinner with me, Leo."

"Oh, I can't, Guy. I'm awfully sorry, but I can't." Not "I never do" or "I have lunch with you on Saturdays," not that any more. "I'm staying here and William's coming over. We're all going out for dinner so that poor Susannah doesn't have to cook."

There went his plan to drive her home . . . But, "I'm really sorry," she said. "It would have been nice. Maeve told me you rang up this morning to ask after Robin. That was kind of you, I do appreciate it."

He dared to reach across the sofa and take her hand. He *knew* she would snatch her hand away but she didn't. She even let the fingers nestle softly in his and she turned on him a look of such sweetness, such compassion, that if Janice hadn't come back at that moment he would have lost control of himself, he would have had to jump up and seize her in his arms. He did jump up, but only to go. There was little pleasure in being here with that fat gimlet-eyed one staring censoriously at him.

"Lunch on Saturday?" he said.

"Yes, Guy dear, of course. Where shall we go?"

"The Savoy," he said. "We'll go to the River Room at the Savoy."

She didn't protest. She was changing towards him, she was changing *back*. He kissed her goodbye, stood up, turned to face the fireplace and saw that the wedding card had gone. It had been there when he came in half an hour before and now it was gone.

Someone had quietly moved it so that he shouldn't see.

CHAPTER FOURTEEN

He had known Leonora for quite a long time before he met her brother. One winter's day, just before or just after Christmas, he went with Leonora into the living room of her parents' house where a boy was standing by the window with a paper in his hand that he was reading. He must have heard them come in but he didn't look round immediately, he read to the end of the page. There was something headmasterly in this behavior or even policeman-like, something deliberate and scornful, though the boy himself looked almost babyish. He was tall enough, a lot taller than his sister, but his face when he finally turned his head was that of a five-year-old, plump, innocent, with toddler's skin and a rose-bud mouth. The voice that issued from those baby lips was therefore all the more amazing. Instead of shrill and lisping, it was deep and rich, it was *plummy,* with an accent that can only be acquired (Guy learned later from Leonora) by attendance at one of those schools within the Headmaster's Conference.

"Is this your beau, Nora?"

Guy had heard the word before, but only on television. He would—then and now—have given a lot to have a voice like that. Leonora introduced him.

"Robin, this is Guy. Guy, this is my brother."

Already, at the age of fifteen, Robin Chisholm was practising that teasing mockery that was such a feature of his unpleasant character. It wasn't clever or amusing, it was just rude.

"Guy," he said. He said it slowly and with a certain puzzlement. He said it again, thoughtfully, as if it were the name of someone he had known long ago but couldn't quite place. "Guy. Yes—don't you find it difficult being called that? I mean, if Nora hadn't said, I'd have put you down as a Kevin, say, or a Barry. Yes, Barry would suit you."

He looked like an innocent child, smiling, wide-eyed, his cheeks plump and rosy, defying the object of his insults to take offence. For they were insults, Guy was in no doubt about that. Leonora's brother was implying that his name was far too upper-class for its possessor.

She defended him. "Oh, shut up. You're in no position to mock people's names. Robin may be all right now while you look like an infant but it'll be no joke when you're old."

Even then, in a very unnatural way, Robin Chisholm was proud of looking younger than he was. Most people are at thirty but not at *fifteen,* for God's sake. Guy, seeing him occasionally, not often but too often for his own comfort, thought he purposely cultivated the baby-face look. He wouldn't have been surprised to see Robin with his thumb in his mouth. Well, he would have been surprised, he'd have run screaming from the room.

The Chisholms had sent their daughter to a state school and a prestigious university. Their son attended a public school with high fees but dropped out of the polytechnic he'd just squeezed into and went instead "into the city." He was twenty-three when he started having those black-outs. They thought it was a tumour on the brain, then epilepsy. There turned out to be nothing wrong with him. Guy privately thought Robin had carefully planned and staged it all to extricate himself from the firm he was working for, an investment company that was plunged into a financial scandal of mammoth proportions a week or two after he entered hospital.

He was the sort of person the world would be better without. Someone else could see to his destruction, though, not Guy. It wasn't he who had told Leonora about Con Mulvanney. Further to that, Guy, who, having failed to get hold of Danilo that evening, had been considering the matter for half the night, decided that her brother, of all those who surrounded her, probably influenced her the least. Of course she loved him, that went without saying—she said it often enough for all that, said it of far too many people, Guy thought—but Robin irritated her, she didn't altogether approve of him.

All this made him dream of Robin. Robin was dead, pushed down all those flights of stairs in Portland Road, his bleeding body discovered by Maeve. This wasn't at all a fantastic or irrational dream, and it therefore alarmed Guy all the more. He couldn't phone St. Leonard's Terrace before eight-thirty or Danilo before nine at the earliest. Making coffee for himself, he kept touching wood as he moved about the kitchen. It was an old habit of superstition he had believed long shed.

If you touched wood, the action fended off disaster. It kept away—what? Evil spirits? His grandmother, from whom he had learned wood-touching, not helping others to salt, not passing a knife to a friend, avoiding the divisions between paving stones, hadn't specified the precise function of these acts. They just kept you safe. Funny he should think of her now when he hadn't for years. Luckily, the kitchen, lavishly refitted in limed oak, was a paradise for wood-touchers.

A sleepy Danilo answered the Weybridge phone at ten past nine. Guy was nearly out of his mind because there had been no answer from St. Leonard's Terrace in spite of his trying ten times between eight-thirty and now. He was sure Robin must be dead, and with his death Leonora lost forever, but he called

Danilo's hit man off just the same. Danilo took his change of heart with a show of ill temper but agreed to meet him for a drink at a club called The Black Spot at six. Certain now that he was too late, that Robin's corpse was even at this moment being identified by Maeve in some mortuary, Guy nevertheless had another try at the Chelsea number.

Rather a strange thing happened. The phone was picked up but before anyone spoke into the mouthpiece Guy heard Robin's voice bellowing from a distance.

"Answer the bloody thing, can you? I'm in the bath."

Then accents like his grandmother's, it must be the Irish cleaning woman, said, "Hallo, who's speaking? Mr. Chisholm's busy."

Guy gasped with relief. He was on the point of saying, "Tell him to go back to bed and stay there," but thought better of it.

·   ·   ·

The Black Spot was all bar and floor. There were no tables, nowhere to sit except on a stool up at the long black-and-silver counter. It was very dark, American-style. The first person Guy saw was Carlo sitting on a stool next to his father and drinking something dark and frothy from a brandy glass. It was probably Coke but the glass it was in made it look sophisticated, even sinister. Guy was rather surprised. Then he reflected that he would very much have liked to go into bars like this one when he was ten, only he never got the chance.

Carlo was wearing junior designer jeans and a black sweat-shirt with BREAD-HEAD'S KID printed on it in luminescent pink. He said, "Hi" to Guy and continued eating prawn fries out of an ashtray. Danilo was in caramel-coloured herringbone silk tweed, a suit with an enormous wide-shouldered jacket, and under it an open-necked crimson shirt.

"You're not looking too good," said Danilo.

Guy shrugged impatiently. That was what Danilo always said every time they met. "It's the light in here, if you can call it light." He asked the barman for a large vodka martini. "We can't talk," he said to Danilo, cocking a thumb in Carlo's direction.

"I can't help it, mate. What was I to do? One of the nannies has got flu, the other's walked out. Tanya's sister'll have the other kids, she won't have him. Last time he was there he put her *Apocalypse Now* video in the microwave. He said he wanted to see what would happen.

"Mervyn," he said to the barman, "take him round the back and let him watch *Mork and Mindy*. Five minutes, that's all I ask."

"It's not on, Dad. There's only *Buck Rogers in the Twenty-fifth Century*."

"Go round the back and watch that then." Danilo had to have another glass of the red wine he favoured. "Don't ever do that to me again," he said dramatically to Guy. "Don't ever."

"Don't ever do what?"

"Bell me with that changed-me-mind crap." He lowered his voice deeply. "You could have made a murderer out of poor old Chuck, d'you realize that?"

Poor old Chuck, whoever he might be, was certainly a murderer already, several times over. Besides, what was the difference? It was either one victim or the other. Guy knew arguing with Danilo was quite useless. He said he was sorry, he realized he'd been a bit thoughtless.

"Immature," said Danilo, "that's what you've been. Call a spade a spade. Now you listen to me, Guy. We've nearly had a very nasty accident in this particular area. I want you to think carefully. Do you or do you not want me to pursue this matter? The original party you wanted wasted I quite understand is out of the firing line, and for personal reasons I'm not sorry, but from what you said on the blower this morning I got a sort of hint you'd someone else in mind. No, don't answer now. Name no names. I want you to think very carefully, like I said."

"I have thought." They were alone in the bar but for a man and a girl kissing up at the far end. Guy thought, that's just what the fuzz would do, it's an old one, that, a WPC and a DS in a clinch but all ears really. Just the same he said, very softly, "Rachel Lingard," and he gave the address in Portland Road. Because Chuck might only need to recognize her and not know her name, he took one of his cards out of his pocket and wrote on it: "Short, round-faced, fat, glasses, dark hair scraped back, about 27," a cruel but accurate description of Rachel, so that there could be no confusion with Maeve or—for God's sake!—Leonora.

•   •   •

In the light of this, it struck him as odd there was no reply at all from their flat when he phoned at nine, at midday, at four, and at ten. In the meantime he also phoned Georgiana Street. No one answered there until ten-thirty at night, when Newton finally replied to his fourth call.

"Leonora's in bed. She was tired and she went to bed early."

"She'll talk to me."

"She won't. I've told you, she's in bed."

"Surely you've got a bedside extension."

Newton said obscurely, "I'm a poor man, Your Majesty," and put the phone down.

It was much the same next day. Guy had to see his accountant, phoned the flat in Portland Road from the restaurant where he was giving the man lunch. He tried Georgiana Street, then St. Leonard's Terrace. Maeve answered.

"I'm living here. I was going to move in with Robin after Leonora's wedding anyway, so we thought I might as well now."

"Do you happened to know where Leonora is?"

"I should think you say that in your sleep, don't you? It'll be on your tombstone. 'Guy Curran, 1960 to whatever, RIP, *Where's Leonora?*' No, I don't know where she is. You're a bloody menace, d'you know that?"

He had to go back to the accountant. Coffee had been brought in the meantime. Guy had a large brandy with his. A taxi took him back to Scarsdale Mews and his own telephone.

The room and the green garden seen through the French windows seemed to turn red, dyed by his anger. To keep his anger down he had to hear her voice; it was like a tranquillizing drug. He needed his fix of her voice.

She wasn't at Portland Road, she wasn't at Georgiana Street. Where does she go, he thought, where does she hide? Probably Rachel hides her, takes her to work with her, anything to keep her from me. Later on he phoned Lamb's Conduit Street. Janice picked up the receiver.

She'd only been out there four or five years but she already had an Australian accent. For some reason the sound of his voice made her giggle. It was as if she and Susannah had just been talking about him—no, more as if she was recalling some trick played on him.

"I'm sorry," she said. "I was laughing about something when you phoned and I couldn't stop. I'll fetch Susannah."

A nice woman, Susannah. You often couldn't understand why people married other people, mostly you couldn't, but in this case he could easily see what there was about Susannah that had appealed to Anthony Chisholm.

"Hallo, Guy," she said with real warmth, putting a thrilling emphasis on his name as if she were really pleased to hear from him, as if he were someone she loved and hadn't heard from for months. "It was so nice to see you the other day. It must be ages since we last met."

He had meant to be cool and light, to make small talk. But her words moved him. He was near the edge today anyway, he was nearly out of control. "Too long," he said, and, "you were always good to me, Susannah. You alone of all of them. Even Leonora's father turned against me."

"Now, Guy, I'm sure that's not true. Anthony and I have always liked you. The thing is . . . Excuse me just a moment." He heard her lay the phone down and go to close the door. This was so that that giggling little Janice didn't hear. "Guy, Leonora's a grown-up woman, she has her own life. I understand how bitter it must be for you to see her prefer William, but if she does, what can anyone do about it? As a matter of fact, I'd like you to know I think your—well, your constancy to Leonora is a very beautiful thing. You've been like one of those knights of old who were devoted for years to their ladies. You really have. But, Guy, my dear, it has to be over now—you see that, don't you?"

"It will never be over," he said, speaking low.

"What did you say?"

"It will never be over, Susannah. You see, I believe, I *know*, she'll return to me. I know we'll be together for the rest of our lives and we'll look back on this as a temporary madness."

"If you like to look at things like that, I can't stop you. I'd just like to save you from prolonging your unhappiness, that's all."

Why not come right out with it? "There was an invitation to the wedding on your mantelpiece yesterday. It was there when I came, but before I left someone had taken it away."

She answered immediately with no hesitation. "Oh, no, Guy. You must be mistaken. Anyway, we wouldn't have an invitation, would we? We're *giving* the wedding."

That was unanswerable. Was it possible he'd imagined it? He thought, Susannah wouldn't lie to me, not Susannah. He asked her if she knew where Leonora was. No, but she expected to see her tomorrow. Leonora was coming to her mother's funeral.

Probably the lot of them would go, Guy thought after he had rung off. Tessa and Magnus Mandeville, Robin and Maeve, William Newton, and even some of the Newton relations. They were all drawn into the great Chisholm spider's web. A little fantasy showed Guy a glimpse of a future in which, now Leonora and he were married, the Chisholms drew in *his* family, or what there was of it, what could be found. They were capable of going hunting for his mother, for his grandmother, if the old girl was still alive. He imagined them all at some vast dinner table, celebrating something. Robin's wedding? *His* wedding to Leonora? Why not? Why not?

He made several more attempts at Georgiana Street and

Portland Road. No reply at either. Newton was preventing her from answering the phone or Rachel Lingard was. The latter was actually more likely, for Leonora would have had to go home to find suitable clothes to wear at the funeral. Still, tomorrow should not only see the end of Susannah's mother but also of Rachel.

No doubt Chuck or Chuck's man had so far had no opportunity of doing the trick. Guy would know if he had. It wasn't that he expected Danilo to phone and tell him the deed was done. Leonora would. Leonora would turn to him in trouble. It brought him a small qualm to think how unhappy she would be. She was really fond of that ugly, fat, ego-tripping Rachel with her superior manner and her ruthless manipulating of other people's lives. Learning that Rachel had died in a car accident (or been lethally mugged or fallen off a river bridge) would upset her so much that she certainly wouldn't go ahead with that absurd wedding. She would turn to him for comfort.

In the morning he phoned the flat in Portland Road as early as he reasonably could, just after eight. He was in his bedroom and he touched wood, this time the Linnell bedhead. Someone took off the receiver but didn't speak. He knew who it was.

"I know that's you, Rachel," he said. "It's pointless pretending with me." He wanted to say what the kids where he came from said when they begged from a woman and got nothing: "Die, bitch, die." But she really *would* die and someone might overhear. "I'd like to speak to Leonora, please."

She put the phone down.

He dialled the number again and let it ring. When it was clear she wasn't going to answer and was stopping Leonora from answering, he laid the receiver down so that the ringing would go on and on to torment her. Perhaps he should go to Susannah's mother's funeral but he didn't know where it was. It was now three days since he had spoken to Leonora. Had it ever been so long, apart from at holiday time or when she was at college? Even when she had the bed-sit and the phone was downstairs, it had never been as long as three days. He panicked when he thought that way, so he made an effort to rid his mind of it. The receiver restored to its rest, he went off in the Jaguar to a paintings sale at Wallington in Surrey.

Driving back, he came to the gates of Croydon Crematorium. This would be the place, he thought, and he parked the car half-way up the pavement and waited. It came to him how wonderful it would be just to see her. If he did, he would leave the car and go in, follow the mourners, sit discreetly at the back of the crematorium chapel. He imagined her the way he would dress her to go, for example, to her own mother's funeral, an event devoutly to be wished for in four or five years, say, after their own wedding. A simple black dress by Jean Muir with a single flounce six inches from the hem, a wide-brimmed black hat, black suede pumps, and gleaming black stockings with seams. He liked the idea of her in a veil, her face mysteriously hidden, disclosed only to him.

They would walk in side by side, he supporting her, she clinging to his arm. He imagined her in the front pew kneeling to pray a little before the service started. The long thin coffin containing Tessa's long thin body appeared, borne by half a dozen bearers—Magnus, Anthony, Michael Chisholm, Robin—but he would be there too, surely, among them? Trying to solve the dilemma of how to be at Leonora's side and at the same time an undisputed member of the inner family, Guy looked up to see a slow sad procession of cars moving out from the gates.

He jumped out of the Jaguar. The first car was full of very old people, white heads like dandelion clocks. He peered, he scanned them. The second car was full of very old people. Two slightly younger grey-headed people sat in the third car. Someone said behind him, "Excuse me, you can't park there."

It was a traffic warden. He drove home. Fatima was still there, polishing. Guy went upstairs and tried to phone Leonora on his bedside extension. It reminded him of what Newton had said, mocking him, calling him "Your Majesty." No one answered, either in Portland Road or Georgiana Street.

She wouldn't forget about lunch with him, would she? They had made no arrangements as to time. But perhaps there was no need for that, they always met at one. The Savoy, he thought, at one. The front door closed as Fatima let herself out. He went down and made himself a large drink, vodka and ice and a few drops of angostura. That wedding invitation kept returning to his mind. It occurred to him for the first time that if they were sending out invitations to this ridiculous wedding, it was odd that they hadn't sent one to him. Odd, that is, in their assessment of things. Not in his. In his it would be grotesque inviting him to Leonora's marriage to someone else. But they wouldn't see it like that. They would see him as an old friend with the same sort of right to be invited as that bitch Rachel—more right, because he'd known Leonora longer. So why hadn't they invited him?

Because they weren't sending out invitations? Because that silver-edged card had never been there. He'd imagined it. He had got into a state and imagined it. The garden was green again, the waters of the pool lay still and gleaming, bearing dense sheaves of lilies, leaves that were green above, crimson-lined, their flowers a veined streaky rose or ivory. He noticed that the roses were over and he walked about removing the deadheads. It was quite quiet out there, tucked away in the mews, the traffic a distant throb. There was peace here and an air of healing. You would never lose your mind, have strange, inexplicable things happen inside your head and to your imagination, if you sat calmly here.

After about an hour the phone rang. Intuition told him it would be Leonora, he knew it would be Leonora. It was years since she had phoned him but he knew it was she. He went indoors so fast that he knocked over the red lacquer table inside the door on which the Chinese vase had once stood. His heart thumping, he picked up the phone. It was Celeste. Had he forgotten he was taking her to her friend's party? There was going to be dancing on a terrace above the river at Richmond. Only he'd said he'd phone her and he hadn't.

Guy had forgotten. He knew he ought to go, it was the sort of thing he enjoyed, he'd accepted the friend's invitation and promised Celeste, but just the same he said he didn't feel like it. He'd got a bug, he thought, some virus, or a migraine coming. She took it resignedly, she didn't try to persuade him. After she had rung off, with the phone still in his hand, sick with disappointment, he thought he might as well take the opportunity and phone Georgiana Street.

No reply. He made himself another drink and dialled Portland Road. He touched the red-lacquered wood—was it wood? No reply. Rachel might be already dead. Chuck would probably do it down in Brixton where Rachel worked. A lot of people said it wasn't safe for a woman, particularly a white woman, to walk about alone in the back streets of Brixton. Guy had never quite believed that but he thought he might start believing it now.

A scenario took shape in his head. The police would want someone to identify Rachel's body. They'd call on Leonora or Maeve—Leonora most likely because she still lived in the same house as Rachel while Maeve did so no longer. Of course she'd ask William Newton to go with her, she'd be beside herself with grief and terror, but Newton wouldn't go because he was squeamish, he was the kind of person who couldn't face the idea of seeing a dead body, particularly a body in the state Rachel's would be in. So in despair she'd turn to the one she could depend on, her own true love, and together they'd go to Brixton. He'd drive her in the Jaguar. Once there, he'd take matters into his own hands. "I know the deceased quite as well as my fiancée does, Sergeant. Leave this matter of identification to me." She'd cling to him afterwards in the car. "It was always you really, Guy. I must have been mad . . ."

After two more stiff vodkas he was perfectly sober but his speech was a bit slurred. He practiced talking to himself in the mirror and confessed honestly that he didn't really want

Leonora to hear him speak like that. When he got back from the restaurant would do for a last try.

He walked. He needed the air. It was very unusual for him to eat alone or in a place where he hadn't previously booked a table. A little way along the Old Brompton Road was an Italian restaurant where he had once had a good pasta with Celeste's predecessor, a half-Chinese girl who was a stewardess on a Boeing 747. Four days since he had spoken to Leonora . . . It was better, safer, to concentrate on Rachel, who might so easily be lying dead somewhere by now, almost certainly was. It was nearly eight o'clock, more than forty-eight hours since he'd tipped the wink to Danilo.

The restaurant was somewhere in this row of shops. A man, a beggar, down and out, whatever you liked to call it, was lying full-length along one of the doorsteps, the threshold of a health-food store, long closed. He was black, a youngish man, tall apparently and thin to the point of emaciation, dressed in blackish rags. A cap lay on the pavement beside him and the single five-pee piece in it was the only indication that this was not simply headgear cast temporarily to the ground.

He lay on his back with his hands folded behind his head, staring upwards. His lips were parted, the teeth very white with a gleam of gold among them. He didn't look at Guy and Guy gave him only a rapid glance but he was sure it was Linus. A Linus terribly changed, brought low, with a growth of beard on his once-glowing cheeks and an ugly jagged scar across his once shapely cheekbone, but the same man. Guy walked on, quite sober now but trembling. His hands shook, he felt as if his legs could scarcely carry him, but for all that he kept walking. He forgot about finding the Italian restaurant and walked unsteadily down the Boltons, along the Fulham Road. All that mattered was to put as great a distance as possible between him and the poor derelict on that doorstep who might have been, who *was*, Linus.

Yet once he was in the restaurant he found in Cale Street, had gone to the bar and ordered a large vodka martini before asking for a table, he wondered almost with a groan why he had run away. Why hadn't he stopped and asked how he could help his friend? That, of course, was to simplify things. But he might have made a start by asking the man if he really was Linus. The precise identity of a black person is no more readily discernible to a white man than a white is to a black. There will not be that instant indisputable recognition. In Guy's mind a slight doubt lingered. When he last saw Linus he was a lithe, fit, beautiful, prosperous, young gangster. He was always well and gaudily dressed. He had a gold tooth, Guy remembered, rather unusual in the young but not so unusual in someone of Caribbean origin.

Guy sat down at his table, ordered some sort of chicken dish and another vodka martini while he waited for the food. The beggar on the step had a gold tooth. Going back in his mind to half an hour before, he saw again the parted lips, full and gleaming, with a bluish tinge, and among the white molars a glint of gold. It was Linus. What had happened to him that he had come to this?

Fifteen years ago . . . The teenage street gangs knew nothing of racism. It was something to be proud of now, something to be pleased about, but in those days none of them thought about it from that aspect, only marvelled when the police and social workers talked about race troubles among the young in Notting Hill. Guy could almost have said—almost but not quite, if he was honest—that he didn't notice another person's colour. He was aware that in some people's eyes to be Irish, as he was, was a liability. Linus had been a young devil. Once, in the Central Line tube between getting in at Notting Hill and getting out at Queensway, he had taken five hundred pounds off three American tourists without their knowing a thing about it.

The food came but he could only pick at it. He drank a carafe of the house wine. Why had he stayed to eat anything? He should have returned immediately to the place in the Old Brompton Road where he had seen Linus lying. He had run away. Getting up now, paying the bill, he told himself he must go back. He must go back and find the young black man on the step and confirm that he was Linus.

He walked down the street looking for a taxi, looking for that glowing golden cube moving towards one that is the most welcome of all street lights. Approaching him along the King's Road, arm-in-arm like an old married couple, were Robin Chisholm and Maeve Kirkland.

Of course it was less surprising that they should be here than that he was. They lived only a street away. The King's Road was their High Street. Guy expected them either to pretend not to see him as on that day in the park or to start a row in the street. He braced himself and stared as they approached. They were going in for that twin-dressing again, perhaps it was a feature of their relationship. Identical pink shirts this time. It was the jeans that differed, hers the brushed sooty kind, his stone-washed blue denim. Robin showed no signs of having narrowly escaped a serious accident, and his eye was no longer discoloured. Guy had to stop himself from putting his hand up to his cheek, where the faint mark of a fingernail still was.

They were both grinning widely. "Bygones be bygones, old man?" said Robin.

Guy had never heard anyone under sixty call another "old man" before. "How are you?" he said, and then, for politeness, "Good to see you up and about again."

"Oh, I'm fighting fit." It seemed an unfortunate choice of words. Knowing Robin, Guy had no doubt it was a matter of choice. "What brings you," said Robin in his fruity tones, "to this neck of the woods?" Without waiting for an answer, he asked Guy round to St. Leonard's Terrace for a drink.

All this warmth staggered Guy. What was Robin up to? "Sorry, I'd like to, but I'm in a bit of a hurry."

"You haven't asked where Leonora is," Maeve said rather spitefully.

It was true. He realized he hadn't thought of Leonora for the past hour. It must be a record. "No," he said. "No. She's at

Portland Road, I suppose. I'm having lunch with her tomorrow."

"She's moved out to William's on account of Rachel not being there. There's no point in her staying in the flat alone."

He felt a thrill of excitement. "What do you mean, Rachel not being there?"

"She's gone away on holiday, hasn't she?"

"On holiday?" he said.

"This morning. She went to Spain with Dominic. Why are you looking like that, Guy? It's Rachel I'm talking about, not Leonora."

A taxi came. He hailed it, told the driver to drop him in Bolton Gardens, said goodbye to them and got in. As it drove off he could see Maeve's face through the rear window, her mouth a little open, her head shaking. So Rachel had escaped him, or rather, had escaped Chuck. Rachel had gone off on holiday with one of those egghead men of hers. The important thing, of course, was not that she should be dead but that she shouldn't be *there*. Well, she wouldn't be there.

The evening had grown windy and no longer warm. Autumn was coming. The concrete of a doorstep was cold and hard, piercing through thin soot-coloured clothes like pain. He got out of the taxi in Bolton Gardens and walked the few yards back into the Old Brompton Road.

There was no one in the doorway. Linus, if it was Linus, had gone. The only evidence of his past occupancy was a cigarette end, a tiny stub, much smaller than that left behind by most tobacco smokers. Guy picked it up and smelt the slightly dizzying scent of marijuana.

CHAPTER FIFTEEN

She was late. He sat at their large round corner table in the gracious room, determined not to look at his watch again. His drink had been ordered and he resolved not to look at his watch until it came. The cigarette he had not been able to resist lighting was attracting censorious glances from a woman in a pink hat. Guy forced himself to look out of the window.

The brandy he had ordered arrived. It was the strongest thing he could think of, short of something totally way-out like absinth or Zubrówka. Even the Savoy probably didn't have those. He looked at his watch. It was twelve minutes past one. He hadn't spoken to her on the phone for days. This date at the Savoy had never been confirmed. He thought, she's not coming. They've beaten me, they've moved her away to Newton's place, they're never going to let her speak to me again. I'll wait till twenty past. If she hasn't come by twenty past—what will I do then? What shall I do?

Go to Georgiana Street, he thought. Find her. He hadn't spoken to her since he saw her in Lamb's Conduit Street on

Tuesday. It was four days. He ought to have persisted, he ought to have found her before this. She might be anywhere, she might have gone with Rachel to Spain. He caught the waiter's eye and asked for another brandy. Of course she wasn't coming, he knew she wouldn't come now. He looked at his watch. It was twenty-two minutes past.

The second brandy was nearly gone by the time the waiter showed her to the table. Guy jumped up. He forgot the agonies of his long wait. She looked *beautiful*. For him and for this special place she had for once dressed up.

But perhaps not for once. Perhaps forever. It was part of the changing process, the change back to him. He forgot the unanswered phone, the silent days. She wore a linen suit. The short skirt was of a rich dark but not navy blue, the long, high-buttoned, tight-waisted flared jacket was dark blue and dark pink in wide vertical stripes. The sleeves were turned back to show the pink-and-blue-spotted lining. She had mauvish stockings and blue suede shoes and her earrings were dark red glass roses.

Her hair shone. It looked as if it had just been cut, and well-cut for a change. There was a glow on her face so that for a moment he thought she was made-up. She kissed him, one cheek, then the other, nothing unusual in that.

"I'm sorry I'm so late, Guy. There was trouble on the tube."

Who cared about the tube? Her eccentric modes of travel made him laugh. "Darling Leonora," he said, "you look so beautiful. I want you to look like that always."

"It was my mother. She said, 'You can't go to the Savoy in jeans.' I'd just bought this suit, so I thought, well, why not?"

"Your mother wanted you to dress up for lunch with me?"

She smiled, the tight smile with the corners of her mouth restrained. "My mother would want me to dress up for lunch with anyone."

That was best ignored. "Have something nice to drink for a change," he said. "Don't spoil things with orange juice."

"All right. I'll have a sherry. No, not a dry one, a lovely dark brown, sticky Bristol Cream."

"So you've moved into Georgiana Street," he said.

She began explaining why. He told her about meeting Maeve and Robin. The apparent truce or detente between him and Robin seemed to bring her great pleasure. She reached across and squeezed Guy's hand. No, she wouldn't eat meat even to please him, she said. She'd have fish. Lobster? Guy suggested. That made her shudder but she would have sole. Creole prawns first and then sole and fried potatoes—why not?—and vegetables instead of a salad. A proper meal, Guy said, he was delighted.

Although he had never contemplated doing so, he told her about Linus. She did remember Linus?

"Of course I do. He didn't like me. I'll never forget it, the first time we met, it was out in the street, Talbot Road or somewhere, and you were nice to me, you passed me a joint—though, God knows, Guy, you shouldn't have—and Linus, he spat into the drain."

She remembered all that. She remembered how he had been that first time. His heart was full. "There was the end of a joint left behind on the step," he said.

"He never liked me," she said again. "There was no reason. He was just one of those gay men who don't like women."

"Linus wasn't gay." He was astounded sometimes by the things she thought of, the *layers* of her, the things that went on in her pretty head. "What makes you say that? He had that girl-friend, Sophette, she was old enough to be his mother, but she was his girl-friend."

"Exactly," said Leonora with a little laugh. "Are you sure it was him on the doorstep?"

"Almost positive."

"You'd better be entirely positive before you start doing something."

She ate her prawns with gusto, she ate all her fish and most of the potatoes. She wouldn't have a second sherry but she shared the Frascati with him. He had to order a second bottle.

"Guy," she said, very serious, "it's very good of you, very kind, to want to help Linus if that's really him and he's down and out, but I think you've got to remember something. Linus was a pusher, he was a dealer in dangerous drugs. That's how he made his living. He's probably come to this state through his own addiction. Had you thought of that?"

He had to stop himself from gaping at her. Didn't she know? Didn't she know that what went for Linus also went for him?

"It would be a bit strong," she said, "to say he only got what he deserved, but you could say he brought it on himself."

"So he's to be left in the gutter? Who gives you these ideas? Newton?"

"You're identifying yourself with Linus, that's why you feel so deeply about him. You see yourself in him, brought low by some means or other. Oh, not poverty or crime now, I don't mean that, but something else. You were in the same line of life, you see, you're the same age with much the same background, the same way of making a living once."

"You've caught that way of talking from Rachel."

She didn't answer.

"What do you know of my way of making a living, Leonora?" he said heavily.

She said innocently, "You sold marijuana, didn't you? I always knew that."

The moment passed, the terror. She drank a second glass of wine, would have no more, but was excitedly prepared to have a wonderful sweet, a kind of sculpture in chocolate with leaf-thin whorls and petals, white, milk, and dark. The decision about the sweet, its arrival shifted them from the subject. He began to think about the two weeks ahead, the wedding that everyone *said* would take place on September 16, a fortnight from today. Of course it wouldn't but . . .

"I couldn't get you on the phone at all last week," he said.

"No, I know. I *am* sorry, Guy. But I'll be in Georgiana Street all the time now." She smiled at him, her head a little on one side. "I do have to go out sometimes, you know."

"You've left the flat in Portland Road for good?"

"It looks like it. With Maeve gone and Rachel away, there didn't seem much point in going back there. As a matter of fact, we're lending it to Janice and Gerry while they're in this country. It's nicer for them to have a place of their own than stay with Daddy and Susannah. Then, when Rachel comes back, we'll exchange contracts and it'll be all hers."

When they had finished they walked down onto the Embankment. He took her hand and she let him hold it. The words were in his head and he wanted to bring them out but he was afraid. They were there, in his mouth now, waiting to be uttered. She talked about the river, the craft on it. There had been an accident to a pleasure boat the week before, the worst river disaster for more than a hundred years, fifty people drowned. She was talking about what it would be like, trapped below deck, shuddering. He said because he had to, because the words crowded into his mouth were choking him, they exploded from him, "Con Mulvanney—the name—what does it mean to you?"

Innocent eyes, an uncomprehending gentle gaze. "Nothing. I don't know. What is it, Guy?"

"A man who took LSD and died of bee-stings."

"Ah." He saw light dawn and his heart dipped. "Yes, I heard about that. A long time ago. I never knew if it was true."

"It was true."

"What am I supposed to say? Do you want to tell me about it?"

"He begged me for the stuff. I didn't want to give it to him. But I was devastated afterwards. Leo darling, I was so ashamed. And I didn't want you ever to know, I knew what it would do to you. To you and me. How you'd feel about me."

"I knew there must be a reason why you did it," she said. "It didn't make any difference."

"It didn't make any difference?"

"To the way I felt about you," she said.

He took her in his arms. She was leaning against a round smooth stone pillar and he put his arms round her and kissed her. There had been no kisses of that kind between them for years, five years, six. It was a long and sweet, open-lipped kiss with tongues meeting, of the kind that precedes love-making, not a kiss for a river-breezy corner with people passing and a ship on the water sounding a long blast on its siren.

"I love you, Leonora," he said. "I've always loved you. I shall love you till I die. Come back to me. I know you'll come back to me one day. Come back to me now."

She said with infinite sadness, "It's too late, Guy."

"Why is it too late? It's never too late. I love you and you love me, and you know you'll never go through with that crazy marriage, that ridiculous marriage. Don't you see it would be a crime against you and me to marry that man? I know you won't, though. I know you love me. You've shown me. I know you love me now."

"Let's walk, Guy," she said.

They walked along the path in the Victoria Embankment Gardens. It was cool and windy and there were little grey waves on the river.

"Promise me," she said, "not to press me about this. It's hard enough for me without that. Things are hard enough."

"My darling, I won't do anything you don't want me to do. I'll do anything you ask. You've made me so happy."

"You do nag rather, you know, Guy. You do go on and on. But you won't any more, will you? You won't pin me down?"

"Now I know you love me, I'm so happy I won't say another word."

"Come and have supper with us on Wednesday," she said. "Would you do that? Phone me tomorrow and Monday and Tuesday and come and have supper with us on Wednesday at about seven-thirty."

What's supper? he might have said if it had been anyone else. Dinner is what you eat in the evening. Tea, of course, was what he had eaten in the old days with his mother, if there had been anything to eat. "Who's 'us'?" he said.

183

"William will be there, of course. Guy, it's William's flat. Be reasonable. Be *nice*."

"I'll be nice. I'll come. I'll get to see you twice in one week. Where shall we have lunch next Saturday?"

She laughed. "We can talk about that on Wednesday."

After she had parted from him he didn't take a taxi. He walked. She had kissed him again when they said goodbye, a warm, sweet, loving kiss. And now he was alone again. She had told him she loved him, that nothing made any difference to that, she had renewed her love for him. Of course she had also said it was too late to come back to him, but she didn't mean that. Probably she thought he wouldn't really want her after her inconstancy, but she was wrong there, she was quite wrong.

It occurred to him as he walked along the Embankment that when people in their circumstances come together again after a split, when they start again, it would be usual for them to go home together. The natural thing would have been for Leonora to go home with him now. But he understood why she couldn't do that. Hadn't she said things were hard for her? "Things are hard enough without that," she had said. Nothing could have declared more plainly the pressure she was under from her family to stay with William Newton. They had found him for her, brought them together, and now they were all united in binding her to him.

All they wanted, and this was very clear, was to get September 16 over and that wedding with it. They were like some royal family in history or a fairy story who locked the princess up in a tower until she consented to marry the— ginger dwarf. He smiled to himself when he thought of it like that. But he was soon angry again, angry for *her*, whom they had made unhappy, his sweet and beautiful love who found "things hard enough" because she was being forced into marriage with a man she didn't love.

It began to rain and he hailed a taxi. Once back in Scarsdale Mews he thought he would check up at once in his engagement book to see what he was doing on Wednesday that he would have to cancel. Nothing—on Wednesday. For a moment he could hardly believe what he read, then believed it only too well. He *remembered* it.

On Monday, her birthday, he was supposed to be driving Celeste to Stratford-on-Avon, taking her to the Shakespeare Memorial Theatre and afterwards staying the night at the Lygon Arms in Broadway. *Supposed* to be? He had the tickets, had made the booking. She had taken his letting her down last Friday very well. He couldn't do that to her again. As he reassessed the next few days he started planning his phone calls to Leonora. On Monday he ought to be able to reach Leonora before he left, and on Tuesday he could phone her from the hotel . . .

•   •   •

Celeste spent Sunday night with him. She arrived in the late afternoon just as he rang off from talking to Leonora. It was necessarily a bland and on the whole meaningless telephone conversation they had, due to Tessa and Magnus being there. Leonora was back in Portland Road for the day, packing up some of her personal possessions, she said, for her mother and stepfather to take home with them in their car and store in their garage. This made Guy reflect to his satisfaction that if she really intended marrying Newton, she would have her things taken round to *his* flat.

"Darling," he said, "I would have brought it all here. Why didn't you ask me?"

He understood she had to speak in a very neutral way, make small talk really, with Tessa there. With Tessa, doubtless, breathing down her neck, noting every word to rebuke her with it later. He could *see* Tessa, that stick-insect woman darting about the flat, picking up this and that, choosing to take things off a shelf just behind Leonora while she was on the phone. He could see her stringy brown hands, a skeleton's bone hands with a bit of dried leather covering them and the nails painted like silver knife blades, her small head with the dark hair scraped back on a neck like a tortoise's questing out of its shell.

"I have to go away on business, Leo," he said. "Just tomorrow and Tuesday." It was untrue, but now was no time for admitting he was taking another woman away for the night. Telling a lie about it would only be bad, Guy thought obscurely, if he had *wanted* to go off with Celeste. "But I'll still phone you; I'll make sure I get to a phone."

It wasn't until very early next morning that, waking up in the Chinese bed beside Celeste, he began to recall what Leonora had said to him about Con Mulvanney. Her kiss, her declaration of her continuing love for him, her disclosures, so revealing, about the pressures she was under—all this had driven those simple remarks of hers from his mind. He hadn't even remembered them when he talked to her on the phone yesterday afternoon. But they were back with him now, in the dark mad small hours. He could see the luminous hands of his small carriage clock showing four-thirty.

"I heard about that," she had said. "A long time ago. I never knew if it was true."

She had heard about that. He had never really doubted, he had never needed proof, but now his belief had been confirmed. Why hadn't he asked her who told her? Because he was so overwhelmed with joy by what she said next that none of it made any difference. Anyway, he knew. Rachel had told her, Rachel who had gone away on holiday to Spain with a man called Dominic. And what a difference that had made! Rachel was scarcely removed from the sphere of influence she had set up, for Leonora to be back in his arms.

He was painfully aware just the same of her not being in his arms at that moment. Only a fool wouldn't have asked why she couldn't just walk out on Newton, get in a taxi and come here to him. But he knew why she wouldn't. Her family's pressures and threats were still too much for her, she had to be liberated from that and liberated by him. If there was any possibility of her arrival, Celeste wouldn't be here now, her sable dark hair spread over the pillow, her brown shoulders emerging from the white ruffled tulle of her nightgown. There had been no occasion for the removal of that pretty garment last night or on any night for a while now. The odd thought came to him that she would never take it off for him again.

When he thought sleep gone until the next night, in some Cotswold bed, sleep came to him and held him until past eight. Celeste was up before him, making the phoning of Leonora difficult in theory, impossible in practice. They were away by ten. At the place where they had lunch he couldn't tell Celeste he had to make a phone call on business. She knew too much, she wouldn't believe him. It was her birthday, she was enjoying herself. He had just bought her a magnificent lunch, promised her a present, anything she wanted from the nicest dress shop in Stratford. She looked wonderful with her beautiful hair plaited and coiled on top of her head, in a cream silk trouser suit and caramel shirt. Men turned their heads, looked at her, then at him. He couldn't go and make a phone call to Leonora now and tell Celeste a lie about it—still less, tell her the truth about it.

It was *Romeo and Juliet* they saw. Guy had seldom, if ever before, seen a Shakespeare play on the stage. Maybe on the TV by accident, but not on the real stage.

"You thought it would be boring, didn't you?" said Celeste as they got into the Jaguar. "But I could see you loved it. You're like a kid that's only done Shakespeare at school and can't believe it's the same thing when he sees it done for real."

"I don't remember Shakespeare at school," said Guy.

"Sweet Guy, they did it on the days you were shuckin' 'n' jivin' round Notting Dale."

"Maybe," he said. "Do you know what that play reminded me of?"

She didn't answer. He could feel her silence, warm and distressed. Then she said, "Yes," with great finality.

It was their own story, his and Leonora's, the star-crossed lovers, the repressive autocratic family. He hadn't killed anyone, of course, but in their eyes he had: Con Mulvanney. Con Mulvanney was his—what was he called?—Tybalt. The play stayed with him as he drove south, reproducing glowing pictures in his mind. That bit in the orchard and on the balcony, he could so easily replace in it Romeo with himself and Juliet with Leonora. He wished he could remember some of the lines, he wished he could talk about it with Celeste. Something about the way she was sitting, her shoulders stiff, her profile bronze-hard and staring ahead of her in the dark, told him he couldn't.

By the time they were in their hotel bedroom it was midnight. The day had gone by and he hadn't phoned Leonora. He had longed and longed to phone, even during the intervals of the play he had thought about phoning her, about escaping from Celeste and finding a phone, but it had been impossible. It wasn't the first time a day had passed without their speaking on the phone. Far from it. In the previous week, though he had seen her at Susannah's, he had spoken to her only once. But it was the first time they hadn't spoken because *he* had failed to call.

Celeste didn't maintain her silence. She was speaking again, talking about the room, the view they would have in the morning. But the confidence that had existed between them, the wonderful way that, though he didn't love her, he had been able to say anything and everything to her, they had been able to share each other's minds, that had gone.

It was lost, he had killed it, it would never come again. What did it matter? He thought, as he lay in the twin bed a yard away from Celeste's, that he would be bound anyway to lose her once he and Leonora were together again.

CHAPTER SIXTEEN

Y ou didn't phone me yesterday."

"Darling, I'm so sorry. Were you worried? I haven't upset
you, have I?" Guy was so happy that she minded his not
phoning her that he couldn't keep the note of excited joy out
of his voice. "I couldn't get to a phone. It just wasn't possible.
Will you forgive me?"

"Oh, it doesn't *matter,* it's not that. I only meant it was odd,
it was so unlike you."

She must have waited in for his call. His heart sang. His
head felt tumultuous, as if someone inside it were doing an
energetic dance. "You stayed in, waiting for the phone to
ring? Oh, Leo."

"I happened to stay in. I'd nothing to go out for."

Ah, yes. A likely story. He almost laughed aloud. "Leo,
will you tell me something? It's about what we talked about on
Saturday. I don't know why I didn't ask you then. You said
you knew all about—well, Con Mulvanney. Do you remember?"

"Who?"

"The man who died of bee-stings. You said you knew all about him, you'd heard about that and it was a long time ago. It was exactly four years ago, as a matter of fact."

"Yes," she said, "it would be about that. I was still living with Daddy and Susannah. It was before I moved into that room in Fulham with Rachel."

"Leo, who told you about it? It was Rachel told you, wasn't it?"

"Rachel?"

It was so clear in his mind, he began to tell her the story as he understood it. "Con Mulvanney lived in South London, in Balham, and so did this woman who was with him when he died. She was some sort of social worker and Rachel's a social worker in South London, so you can see how she came to tell her. She said she'd tell everyone . . ."

"Guy," she interrupted him, "what are you talking about? Do you know what you're talking about? Because I don't. It was Susannah who told me, *Susannah*."

The name exploded in his ears. *Susannah*, whom he had thought of as his friend, the woman who, of all Leonora's family and friends, had been kindest to him—it was she who had betrayed him and alienated his love. He should have thought of it before. Why had he been such a fool?

"Of course." He heard himself stammering. "Susannah's mother lived in Earlsfield, which is east Wandsworth, which is next to Balham, she was in hospital there."

"Guy, I honestly don't know what you mean. It wasn't like that, Susannah's mother never came into it. I suppose I'd better tell you, though I promised myself I never would."

"Tell me what?" He touched the wooden frame of the French windows and held on.

"A woman wrote to Susannah—well, she wrote to Susannah and my father, I mean to Mr. and Mrs. Anthony Chisholm. I was there when the letter came. I suppose she thought they were my parents, I mean that Susannah was my mother. She wrote warning them off you, for my sake, I mean. Look,

Guy, what is this? What does it matter? I've told you it didn't make any difference. I have to go, we've been talking for half an hour."

"Please don't go, Leo, please don't ring off. This is terribly important to me, I have to know. Who wrote to your parents?"

"To Daddy and Susannah," she said. He could hear a growing impatience in her voice. "Well, I'll tell you quickly and then I must go. I've told you it made no difference to the way I felt about you and you must believe that. This woman's name was Vasari, I've always remembered because it's the same as the man who wrote about the lives of the artists." He didn't know what she meant, he was lost. "Vasari," she said, "Polly or something. She wrote to them to tell them they shouldn't let me marry you. My God, I was twenty-two years old. They were to stop me marrying you because you were a social menace and you'd given drugs to her boy-friend. It was something like that. Susannah opened the letter because it was addressed to both of them and Daddy had gone to work."

"And she told you just like that?"

"I was there when she opened the letter. Of course she showed it to me. Look, phone me later if you want to, but I do have to go now, this minute."

He said he would phone her at seven. She said goodbye quickly and put the phone down. He sighed. Clarifying the mysteries of the past and the present only led to further complications. Of course it was easy to see how Poppy Vasari had found out about his association with Leonora and found out, too, who Leonora was. In those days they were often together, he was always calling at Lamb's Conduit Street. She would have followed him, read the name by the bell-push on the door. How that vindictive woman must have enjoyed writing the letter that would ruin his life!

And Susannah, that treacherous woman, that snake in the grass . . . Surely a nice person with any idea of loyalty would have thrown that letter away in disgust after reading the first line. The sort of woman he had thought Susannah was wouldn't have believed a word of it, the last thing she would have done was show it, and show it immediately, to the girl it was intended to caution. The hypocrisy of it made him indignant. It wouldn't have been so bad coming from Tessa, who had never pretended to like him, who had never concealed her hatred. He remembered Susannah's kindly proffered advice, her Judas kisses.

He phoned Leonora again at seven. It was Newton he expected to hear and he braced himself for the man's exasperated, superior-sounding voice—after all, he was going to have to spend tomorrow evening with him—but Leonora answered the phone.

"Can he hear what you're saying?" he asked her.

"If you mean William, he's not here. He's been in Manchester all day and he's not back."

"Will he be back by tomorrow evening?"

"Yes, of course. He'll be back tonight, any minute now, I should think."

"Leonora, tell me about the letter Poppy Vasari wrote to Susannah."

"Oh dear, I wish you'd forget it. I wish I'd never told you. You're making far too much of it. Poppy—is that her name?—Vasari wrote to Daddy and Susannah and told them you made your living by selling dangerous drugs. I think she called them Class-A drugs. She said you'd given a hallucinogenic tablet—those were the words she used—to this Mulvanney man and he'd gone crazy and stuck his head in a beehive. Well, that part had been in the papers. There was a photocopy in with the letter of an account of the inquest from a newspaper. Susannah showed it to me—well, I was sort of reading it over her shoulder. She said she didn't think she'd even tell Daddy. She was quite upset."

"What did you say to her?"

"As a matter of fact, I said I thought it was probably libel putting things like that in a letter."

"Did she tell your father?"

"I don't know. I didn't ask and he never said. She told Magnus."

"She did what?"

"Guy, please don't get in a state. She told Magnus because he's a solicitor. She rang him up at his office and asked him what one ought to do about letters like that. She meant should she tell the police, I think."

"Oh, Christ," said Guy. "Christ."

"Anyway, you needn't worry because he said the best thing to do with it was burn it. I suppose he thought it was a poison-pen letter, though it was in fact signed."

"No doubt old Skull-face told your mother."

"Possibly. Well, yes, I expect he did. My mother and I never discussed it. I wish you wouldn't call Magnus that. Susannah and I talked about it quite a bit. She's very understanding, you know. I told her we all smoked grass in those days and she said she had too, and I said I expect you *had* dealt in drugs when you were younger. It was the background you came from and the people you associated with—you didn't mind my saying that, did you, Guy?"

"I don't mind anything you say," he said.

"All Susannah said was that it might have mattered if I was seriously thinking of marrying you but I wasn't."

"She said that?"

"There isn't any point in going over and over it. *It made no difference to the way I felt.* Guy, you *know* how I feel, I've told you often enough. Listen, I can hear William coming in. We'll see you tomorrow night, right?"

"I'll phone you first thing in the morning."

"No, don't do that. I shan't be here. I'll see you about seven-thirty tomorrow."

He was going out to dinner with Bob Joseph and a man who was chairman of a Spanish hotel chain. They were meeting at a restaurant in Chelsea not far from the one where he had dined on the evening he had seen the street person who might have been Linus. Guy walked down to the Old Brompton Road. What had Leonora meant, she wouldn't be there "first thing in the morning"? She was there now. Where could she possibly be going? Then he realized. Tomorrow would be

September 6 and very likely the first day of her school term. The children would be returning to school tomorrow. She would be going to work.

But, wait a minute. That was a bit odd, going back to school as a teacher when you intended to get married less than two weeks later and take a fortnight off. Teachers never did that. Teachers were expected to get married and go on honeymoons in the long school holidays. But of course, it meant only one thing: she wasn't getting married, she had never really intended to get married. It was all a fantasy. Was it perhaps designed to make him jealous? If so, it had certainly succeeded. He smiled to himself. Women, he thought, were like that.

He turned out of the Earl's Court Road and began looking for Linus. In a doorway, though not the doorway of the health-food shop, a man lay asleep, curled up in the foetal position, his face and head covered by a newspaper. Guy thought it was the same man but he couldn't be sure. Nor could he bring himself to wake the man. The realization he had come to about Leonora and her fake or dream wedding made him feel so happy and buoyant that his interest in Linus was temporarily weakened. There was nothing anyway that he could do about it. To lift up the newspaper and look at the sleeping man's face seemed to him an outrageous act, a piece of insensitive impertinence. This evidently was Linus's beat. He would find him again.

A taxi came and he got into it. He thought of Susannah with hatred, picturing her in that flat in her smart black trousers and top. She was leaning over the banisters and smiling. He followed this welcoming presence into the living room. The white card with the silver border was on the mantelpiece. It was probably an invitation to someone else's wedding. Yes, that would be it. It was an invitation to another couple's wedding, the ceremony had already taken place, and because the card was now therefore useless, Janice had picked it up and thrown it out as she went to make tea. This explanation satisfied him completely.

Flowers, chocolates, wine—or a real present? He had never seen her eat chocolates. She was a health foodie. Flowers had to be put in water, which would mean her going away and leaving him with Newton. A real present could only be jewellery for her, earrings, for instance, and he sensed this would somehow be out of place, over the top, ostentatious. After all, unimportant as William Newton might be, a mere stooge or puppet set up by Anthony and Susannah, it was his home, he still no doubt thought of Leonora as engaged to him, even as due to marry him on Saturday week. Guy didn't think he could give Leonora a pair of earrings worth, say, three hundred pounds, in Newton's presence.

He settled for champagne. A single bottle of Piper Heidsieck. Should he wear a suit? He couldn't imagine Newton even possessing a suit. Maybe designer jeans and a sweater would be best. It wasn't going to be warm. Guy realized he was as nervous and uneasy about the evening ahead as if he had never dined out in his life. Would there be other people there? If only he could phone her. There was an idea in his mind of finally winning her away from Newton on this evening, carrying her off under his nose, a happy victim of kidnap, bringing her home here forever.

A night's sleep had cooled his anger. He no longer felt he hated Susannah. He blamed her, he never wanted to see her again, if he had met her in the street he would have passed her by with head averted, but his hatred had gone. After all, she had failed. In spite of her vindictive motives, she hadn't succeeded in turning Leonora against him. Leonora herself said it had made no difference. Susannah had interfered inexcusably in his life, but her interference no longer mattered, had never mattered, it was simply of no account.

Yet his discovery altered the situation. Rachel, designated Chuck's victim, was very obviously not guilty. Rachel had never spoken to or even heard of Poppy Vasari, Rachel had never been told about his activities as a dealer, so

Rachel did not merit death. But Guy, not usually cowardly, balked at saying so to Danilo. Having changed his mind about Robin Chisholm and been roughly handled by Danilo on account of it, he hesitated to ring Danilo up and say he had been wrong about Rachel too.

It wasn't as if he could even say, "Forget Rachel Lingard, Susannah Chisholm is the one." Susannah *wasn't* the one, he didn't want Susannah killed, he just never wanted to speak to her again. Dressing for the dinner party ahead, deciding finally—the sun having come out—on a pair of white linen trousers and a black silk shirt with white-and-cream-patterned V-necked silk pullover, Guy came to the conclusion that there was no need, at least at present, to tell Danilo anything. Rachel, after all, was out of the country, safe in some Spanish resort. Chuck probably knew this, or knew she had gone away, and would do nothing until she returned on September 15.

Just before he left, he poured himself a stiff brandy, then another. He needed it and there might not be much on offer in Georgiana Street. The taxi waited while he went into the wine shop and bought the champagne. He was going to be early. He got the driver to set him down in Mornington Crescent and began to walk the rest of the way, cradling the heavy bottle that was wrapped up in mauve tissue paper. It was still only twenty past seven when he got there. The houses here had scrubby front gardens, tiny plots of brown grass and dusty bushes. Steps went up to the front door and there was a deep basement. In the front garden of the house where Newton lived was planted a pole with an estate agent's board attached to it on which was printed: ONE-BEDROOM LUXURY FLAT and SOLD, SUBJECT TO CONTRACT.

There were five flats, one on each floor. Guy, before he even rang Newton's bell, had a very good idea what the "luxury," as described by the estate agent, would amount to. A bathroom that actually had tiles on the walls, and some sort of central heating. He didn't much like to think of Leonora living in this place, a back street that looked as if it would be unsafe at night, a grey brick house whose paintwork needed renewing.

Newton's voice, coming out of the grid, instead of asking who it was, said, "Come up," and the lock on the door buzzed.

A steep staircase and two long flights to climb. Another one of those dreary walk-ups. Newton was on the landing, outside an open front door, waiting for him. He said, "Hi," and held out his hand. After a moment's hesitation, Guy shook hands with him. He was glad he hadn't put a suit on. Newton wore jeans and a grey jumper with a hole in one of the elbows. His longish ginger hair stuck up like a punk's, only it grew that way, the effect hadn't been achieved with styling gel.

Leonora was in the living room, looking awkward, Guy thought, or embarrassed perhaps. As well she might in this barn of a room with a surprisingly low ceiling and two small sash windows giving onto the grey façade opposite. He had got over all his heart-turnings on the way upstairs and advanced towards her with no more diffidence than if she had been Celeste. She kissed him, a light peck. Of course she would, with Newton watching. He handed the champagne to Newton, who said, "How grand. What are we celebrating?"

That made Guy smile. The little red-haired man was really very unsophisticated. Guy felt powerful, in control. He said kindly, "Quite a lot of people drink champagne as an aperitif these days, you know. There doesn't have to be anything to celebrate."

"Oh, I see. Then it would be appropriate to drink it now?"

"Don't be absurd, William," said Leonora, looking uncomfortable, though Guy couldn't see what was absurd about what he'd said.

He was taking a good look round the room. The furniture was the kind of thing rejected by comfortably off middle-aged achievers and passed on to poor young relatives. He assessed the carpet as coming from one of those sales held after a store fire. You could even see the burnt patch in one corner. Up on the wall, above a Victorian fireplace of cast iron and floral tiles, a fireplace that was there not because Newton had found it in an antique shop but because it had been put in with the rest of the dilapidated fittings in 1895, hung the swords.

They were crossed at the point Guy remembered was called the forte. One was bare, the other in a rather worn and shabby embroidered scabbard. They recalled to Guy that dream he had had in which he was fighting Con Mulvanney with swords in Kensington Gardens and had stabbed him through the heart. He remembered Newton had said he wanted to sell the swords. He had also, on that occasion after the cinema, said something about selling his flat.

"Is that this flat that's been sold?" he had begun to ask when Leonora came back with three glasses (one champagne flute, one hock glass, and something that looked as if designed to hold half a grapefruit) on a tray. Guy nearly offered to open the champagne, but stopped himself because he wanted to see Newton make a mess of it and in Leonora's presence.

She was looking worried and far from her best. Gone was the elegant fashionable young woman in the dark-blue-and-pink linen suit, the pretty stockings and shoes. Being with Newton simply didn't suit her. That was an inescapable conclusion, anyone would see it. Those white pants would only look good if freshly laundered each time they were worn, and as for that faded sweat-shirt . . . Her hair was hauled onto the back of her head with one of those awful crocodile clips. The red glass roses hanging from her ears looked ridiculous with the rest of the get-up.

Newton opened the champagne without mishap. It must have been one of the easy bottles, Guy thought, you sometimes got them. They began to talk about the sale of Newton's flat and Guy asked him where he was going to live. He asked where *he* was going to live but Newton said, "I expect we shall buy a house."

Guy ignored that "we." "You don't want to leave it too long. Remember, property's the best investment. Even in a recession in the property market it's a great mistake to sell your home and invest the proceeds in something else."

"I'll remember that, Guy," said Newton.

Guy was quite well-informed about the property market and he talked some more about it. He said something about his own plans for moving, perhaps of buying a house at the "best end" of Ladbroke Grove. What did Leonora think of Stanley Crescent, the abode, he had heard, of TV personalities and one world-famous singer, a million-pound Italianate villa in fashionable Stanley Crescent? William said he hardly supposed what Leonora thought would make any difference to whether Guy bought or not. He said it coldly and Guy wondered if the two of them had been quarrelling before he arrived. Leonora went off to do the final dinner preparations and Guy changed the subject. He intended to be tactful, to behave well while he could.

"Very autumnal this evening," he said, looking towards the window.

"The nights will soon be drawing in," said Newton.

Guy looked narrowly at him to see if he was mocking him, but it was all right. Newton's expression was both serious and pleasant. He began to talk about the summer that was past, the sunniest of the century.

It wasn't much of a meal. If people couldn't or wouldn't cook properly, Guy thought, it was better to buy smoked salmon and a cold roast chicken for guests than attempt strange meat loaves. He was even more dubious when Leonora told him there was no meat in the loaf, it was all soya and herbs. The only good thing was the wine, a surprisingly good claret, of which Newton actually produced two bottles. Guy complimented him on the wine. Drink, as it always did, made him feel a lot better. Just the same, he knew it would be impossible for him to pass a passive evening here and to go home alone. The brandy, the wine had wonderfully clarified his mind. He saw that this was the crunch, the time had come. But it wasn't this decision of his that was responsible for the change in atmosphere, the rapidly ensuing trouble. It was the question he asked Leonora, in all innocence, about her first day back at school.

"It's a shame you've had to cook. We could have gone out to eat."

This remark was partly prompted by the dessert she served, a home-made sorbet, the colour and texture of three-day old snow but with large ice crystals in it like splinters of glass. The sorbet was as tasteless as snow too, though Guy guessed it was supposed to be lemon.

"Why is it a shame, Guy? Because the food's so awful? I'm sorry, I know I'm not much of a cook. But William's worse except with curry. His curry's marvellous, only we didn't know if you liked it."

The idea of a man possibly being expected to cook for guests rather shocked him. But he didn't say so. He hastened to assure his Leonora—that she should apologize to him!— that he only meant she must have had a hard day at school, today being the first day of the new term.

She reddened. It was years since he had seen her blush like that. Newton didn't seem to notice. He was busy with the mousetrap cheese, which was all that was on offer. But he looked up and said, with his mouth full,

"She hasn't been in today. She's given up—remember?"

Remember? What did the man mean? "Leo, have you left your job? You didn't tell me."

"I resigned," she said, "as soon as I knew . . . I mean, I resigned in June."

"What were you going to say?" he said. "As soon as you knew what?"

Newton picked up the wine bottle. He looked at Leonora, who shook her head, filled Guy's glass and then his own. He took a long slow drink, said, "As soon as she knew I was going to work for BBC North-West."

Guy looked at her. "I don't understand."

"There's no particular reason why you should need to."

Newton could be quite simple and innocent-sounding and, suddenly, he could become crisp. The crispness was starting to gel into ice. "I have a new job. In Manchester. BBC North-West Studios are in Manchester. Therefore, in the nature of things, since I'm not a happy commuter, I shall live there. Are you answered?"

"*You*, yes," Guy said. "I don't see why Leonora has to give up her job because you're going to live in Manchester."

"Don't you? You're rather slow sometimes. I've noticed it before. Let me explain in simple language. Leonora has given up her job in West London because she intends to get another one in Manchester. She is going to live in Manchester with me. From the end of this month. Leonora is going to live with me because she *will be married to me.*"

"Why didn't you tell me about this, Leonora?"

"Because she's afraid of your reaction. She's afraid of what you'll do. And who can blame her? Now let's talk about something else. Let's change the subject. We can revert to any of those things you're so fascinated by, house buying or the autumnal weather, any bloody thing, only for God's sake let's not get our tempers running any higher."

He was hardly going the right way about reducing Guy's temper. Guy jumped up. Before he could speak, Leonora said, "Please stop quarrelling, the pair of you. Please stop now. I should have told you, Guy, but William's right, you're so *violent.*"

"Would you expect me to take it lying down? That he's preparing to take you away? To take you up to the north of England?"

"Why not? She'll be my wife. I'll be her husband. If she'd got a job in Manchester, I'd have followed her. The idea of being married surely is that you share each other's lives."

"I want to hear what Leonora has to say, not you. Let her speak for herself. She's quite capable of that, I assure you. Now you tell me, Leonora—you weren't going to leave me, were you? You weren't seriously contemplating going to Manchester?"

"What do you mean, 'leave me'?" said Newton, very cold now. "You can't leave someone you're not with. Leonora left you seven years ago."

"It's a lie!" Guy shouted. "She loves me, she's told me so a hundred times. She isn't going to marry you. What makes you think she is? Her family found you for her and pushed her onto you, but they can't control her mind, they can't touch her heart. She's mine and she always will be . . ."

"Guy . . ." Leonora came round the table to him. Newton still sat there staring, calm, as cold as ice. "Guy," Leonora said, "you must stop this, you must."

"Get him to stop lying to me and then I'll stop all right."

"He isn't lying. I'm going to marry him and I'm going to Manchester with him."

"I don't believe it. I *won't* believe it. I'll see you dead before I let you go away with him."

"Do you wonder I didn't tell you about it when you go on like this? The reason I didn't tell you was to avoid you going on like this."

Guy looked at her, feeling a tide of misery gathering and mounting inside him. He had never felt more like weeping in her arms. He wanted to take her in his arms and beg her not to go. "You won't go, will you, Leo?"

She made no answer but her face was twisted as if she was in pain.

"That's why you're selling your flat," he said. "That's why he's selling his."

"Please don't, Guy, don't go on. Please stop shouting."

It was slowly becoming clear to him. "That's why he's getting rid of"—he flung out an arm—"all this shit. All this rubbish," he said, ". . . these swords. He said he wanted to sell his swords."

Guy was trembling. He took two steps to the fireplace and pulled down the swords from the wall. Newton sat there, looking incredulous. Guy threw the naked sword down on the table and tugged the other from its scabbard. Leonora seized his arm. He flung off her hand and leaped back, brandishing the shining sabre.

"I'll fight you for her! We'll fight a duel." He was trembling no longer. Adrenaline poured through him, quenching misery. "I'll fight you to the death!"

CHAPTER SEVENTEEN

William Newton picked up the sabre from the table and stood looking at it as if it were some strange implement he had heard of but never seen before. He laid it down again, said to Guy, "Why don't you put that down and go home."

"He's afraid to fight me, Leonora," Guy said.

"It might be unwise." A little smile, probably nervous, had appeared on Newton's horsy face. "They're old fighting sabres, they're not ornamental."

"You coward," said Guy. "Where's your honour? Admit it, you're chicken. This is the man your parents chose to be your husband, Leonora. Pathetic, isn't he?" He raised the sabre. It was years since Guy had taken his fencing lessons, but he was strong and fit. He held the sword at an angle, the point level with Newton's eyes.

Leonora said in a breathless voice, "I'm going to phone the police."

"Why?" said Guy. "Nothing's going to happen to me."

"I'm going to phone them unless you put that sword down *now*."

"No, you're not, my dear."

The phone on a small side table had a long trailing lead. It wasn't the kind you can plug in. Guy brought the sabre down with a long slicing movement across the lead six inches from where it emerged from the wall. The phone bounced off the table but the lead remained intact. Guy made a grab at it, pulled the lead and wrenched it out of the wall socket.

"For God's sake. Are you mad?"

"Don't say that to me, Leo. You shouldn't have talked about phoning the police. Stand back, please. Go in the other room, if you want." He added contemptuously, "If there is another room." He turned back to Newton, who had said nothing, who had responded to none of Guy's insults, but merely stood there, the smile still twitching his lips. "Ginger dwarf, miserable runt. Fucking prig."

Casually, Newton picked up the sword. Its blade was dull but it looked sharp. For all their shabby appearance on the wall, the swords had been kept in good condition. The two men faced each other, each holding his weapon, but not crossing them, not performing any preliminary ritual. They looked at each other and Leonora watched them, one hand up to her open mouth.

Guy was the first to make a move. He swung his sword in two sideways sweeps, to the left and to the right, then made a swift fierce stab at Newton, but the other man skipped quickly round the table, avoiding the lunge. Guy stabbed again, over the table-top, knocking over the wine bottle. Newton ducked, then sprang up at the end of the table where he had been sitting. His sword and Guy's clashed with a high-ringing sound. Guy thrust again and the swords crossed and recrossed. Playing for a moment or two, like a tennis player in a knock-up before a match, Newton suddenly made a sweeping movement that turned Guy's weapon aside.

"Pimp," shouted Guy, "ginger dwarf, yes-man, wimp, egghead."

Newton started laughing. "I have to tell you," he said, "that I've done quite a bit of this, so if you want to stop now, that'll be okay."

"He's trying to say he's good," Leonora shouted. "He fenced for his university."

"So did I," said Guy, "the university of life! Now wipe that grin off your face," he yelled at Newton and lunged at him.

Leonora put her head in her hands. The swords were simply clashing now, Guy smashing his this way and that, in wild movements without any finesse or control. He sprang back and drove his weapon at Newton in a scooping movement like an underarm serve. Newton didn't skip aside this time but deflected the blade with a single sweep. Guy could feel Leonora behind him. One of her hands clutched at his shoulder. He shook it off. He backed, defending himself. She cried out, "Please, Guy, please stop. I'll get the neighbours, I swear I will. I'll go down to the street and phone the police. You must stop."

"For Christ's sake, keep out of this!" He had never spoken to her like that before. She gave a sob. "I love you," he shouted. "I'll always love you. I'll win you!"

Newton stood there, legs apart. He wasn't smiling any more. He threw back his ginger hair. For a moment they faced each other, perfectly still. Guy had the feeling Newton would like to stop, would welcome a truce. That made him spring forward and whirl his sword in a movement that, if successful and the blade sharp, would have severed Newton's head. Leonora screamed. But the stroke wasn't successful. Newton parried it. He did so easily, and in a way that maddened Guy, it was so smoothly done and with a grace that made the ringing clang of the blades the more shocking.

Newton made a quick riposte, a feint really. He was teasing Guy. He danced with his sabre, making swift covering moves as Guy's sword lunged wildly. Leonora was struggling to raise one of the window sashes. Guy forgot everything he had learned about fencing. He was just a man with a stabbing, cutting weapon. He was doing what an unskilled man with a sword will do, pushing it back and forth to the right and left, and yelling curses with each attack. He could hear himself roaring.

She couldn't shift the window but collapsed against it for a moment, her head on her hands. Guy beat at the air, at Newton's blade when his came into contact with it, once striking the shade of the central light and setting it swinging wildly. Leonora's coming away from the window, standing there and watching them as if hypnotized, gave him a fresh impetus. But the silent Newton was no longer menaced by anything Guy did. He was in absolute control of the bout. Sometimes his weapon grazed Guy's, sometimes beat lightly on it. Guy's rage, at boiling point, rose another inch and spilled over. He leaped outside the range of Newton's sabre and made a wild attempt to run him through from the side.

The blade missed Newton, not because he parried it with his own but because he contracted his muscles in the nick of time. The sabre point went through his sweater at the waist and ripped the wool from hem to neckline.

Newton growled like a bear. His sweater flapped open like an unfastened strait-jacket. He pulled his arms out, stood there in a grubby white T-shirt, his breath rasping angrily. Guy was laughing in triumph. He pulled off his own jumper and threw it across the room. From his success he had gained skill, or at least energy. He began to mix slashes and stabbing, crowing and making Wild West yells. Leonora was watching wide-eyed, like a first-time spectator at a bullfight, horrified, yet compelled.

Guy began directing his blade in a low line, pointing at Newton's genitals. He twirled the point. He laughed. Shouting insults, he danced up and down, the sword jumping and bobbing in a half-circle at thigh level. It was designed to lull Leonora's lover into a state of unpreparedness, and if the surprise thrust he now made had hit its target, Newton would have got to his feet a eunuch. But this was the last blow Guy was to attempt. It was all over with a frightening suddenness.

Newton parried the lunge with a neat turn of his wrist in a lateral defensive movement, riposted at once and caught Guy on the left arm. The point of the sabre cut him in a straight line from wrist to elbow.

Guy's sword fell from his hand. With blood fountaining from his wound he toppled over, seizing what first came to hand to break his fall. It was the edge of the table-cloth and with it came plates and glasses, wine bottle, knives and forks. He collapsed onto the floor covered in a litter of sticky china and glass. He could hear Leonora screaming, a manic animal sound. She dropped the window sash and ran to him. Guy shut his eyes, opened them and sat up. His arm was streaming with blood.

"Oh God," Leonora sobbed. "Oh God, oh God."

"It's all right," he whispered. "I'll be all right."

He held the wound but his hand wasn't large enough to cover it. Leonora started ripping up the tablecloth, tearing it into strips. The first bandage she put on was immediately soaked in blood. She was sobbing and gasping.

"Don't worry, darling," Guy said, "it's only a flesh wound."

This, for some reason, evoked a crow of laughter from Newton, who with ridiculous coolness was wiping the sabre blade and replacing it, unwashed, in its scabbard. He hung both swords back on the wall.

"Still want to buy them?" he said.

"Oh, William, don't. Haven't you done enough?"

"I'm sorry," Newton said. "I shouldn't have fought him."

"No, you shouldn't. It was awful. Look what you've done. Phone for an ambulance, now, please."

"I can't phone for anything, can I? Not now he's buggered up the phone."

Leonora unwrapped the table-cloth bandage and started applying a fresh one. Guy was still sitting on the floor. He got to his feet. His left arm felt rather numb, without pain. There had been no pain, only the initial sting, like an insect biting, when Newton's sword point ripped the skin. Newton sighed and said, "I'll drive you to hospital. I'm sorry about this, Guy. It's a mess. All we can do now is go and find some casualty department."

"Thanks, but I'd rather die than have you drive me anywhere."

"Okay, be like that, but you'll have to have something done about your arm."

"I'll drive him," said Leonora. "I'll drive you, Guy."

Everything that had happened was worth it to hear her say that. She had another go with a fresh strip of table-cloth, binding it more tightly this time. One of her scarves made a sling for his arm. "Put your sweater round you." She picked it up off the floor. "Do you want a coat? I expect I could find you a jacket."

"Not one of his," said Guy.

Newton grinned. "He'd rather die of cold."

That made Guy start for him, fists up, in spite of his bleeding arm. Leonora grabbed him, pulled him round, and then the wound did start to hurt, a deep throb beginning. Guy groaned. Leonora's face was wet with tears. She wiped it on another bit of table-cloth. Newton touched her arm and she looked at him, but Guy couldn't read that look. He would have liked to hold on to her going down the stairs but pride forbade it.

At the bottom a front door opened and a man, a sleek yuppie with a small moustache, put his head out.

"Everything all right?"

"Only a duel," said Leonora, with an hysterical edge to her voice.

The man didn't seem to take this in. "I thought I heard something. My wife said it was builders."

They found a casualty department open in a big hospital half-way up a hill. Guy didn't know the name of it. He didn't really know North London. It seemed to him he must have lost pints of blood. His shirt was soaked with blood. It had cost him nearly two hundred pounds, a deceptively simple and casual garment. The blood would never come out. Some of it had got onto Leonora's track-suit top and there were smears on her white trousers. The pair of them looked as if they had come off a battlefield.

He was happy. Of course he realized that it was awful, what he had done. He would be scarred for life. But she loved him. He had won her. Hadn't she reproached the wretched Newton? Hadn't she rushed to him and sacrificed a perfectly good table-cloth to bind up his wound?

"I'll pay for the phone to be re-connected," he whispered.

She started laughing. It was humourless hysteria. Sobs punctuated it.

"Come on," he said. "Everything'll be okay. You'll see. I'll buy him a new sweater."

After that his name was called. A weary doctor cleaned the wound and of course wanted to know what had caused it. An accident with a carving knife, Guy said, an explanation that wasn't believed, but the doctor said no more for the time being. He gave Guy an anti-tetanus injection, put half a dozen stitches in the wound. It was no more really than a deep scratch.

"Do you know what that looks like to me? Just as a matter of interest? As if someone quite skilled with the sabres wanted to, if you'll forgive the pun, make his point. Show he meant business but that was enough for now, right?"

"I don't know what you mean," said Guy.

"I do a bit with the sabres myself, or I used to, in the days when life was normal and I had, you know, what's it called, leisure. Run along now. You can come back next Wednesday and have the stitches out."

In the car Guy said, "Are you angry with me?"

"I don't know. I think I'm just tired, fed up, sick of the whole thing."

"My darling, I understand. I know how you feel."

"No, you don't, Guy. That's the trouble. You don't know

how I feel, you never have and you never will. Now I'm going to drive you home. Will you be all right on your own?"

"I hoped you'd stay with me."

"I can't do that. What good would that do? Shall I phone Celeste?"

He shook his head. They were waiting at a traffic light and he reached out to take her hand. "Stay with me."

"Guy, I'll come in with you and see that you're okay and make you a hot drink. I'll phone you in the morning."

He understood she couldn't leave Newton just like that. Newton, who was a madman, a psychopath, was capable of coming round to look for her, armed probably. Besides, she probably wanted to be alone with Newton and tell him in no uncertain terms what she thought of his violent behavior.

He said it again and this time she didn't argue. "Have lunch with me on Saturday."

"I always have lunch with you on Saturdays."

That she came in with him as she had promised nevertheless surprised him. "Your lovely house," she said. "It's the nicest house I know."

"Is it? It'll be yours one day."

He waited for the denial but it didn't come. "I can't remember where the kitchen is."

"You don't need the kitchen. I don't want a drink, not that sort anyway. You shall sit down, my darling, and *I'll* make you a drink. Something strong, you need it after all that hassle."

"I'm driving," she said. "Remember?"

"Oh, come on. No one's going to breathalyse you."

She took the glass from him, poured soda water into it. He was impeded by his disabled left arm. Something from the evening past came back to him. Perhaps it was the sight of the television set in the corner that he hardly ever switched on. He poured his brandy, a generous measure.

"Haven't you got an uncle in television? Something with the BBC? Haven't I met him?"

She nodded. "My father's brother, my Uncle Michael. He's the chairman of TVEA. Why?"

"I suppose it was through him Newton got this job?"

"Of course it wasn't, Guy. It had nothing to do with it. William's going to work for BBC North-West. He *told* you."

"It all comes to the same thing, though, doesn't it? Back-scratching. What's the word? Begins with an *N*."

"Nepotism. Only it isn't. Guy, are you all right to be left? I ought to go."

"Where shall we have lunch on Saturday?"

"Anywhere you like."

"D'you know, I thought for a while in the car that you might say you wouldn't have lunch with me, you might be too cross."

She smiled, got up. "Well, now you know. I'm not. Too cross, I mean."

"Clarke's again?" he said.

"Could it be—well, more central? Didn't we once go to a nice fish place in the Haymarket?"

"The Café Fish in Panton Street."

"That's right. One o'clock? Guy . . . ?" She took his hand. They walked out into the hall together. He stood inside the front door looking at her, his left arm still supported in her red-and-black silk scarf. "Guy—I don't know how to say this." She was trembling. The light in the hall was dim but he could see she had gone pale. Her eyes glittered. "I want to—could we spend the day together on Saturday? I mean, could we have lunch and be together for the rest of the day? Maybe go to the theatre or the cinema, have dinner—oh, I don't know. I'd just like to—but your poor arm! Perhaps you won't feel like . . ."

"Oh, darling!" He put his good arm round her. She nestled against him. "I wouldn't have minded if he'd cut off my arm if this is the result. Don't you know by now you don't have to ask if we can spend the day together? Don't you know it's what I long for?"

"That's all right, then." She put up her face.

He kissed her as he hadn't kissed her for years, not even that time by the Embankment Gardens. Her warm, responsive lips opened under his. He felt her breasts press against him. His heart knocked and made his hurt arm throb. The strangest thing of all was that he was the first to draw back, to pull away. He had to because of the pain where her body crushed against his wound. She wasn't smiling but gazing at him with a curious, half-hypnotized concentration.

"I must go," she said at last.

"You said you'd phone me in the morning."

"Of course I will."

He stood watching the car turn on the cobbles. The night was chilly, very clear. For once, as very seldom happened, stars could be seen up there in the radiant purple, swimming points of light. She waved from the open car window, rolled it up, disappeared rather quickly. It was almost midnight. He went indoors and drank some more brandy until he began to feel light-headed and his arm no longer hurt.

CHAPTER EIGHTEEN

He overslept. He had been dreaming he was going to be married. It was Leonora he was going to be married to and in church, or he thought it was, he couldn't be entirely sure. He arrived at St. Mary Abbots in a taxi and hurried into the church alone. He was late and the guests, hundreds of them, were already there. Breathless, he arrived at the chancel steps, only to realize he had forgotten the ring. He stood, wondering what to do, while behind him a swell of giggling arose from the congregation. It gathered force and became a long sustained roar of laughter. Guy looked down and saw he was dressed in the costume of a fencer, the tight jacket, gloves, breeches, and white stockings. For the first time he was aware he had a mask on his face.

The phone ringing pulled him out of this dream before worse humiliation could happen. He reached for the phone and, turning over, felt pain from his sore arm. Memory of the previous evening returned as he lifted the receiver, and with it came a surge of panic. What had he done? He said a cautious "Hallo?"

"How are you this morning, Guy?"

He could hardly believe it was Leonora's voice he was hearing. How long was it since last she had phoned him? Years. But, of course, things had changed. He remembered more about the night before. Almost incredulously, he began remembering what she had said.

"Guy? Are you all right?"

"I'm fine, darling. I'm perfectly okay."

"Did you get some sleep?"

"Like a log. I died. As a matter of fact, the phone ringing woke me."

"Oh, I'm sorry. I did wait till nine. I was anxious about you."

He closed his eyes at the bliss of it. He said softly, "It's wonderful to hear your voice."

"Do you think you should go and see your own doctor today?"

"Why? Everything's been done that can be. It's only a bit sore." Downstairs he heard Fatima let herself in and the front door close. "It really *is* nine. Listen, Leo, did I dream it or did you say you'd spend all Saturday with me?"

"You didn't dream it."

"Thank God. I've had such strange dreams I don't know what's real and what isn't. If I get tickets for a show, what would you like to see?"

He remembered too late that she didn't like that word "show" but preferred "play" and he waited for her to correct him. She only said, "I don't mind. You choose."

"I know you don't like musicals. I won't get a musical. Leo?"

"Yes, Guy."

"Afterwards, in the evening, will you come back here with me?"

He knew she would say no. She always did. Her hesitation meant nothing, only that she was looking for the kindest way to say no. One day she would say yes, but he wasn't absurdly optimistic, he knew it would be a long time. He waited stoically. The pause was a long one. He heard her sigh.

"Yes, I will," she said. "Of course I will. Anything you say."

"Leo, did you really say that? Did you really say you'll come back with me? You'll stay with me?"

"I did say that."

"Leo, I'm so happy. I'm so happy, darling. I know I've said it before. I can't help it. I'm so happy. Leo, you're not crying?"

"Guy," she said, "forgive me."

That made him laugh. "There's nothing to forgive. Say you love me. Say I'm the only one for you."

"You're the only one for me. I love you. One o'clock on Saturday, then?"

"One o'clock on Saturday, darling. Goodbye till then. Take care, save yourself for me."

It had happened. She had come back to him. Not a promise of next year, not years ahead, but now, the day after tomorrow. He could confess to himself now that he had doubted, he had sometimes lost hope, but the constancy, the struggle had not been in vain. He had won her. He had fought for her and he had won. The battle scar on his arm he looked at with pride. If he had lost his arm, it would have been worth it.

• • •

When he had had a bath, for showers must be avoided for the time being with that arm, he wondered if it would be wise to keep the sling on. No blood had come through the dressing. His arm was sore but no more than that. Slyly, he saw through his own doubts about the sling. What he really meant was that he wanted to go on wearing Leonora's scarf. Wasn't that what knights of old did—well, they did in movies—wore their ladies' favours? Susannah had called him Leonora's knight, had said his constancy was beautiful.

The scarf Leonora had given him was a silky woven

red-and-black thing. He dressed carefully in blue jeans, a pink shirt, a sweater he hardly ever wore but which was coincidentally very much like the scarf, a ribbed pattern in vertical stripes of dark grey and Venetian red. Guy found himself looking into the mirror for longer than he usually did. He was so much better-looking than William Newton, so superior a physical specimen, that it was almost a joke.

What he would have liked to do was spend the morning at the rifle club but that would only make his arm worse. He started phoning theatre box offices. Andrew Lloyd Webber's *Aspects of Love* was what he would have preferred. The price of tickets in the black market would be astronomical but that never bothered him. Leonora didn't like musicals, so that was out. Celeste had told him what *M. Butterfly* was about and he thought he might have enjoyed seeing it with her, but it wasn't the kind of thing you could take the woman you were going to marry to see. In the end he settled for Ayckbourn's *Henceforward* and booked two seats on his American Express Gold Card in the third row of the stalls.

Next day Celeste phoned to remind him they were dining with Danilo and Tanya and some American friends of theirs who were in London. Guy considered refusing on the grounds of his injured arm but thought better of it. It would pass the time until tomorrow. The dinner party was at the Connaught. The obvious thing would have been to call for Celeste in a taxi. He decided instead on the Jaguar. The idea appealed to him of driving it one-armed. He was going to tell everyone the truth, that he had got his wound in a duel.

"You're kidding," Danilo said.

The Americans looked to Guy like a couple of gangsters. They were both short, dark, Italianate, showily dressed. One of them had a scar on his cheek the circular shape of the broken-off base of a wine bottle. Tanya was up to her old trick of forgetting to change her shoes and wearing white sandals with her smart black minidress and black stockings. She gave one of the Americans a wink.

"Someone got fresh with Celeste, did they?"

"It had nothing to do with Celeste." Guy saw her wince, though he had already explained everything to her in the Jaguar on their way there. "A private matter."

"Be honest," said Danilo the abstemious. "You did it yourself when you were pissed."

It wasn't a very successful party. Tanya talked about her children. The Americans responded as if children were a rare species of mammal and one in which they were uninterested. This didn't deter Tanya, who told anecdotes about Carlo putting red dye into the swimming pool and telling her the gardener had cut his throat before falling in. Guy drank a lot. He moved on to brandy. He had promised Celeste they would leave by ten-thirty at the latest. She had to be at a photo-call in Kensington Gardens before eight in the morning. When it got to ten forty-five, she said she had to go.

"Just half an hour and I'll be with you."

"No, Guy. It's all right, I'll get a taxi."

"I'm not letting you do that." He struggled to his feet and suppressed a cry at the pain in his arm. "I'll drive you like I said."

"You're not fit to drive and I really have to go. I've already asked them to get me a taxi."

He was aware of only one thing. This way he wouldn't have to have her back to spend the night with him. Her hand rested lightly on his shoulder. "I'll see you tomorrow night," she said.

They must have made some arrangement. He would phone tomorrow morning and stop her, he couldn't come out with it in front of everyone. Feeling guilty, feeling obscurely ashamed, he touched the lightly resting hand. She said goodbye and was gone.

"Nice little looker," said one of the Americans, unbelievably to Guy.

Guy thought how extremely embarrassing it would be to take Leonora home with him and find Celeste there. Or for poor Celeste to arrive while he and Leonora were there together. He must give some serious thought to explaining to Celeste the turn events had taken.

"We'll drive you home," said Tanya. "I mean, we'll drive your car. We came in a cab, so we can take you home and get a taxi to take us on."

Danilo didn't say anything. His frog face was set in grim lines. Guy couldn't remember where he had parked the car and they trudged the dark empty Mayfair streets looking for it.

"I'm going to love you if they've clamped it," said Tanya.

They hadn't. Guy got in the back. The fresh autumnal air had brought him round. It was nearly midnight, nearly the day that would mark the beginning of his life with Leonora. What would Danilo and Tanya have to say to that?

He could have driven himself. He felt perfectly all right apart from his aching arm. They were driving along Knightsbridge when he remembered about Rachel Lingard. Tanya knew all about Danilo's activities—or as far as he knew she did.

"Can you put a stop on Chuck, Dan?"

"Can I *what?*"

"Just call it off, will you?"

Danilo was silent. Guy could tell he was upset. He went the wrong way and got them into the Fulham Road. With a little shrug Tanya said, "Don't mind me. I've had to learn when to shut my ears."

"Turn right when you can," Guy said. "Look, I'm sorry. I don't want the three grand back."

"I should fucking think not," said Danilo.

"But you can do it?"

"Ah, shit, Guy, I can live without this."

"But you can manage it?"

"Frankly, I don't know. I don't know who Chuck's put on the job and Chuck's been in Ireland. Maybe he's still in Ireland. I don't even know if Chuck's boy's doing it or Chuck's boy's boy."

Danilo turned left along the Old Brompton Road. Guy said, "You've got a fortnight. Well, two weeks tomorrow. She's

219

away for another two weeks." He was suddenly aware of where they were and what they might see.

Danilo said in a bad-tempered way, "Yeah, yeah, okay. It'll take time but maybe not that long. Only don't reckon on doing that kind of business with me again, right? Christ, what is it now?"

Guy was tapping on his shoulder. "Please stop, will you? Just for a minute. Just park over there. It won't take long, I promise."

"What is all this, Guy?" Tanya was losing patience with him now. "I have to be in the shop tomorrow morning."

"Please pull in over there, Danilo."

They had to walk back. The tall thin man lay stretched out on the doorstep of the health-food shop. He was dressed in the same soot-coloured rags, but this time he lay on his back, with the cap, which had been a receptacle for alms, covering his face. Guy said, "It's Linus."

"You're joking."

"No, I'm sure it is. This is the third time I've seen him. I know it's Linus. It's been worrying me, on my conscience, you know. Dan, we can't just leave him here. We'll have to do something for him."

Danilo went across the pavement, took hold of the cap and lifted it from the man's face. It woke him. He sat up and began screaming at them, his face contorted, his bright, white, perfect teeth bared. A stream of meaningless obscenity poured from him.

"Ah, for Christ's sake," said Danilo. He stuck up two fingers at the screaming man.

Guy could see now that it wasn't Linus. He was no more like Linus than he was like Danilo. "At least give him something."

"Give him something yourself," said Danilo and he walked back to the car, followed by Tanya.

Guy felt deeply disturbed. What was going on in his mind that he had confused this derelict with his old friend? He gave the man a tenner, which had the effect of shutting him up but not of eliciting thanks. He took the note, thrust it into his trouser pocket, and rolled back onto the doorstep, once more covering his face.

"Linus is dead," Danilo said when he was putting the Jaguar away in Guy's garage. "They strung him up in Kuala Lumpur. Have you ever thought of joining the AA?"

"I've been a member for years."

"Danny didn't mean the Automobile Association," said Tanya, by this time laughing helplessly. They went off together to find a taxi.

. . .

He would drink less when he was with Leonora all the time. If she wanted him to give up smoking, he would have a go at that too. In a month's time he would be thirty and it wouldn't be very many more years before he'd be unable to hold the drink as he could now. When he was happy all the time, leading a contented life, he wouldn't need the drink to cushion him against blows, he wouldn't need his consciousness changed from misery to limbo.

He felt none the worse for the excesses of the night before and his arm was much better. The sling wouldn't be needed any more but he wanted to wear it because it was hers. Sentimentally, he thought of wearing her scarf today for the last time and then, when she was back here with him, returning it to her ceremoniously. She would smile her Vivien Leigh smile for him and at last it would be full and unrestrained.

What to wear this morning was something of a problem. Although he knew she had never been that keen on Newton, although he had been procured for her and she persuaded to take him, there was something about the man that appealed to her apart from his conversation. And Newton always dressed in clothes that were a combination of the Housing Trust Charity Shop and Dirty Dick's. It had to be faced that nice clothes didn't interest her, either for herself or her man. Perhaps he should start learning to care less about them himself. With that end in view he chose the jeans he had worn the day before, a plain blue shirt in sea-island cotton, and a blue-and-grey-striped seersucker jacket. It still looked over the top, or would to her. Changing the jacket for yesterday's sweater was a real sacrifice for him, but he made it. Carefully, he reknotted the ends of the scarf and arranged it around his neck to support his arm.

He was on the point of leaving when he remembered the ring. He still had the engagement ring he had bought for Leonora all those years ago. It was in the safe. He hadn't used the safe, hadn't opened it, for four years, there had been no need to do so. The last time was after Con Mulvanney's visit. He went back upstairs, opened the safe and took out the ring. It was in a small blue leather box and the ring itself, a large square-cut sapphire with "shoulders" of diamonds, sat in a bed of midnight-blue velvet. Guy put ring and box into his pocket.

It was twelve when he left the house, much too soon for an appointment in the West End at one. But he had nothing to do. He had already made a careful tour of the house, checking that everything was as it should be to receive her. He had refilled the ice trays in the fridges in the kitchen and the drawing-room bar, arranged on the coffee-table *The Guardian, The London Review of Books,* and *Cosmopolitan,* which, wonder of wonders, the newsagent had remembered to deliver, and put into the bathroom that would be *her* bathroom the various Paloma Picasso toiletries he had yesterday sent Fatima out to buy. There was nothing left to do, and sitting about reading the paper was intolerable. He had made several attempts to phone Celeste and stop her from coming before he remembered she was out being photographed somewhere. At twelve he left to walk part of the way, stopped to look in an estate agent's window, and on an impulse went inside.

On their books they had a beautiful house in Lansdowne Crescent, Notting Hill. The price, they said, ran into seven figures. When they saw he didn't flinch they told him precisely what the price was. Photographs of interiors were produced: a grand staircase, swan-neck-shaped; a magnificent drawing-room forty feet long; octagonal bathrooms in each of the turrets. Guy made an appointment to view for Monday afternoon. By now it was twenty minutes to one, nice time to get there punctually in a cab.

The traffic was less dense than usual and the taxi put him down outside the Café Fish. It was two minutes to one. She might be there already, it had been known, and those familiar sensations repeated themselves—the little jump his heart gave, his insides tightening, pressure in his head. He paused on the pavement for a moment, gathered himself, went into the restaurant.

It was crowded but she wasn't there yet. The girl who came to show him to his table told him that. Smoking or non-smoking? One day he would choose non-smoking to please Leonora but that time hadn't come yet. He lit a cigarette the moment he was sitting down.

Obviously it had been a mistake to come here. The food was good and there was a big choice, but unfortunately a hundred other people knew it too. Of necessity the tables were close together. They wouldn't be able to talk intimately. Guy flicked his fingers at a waiter and when the man came over ordered a large gin and tonic. Brandy would have suited him better but he also realized brandy might not be a good idea at this stage.

With careful thought, he had chosen his theatre tickets for the matinée. The performance began at five-thirty, which meant they could have dinner soon after eight. There was plenty of time for everything—it would all be leisurely and beautiful. If there was any time left this afternoon between leaving here and the theatre, she would surely let him take her shopping. The engagement ring he already had, but perhaps a bracelet? Cartier? Asprey? Or perhaps some earrings. He imagined diamonds close up against her glowing face. When they were no more than children and she had first had her ears pierced, he had dreamed of the day when he could buy her diamond earrings.

The gin came, it was very welcome, he was thirsty for it. The first sip of the day was always wonderful. It spread peace through his body on long, divergent feelers. He sat back in his seat, looking at the pattern in the weave on her scarf, then at the menu, which was written on the card as well as up in chalk on blackboards. What would she have? She was eating more fish lately, he had been glad to see. She didn't get enough protein. He adjusted the sling on his arm and in doing so caught sight of his watch. It was nearly a quarter past one.

That was what came of trusting to the Northern Line instead of taking cabs. It was going to be the Savoy experience all over again, but in less luxurious surroundings. He finished his gin and ordered another. She had been over twenty minutes late, he remembered, for their lunch at the Savoy. It would be just like her to walk here from wherever the nearest Northern Line station was, Leicester Square probably.

The people at the next table, four of them, were laughing immoderately. It wasn't coarse laughter or particularly raucous, but it irritated him. His second gin went down very fast. If only you could ask for the bottle in these places and just help yourself as you could at home. He didn't quite like to ask for the bottle. Danilo and Tanya's remarks of the previous evening about Alcoholics Anonymous repeated themselves unpleasantly. The time was twenty-five past one. A waiter came up and asked him if he would like to order. Guy said no rather abruptly. More gales of laughter shook the table next to him. They were drinking champagne, evidently celebrating some anniversary. He had begun to feel hungry in the taxi going round Hyde Park Corner but his hunger had left him. In spite of the gin his mouth was dry. He asked for a large glass of white wine.

At twenty to two he began to feel sick. She was forty minutes late. He couldn't remember her ever having been more than twenty-two minutes late. She wasn't coming. He couldn't delude himself any longer that she was coming. Either something terrible had happened and she had met with an accident or she had been prevented from coming. Some member of that awful family of hers had found out what she planned to do, to spend the day, then the rest of her life, with him, and had stepped in to stop it. For another ten minutes he sat on, staring at the street door. Then he got up.

He told the imperturbable sullen-faced waiter he didn't want anything to eat after all, a remark to which the response was a Gallic shrug. He paid for his two gins and his wine. Luckily and for once he had a pocketful of small change. In the first empty phone-box that he found he dialled the Georgiana Street number. It was years since Guy had used a phone-box, they had changed in the interim and he had to read the instructions carefully before getting it to work.

The ringing began but there was no answer. He dialled again to make sure. Still no answer. He closed his eyes and imagined opening them to see her walking down the street towards the restaurant, running rather because she was in a panic at being late.

Of course she wasn't there. He scooped out the money that had come back and dialled Lamb's Conduit Street. All these numbers were stamped on his memory. He knew them better than his own phone number, bank account number. The bell rang and rang, but no one was answering there either. There was no reply when he dialled the St. Leonard's Terrace number and none from Portland Road, though that was a long shot, unless one of them had somehow contrived to imprison Leonora in her former home. The last place he tried was the Mandevilles' house in Sanderstead Lane and he tried in vain.

They couldn't *all* be out. It was plain what was happening. They had ganged up to stand solid against him. They were all refusing to answer their phones. She told them what had happened on Thursday night, told them in all innocence, still believing she could make her own choice as to her future life. Somewhere she had been made a prisoner. No doubt, it was principally her father who had done that, her father who, once his wife had poisoned Leonora's mind against her lover, had produced a husband for her, a tame lackey, an ugly egghead, and then, to make absolutely sure, with his brother's help, found him a job up north where his wife would accompany him.

Only it wasn't going to happen that way, Guy thought. Where would they keep her? Portland Road or Georgiana Street? He went back to Scarsdale Mews in a cab. Although he had drunk quite a lot and eaten nothing, he felt clear-headed and very calm.

At home he tried phoning again. Methodically he tried each number: Lamb's Conduit Street, Sanderstead Lane, St. Leonard's Terrace, Georgiana Street, Portland Road. Again there was no answer from any of them. He imagined all the phones unplugged, or those people—Anthony and Susannah, Tessa and Magnus, Robin and Maeve, Newton himself—sitting there listening implacably to the continuous ringing. The time was two forty-five.

He tried all the numbers again, to unnerve them, to make them jumpy. Then he went upstairs and took his .22-caliber rifle from its case.

CHAPTER NINETEEN

On the way to Portland Road he tried to find an explanation. At last he thought he could understand. It was the duel he had fought with Newton that was responsible for all this. The last straw, her family would call it. He couldn't imagine Leonora telling them about it but Newton would have. While Leonora was out taking him to the hospital, Newton would have been on the phone to her father and then her mother with an account of what had happened. He could hear Tessa's voice: "He's mad, of course. He's a violent, dangerous madman. He'll stop at nothing to get Leonora. The only thing is to keep her away from him until the sixteenth and then you can take her up north and he'll never see her again."

And Anthony Chisholm: "He attacked you with a sword? That's a bit much, isn't it? No, I quite agree, it won't do for Leonora to see him again."

And Magnus Mandeville: "Leonora should have gone for the police. Of course you couldn't have left her alone with him, I quite see that. But you should have made *her* go. That was assault, you know, it might even be called attempted murder."

And Susannah: "Poor Guy, he's so emotional, so *violent*. But there's such a lot of good in him too. He's really bad for Leonora, the last person for her. If there's no other way—well, it's very regrettable, but she'll have to be kept away from him by force."

He double-parked the car, hoping that its being Saturday afternoon would make that all right. The rifle was in the boot in a black leather golf bag. He was already coming to see it as an awkward sort of weapon to carry on a mission of this kind. Leaving it where it was, he went up the steps and rang the bell, which was still marked LINGARD, KIRKLAND, CHISHOLM. No one answered. He wasn't surprised.

His arm felt fine if he didn't move it much, and with automatic transmission there was no need to. He rested it lightly on the wheel. The traffic had thickened up since the morning and it took a long time getting to Camden Town. This time he took the rifle in the golf bag with him. After he had rung the bell and was standing there waiting, he had the sensation of someone looking down on him from above. It was very strong, this sense of being watched. He stepped back, went down a stair or two and looked up. No one was there and all the windows were closed, though it was a mild afternoon.

Lamb's Conduit Street next. That wasn't so far away. A parking space was empty directly outside the house. Susannah's window-boxes had just been watered. Water was dripping from them onto the flagstones below. That told him they must be in, someone must be. No one answered the entry-phone. He pressed the bell again and heard footsteps on the stairs. A woman Guy had never seen before opened the door. He didn't know her but even before she spoke he sensed that she had been expecting him.

"Laura Stow," she said. "I'm Susannah's sister."

He could see the likeness. She was a bit older, dressed in jeans and a shirt, a towel twisted turban-wise round her head.

She had been washing her hair. He hadn't known Susannah had a sister but he wasn't surprised. Did they have any *friends,* these people? Did they know anyone who wasn't family? Everyone you met at their houses, everyone you were introduced to was a relation.

He said bluntly, "Guy Curran."

She nodded, looked at the golf bag in his hand. Anyone with a grain of intelligence could see it was a rifle in there or a shotgun.

"I'm looking for Leonora." And then, "You do know who I mean?"

"Yes, of course I do. She isn't here. No one's here but me. I'm looking after the house while they're away."

"Away?" he said.

"On holiday. They've gone away on holiday today." She was patient with him but her eyes went to the golf bag again. "I'm sorry, but I'm afraid I can't help you."

It was rehearsed. Someone had prepared her for his visit, taught her to say all this. "Are you sure she's not here? Are you quite sure she's not upstairs somewhere?"

For a moment he thought he had frightened her. She had retreated a little. He made his voice gentler, he tried to smile. "Do you think I could come in and—well, look? I'm an old friend of the family."

"Look for *Leonora?* I've told you she's not here. Of course I can't let you in."

"I'm going to marry Leonora," he said patiently.

She stared, a nervous smile now trembling on her mouth.

He shouted in the direction of the stairs, "Leonora! Leo! Are you there? Leonora!"

She made an incoherent sound and shut the door in his face. Without being able to see, he sensed she was leaning back against the door, gasping.

He hadn't really believed Leonora was in there. She would have come down long before. Even he couldn't believe she was actually imprisoned, tied up, locked in a room. They wouldn't do that—or would they? He imagined this Laura

Stow getting on the phone at once to Anthony and Susannah in their holiday hotel. She would probably phone them all to report his visit. Perhaps she'd make her first call to Robin and Maeve, at whose flat it now seemed Leonora was most likely to be.

He drove home, left the car in the mews, and went upstairs to replace the rifle in its case. It had been an unwise choice, that cumbersome weapon. The time was five-thirty.

His hunger had come back. There was never much food in the house, no more usually than the basic materials for breakfast: bread, various cereals, eggs, Dutch cheese, marmalade, orange juice. Having poured himself a vodka and filled the glass with orange juice, he wondered if he knew how to cook an egg but decided against it. He had some bread and Gouda, finished his drink and dialled the St. Leonard's Terrace number.

They still weren't answering. They were still letting the phone ring. Guy cut himself more bread, poured some vodka. He dialled in vain Sanderstead Lane, Georgiana Street, and—out of devilment, as he told himself—Lamb's Conduit Street. Laura Stow answered. She sounded nervous. He laughed in a sinister way and she slammed the phone down. By now he was feeling enormously better. To say he felt fighting fit, in spite of his arm, wouldn't be an exaggeration. A challenge had been made to him. It was as if they had thrown down a glove in front of him and dared him to fight them all.

He was suddenly involved in a savage fairy story or cloak-and-dagger adventure. The beautiful princess had been imprisoned in a tower by her cruel father and stepmother. Marry the ginger dwarf or stay there forever! But her rescuer was coming, in his armour and with his weapons, if not on a white horse, in a golden car.

He went back upstairs and took out of the wardrobe the new handsome jacket in battleship-grey calfskin he had bought from Beltrami in Florence last May. He changed his shoes for grey leather half-boots. Reluctantly he took off the sling, but he hardly needed it any more. There was no reason why he shouldn't wear the scarf wound round his neck.

In the third bedroom, one of the two at the back that looked onto the back of houses in Abingdon Villas, he went to the bureau that stood against the rear wall between the windows. From the top drawer he took the heavy .45 Colt that had been in his possession since he was seventeen but which he had never used.

· · ·

Danilo had got that gun for him. It was while he was protecting the shopkeepers of Kensal. He had let it be known discreetly that he would like to possess a real gun instead of the convincing-looking replica he carried about with him. Danilo brought it into the pub in Artesian Road one night, showed it to him in the men's, and by the time Danilo had pulled the flush, Guy had paid cash for it and the ammunition that came with it. Leonora had seen it and called it a ghastly weapon. He saw what she meant.

He hadn't a holster for it. That had seemed unnecessary. He put it on the passenger seat of the Jaguar with his leather jacket on top of it.

The evening was growing cold. It was already dusk. For the first time for months he was using the car heater. He lit a cigarette. It took no more than ten minutes to reach St. Leonard's Terrace. Guy couldn't remember if he had actually ever been in this street before but now he was here he was impressed. Robin was evidently doing better for himself than the rest of that family with their shabby duplexes in Bloomsbury and their suburban villas. The flat was in an elegant but substantial house, its architecture classical, with a noble dark blue front door set under a portico whose domed roof was supported by Corinthian columns. Guy wouldn't have minded living there himself.

The framed card above the bell was printed MS. M. KIRKLAND, R. H. CHISHOLM. Very formal. The flat he thought must be theirs had a huge bow window. He had put on his

231

jacket and stuck the gun in the right-hand pocket, which was luckily large. No one replied on the entry-phone when he rang the bell. Guy tried again and then once more. He was coming down the shallow steps when he saw Robin and Maeve approaching from the end of the street.

They were arm in arm, closer than that, somehow intertwined, her head turning onto his shoulder, and they were in high sprits, laughing, squeezing each other. But more remarkable to Guy was the way they were dressed. Gone were the jeans and twin sweat-shirts, gone the socks and running shoes. Maeve was in a pale pink silk suit, very low-cut, the neckline plunging in a deep V, the puffed sleeves ballooning from padded shoulders, the skirt very full and very short. It revealed her long legs in white lace stockings from half-way up the thighs. Her shoes were pink and high-heeled and in her left hand she carried a white cart-wheel hat covered in pink roses.

Robin wore a pale beige suit, probably wild silk. His tie had obviously just been removed. The tail of it, bronze-and-cream-patterned silk, protruded from his jacket pocket. When they saw Guy they stopped, looked at each other, and burst out laughing. More rehearsing had been going on, he thought. They began to walk towards him, smiling broadly.

Guy said, "Where is she?"

This had the effect of almost doubling Maeve up. She crowed with laughter, she clutched at Robin, gasping. They were both very much the worse for drink. Robin giggled foolishly.

"Tell me where she is, please."

Guy could feel the gun in his pocket, heavy, cold, weighing down his jacket on the right side. He rested his hand on it through the leather.

"I know you've hidden her. You've no business to do that. This is a free country. You can't keep people prisoner against their will."

They made their way up the steps to the front door. Robin had his key out. They were still laughing. Maeve actually had tears on her face. Guy could see Robin smiling at her indulgently, amused in spite of himself by her amusement, trying in vain to achieve a straight face. He let out a final, apparently irrepressible, burst of shrill laughter, the neigh of a skittish horse, got his key into the lock, said to Maeve, "Go in, go in, for God's sake. You're making me worse. Every time I look at you it starts me off."

Guy was very cold. The adventure story he had been living in for the past half-hour began to dissolve, to melt and flow away. They were real people in a real street and this was reality. He would have liked to take out the gun and shoot them both, there on the steps. He would have loved to do that. If he did, he thought, he would never see Leonora again. That stopped him—that and the fact the gun wasn't loaded.

"Where is she?" he said again.

Robin, who had stopped laughing now Maeve was inside the house, said like a little boy, "You'll have to ask Mummy."

"I'll *what?*"

Growing up suddenly, Robin drawled, "That's what we agreed on. If you turned up, I mean. We decided my mother was the one to tell you. Right?"

He went into the house and shut the door.

•   •   •

By the time Guy crossed the river it was dark. He chain-smoked as he drove. A drink was what he would have loved, but the drink must wait. He had his leather jacket on with the .45 Colt in the pocket and Leonora's scarf wound round his neck. It smelt very slightly of her scent.

At the northern end of Sanderstead Lane he stopped, parked the car and loaded his gun. The street lamps were alight, smoky yellow globes, some half-burned in the thick dark foliage of the trees with which this long street was lined. The surface of the roadway gleamed. No cars were parked along it. All the houses had garages. No one was about, no dog walkers, no girls walking quickly and fearfully on their way to an evening date. A car passed, then another. The place was silent, still, and colder than inner London.

He drove on to the Mandevilles' house. There it lay at the back of its long front garden and it was ablaze with light. There were lights on in the bedrooms as well as downstairs, but Guy had no sense that the house was full of people, that, for instance, a party might be in progress. The house looked all the more incongruous because the one next to it, the unoccupied one joined on to it, was in total darkness. Not another car was in sight. No shadow moved against the light behind the drawn but transparent curtains. Yet he had the feeling that he was expected, they were waiting for him.

No doubt Robin had phoned his mother and she was prepared. She and Magnus were prepared. Perhaps she had also roped in a bodyguard. He felt the gun in his pocket, patted it like a patrolman in a film. The iron gate clanging shut made a loud clear ringing sound in the quiet. He began to walk up the path. The lighted house seemed to be looking at him.

He wasn't to have the chance of getting all the way there, of ringing the bell or using that lion's-head knocker. When he was half-way there, when he had just passed the point of no return, Tessa Mandeville opened the front door. She stood looking at him, silent, unsmiling, apparently unafraid.

"Where is she?"

Maeve had said that would be on his tombstone. Maybe. Perhaps it would be the last thing he ever said, his dying words. He didn't care. It was all he wanted to say. He repeated it. "Where is she?"

"You can come in," Tessa said. Her tone was remote. She seldom used his Christian name, she hardly ever had. "Come in, please. We may as well get it over."

Magnus was behind her. Tessa was as elaborately dressed as Maeve had been, in a copper-coloured close-fitting dress with a scroll pattern at neck and hem in bronze and gold beads. Her wrinkled neck with the prominent tendons was hidden under ropes of amber beads. But Magnus was in a pair of old serge trousers and a grey jersey, as if stripped for action. For all that, he had the transparent, fragile look of a grasshopper.

They went into an airless, over-furnished living-room. It was intensely hot. Two huge vases held bouquets of flowers that were wilting in the heat.

"You'd better sit down."

"I prefer to stand," Guy said.

"Just as you like. You asked me where Leonora is." Tessa looked at her watch in an over-acted ponderous way. She raised her eyes to his. "As of this moment I imagine they're twenty thousand feet over northern France. Leonora got married at one o'clock today."

CHAPTER TWENTY

The flowers in the two vases seemed to be wilting visibly. They were pale, exotic, full-petalled. Guy could see they were wedding flowers, formerly bouquets or table decorations. His head swam. Although he had said he wouldn't sit down, he did so. The scent from the flowers was sweet and stale, there was something obscene about it. It was like perfume on an unwashed body.

Tessa said, "That's my daughter's scarf you're wearing!"

"She gave it to me."

He was aware that his voice sounded weak, barely under control. He cleared his throat and said it again. "She gave it to me."

"I suppose you've come here for an explanation."

Tessa had seated herself opposite him on a sofa whose chintz cover was patterned with flowers curiously like those in the vases, pale pinkish, whitish, pallid lilac, and peach-coloured blown roses. She was a little, sharply cut figure, sitting upright with her hands clasped about her knees. Because of the bright brown of her dress and the gloss on the material, her dark hair shiny and her skin walnut colour, she looked as if cast in metal or carved from wood. Her eyes were very bright, sparkling with satisfaction, with triumph. Guy had taken too hard a knock, been too bludgeoned by it, to stand up to her and fight. His energy had gone and he could feel pressure inside his head. A chill, in spite of the heat of the room, drew his skin into goose-flesh. Hovering nervously, with a kind of ghoulishness, Magnus must have seen this, for he said hastily, "Would you like a drink?"

Guy shook his head. Later on he wondered if this was the first time in his life he had refused an offered drink. He summoned from somewhere a voice that approximated to his normal voice. "Is that where you all were? At her wedding?"

"That's right," said Tessa. "You've got it right first time. She was married at one, then we had lunch." She was unable to keep herself from smiling, though he could see she tried. Her lips twitched and she sat up very straight. "We've been partying ever since. It was a lovely wedding, everyone said so. We saw them off on their way to Heathrow and Robin tied a shoe to the back of the taxi! He's so naughty, there's no stopping him. I'm sure you'll want to know where Leonora and William have gone. Greek islands—Samos, actually."

He didn't believe her. It was to Samos that Leonora had been going with him. Tessa's eyes flickered when she told the lie. He understood she wouldn't dare tell him where they had really gone. He said desperately, though he hated showing them how terribly he had been hurt, how wounded almost to death.

"She said she was getting married on the sixteenth. She told me over and over it was the sixteenth, *you* said it was."

Even as he spoke he understood about that wedding invitation on the mantelpiece in Lamb's Conduit Street. It *had* been to Leonora's wedding, Janice and her husband were no doubt the invitees. The true date of the wedding would have been on it, the ninth, one week earlier than they had deceived him into believing. They had rushed to remove it. If he had seen it, the whole plan would have been spoiled.

"Why did she tell me the sixteenth?"

Tessa was smiling now, an arch smile with her eyebrows up. He had never seen her look like that before.

"Why did she say she'd meet me for lunch as usual today?"

The rest of the promises she had made he couldn't bear to utter. Tessa's face had relaxed a little. He sensed, with a kind of shame, that his feeble voice had touched her, that she, savagely triumphant though she was, had begun to *pity* him.

"You have to try putting yourself in our position. Try to think of others for once. My daughter was very seriously worried that if you knew the date of her wedding, you'd go to it and make trouble. I mean, she *knows* you. We all know you. We know what you're capable of. Look what happened last week when you got drunk and started fighting William. With *swords*. I mean, it's unbelievable. Fighting someone with swords in this day and age. You're capable of going to a wedding and breaking the place up. You might have forced your way in and shouted to the registrar to stop it—anything. You might have done anything. My daughter has been *afraid* of you for literally years. She's been living in a nightmare of terror about what you'd do next."

By a subtle rearrangement of hope and inhibition, Leonora had become "my daughter." Guy sensed Tessa would never again refer to her by her name when speaking to him.

Magnus said in his mild, dry way, "That is why, if my advice had been taken, we would have sought legal means to prevent you from annoying my stepdaughter. No doubt, it would have been an unpleasant step to take initially, but in the long term it would have saved a great deal of trouble and distress."

Guy lifted his eyes, which felt heavy, as if full of unshedable tears. His eyes felt swollen. He looked at Magnus. Through the fine soft leather pocket of his jacket he could feel the uncompromising shape of the gun. But it was distanced from him, it was as if he lacked the strength not only to use it but even to lift it out of its hiding place. The numbness that comes with shock wasn't unknown to him, but it was a long time since he had felt it. "Forgive me," she had said on the phone yesterday morning. He understood now why she had said it. "Forgive me." Her voice had been thick and unsteady as his eyes were now, full of tears. "Forgive me for the lies they've made me tell you, for deceiving you, for this ultimate terrible lie that I will meet you tomorrow and be with you forever."

Tessa had been speaking. Words, sentences, whole paragraphs had flowed out of her unheard by him. He picked up a word or two here and there: "cream silk," "yellow roses," "white gold." He turned to her. Again the feeling he had was unfamiliar, a sense of agony that people are capable of such refined and calculated cruelty.

"I don't want to hear about that," he said, and his voice was stronger. In a curious way it was a new voice, hard, clipped, stiff with contempt. I have died, he thought, and been born again differently, with a new voice, a new set of values. "I don't want to hear about that." Anger was beginning to return, and that was the same, the same old anger. "Don't give me that rubbish, what she wore, the fucking flowers, don't give me that shit."

"And don't speak to my wife like that!"

"Are you going to stop me?" He felt the gun again. Magnus made a pettish sound, a "pshah!" sound, and Guy knew he was afraid. He could have laughed if laughter had been something he were capable of. But his head felt heavy, his eyelids were heavy. "Whose idea was this?" he said.

"I beg your pardon?" Tessa sounded very sarcastic, all superiority and Lady Muck, the short-lived pity vanished.

"I asked you whose idea it was, to con me into thinking Leonora was getting married a week later than she was. It wasn't her idea, was it? She didn't think that up."

"What does it matter whose idea it was? I can't remember whose idea it was. It wasn't mine. I wish it had been, I wish I'd thought of something so—well, so simple and so effective.

Let me tell you, my daughter may not have thought of it herself, but she was extremely happy to go along with it. She jumped at the chance."

"She was corrupted," he said. "All of you, you corrupted her."

"If getting someone away from a person who's frightening them to death is corrupting them, then long live corruption."

"Leonora wasn't frightened of me. She loved me. She asked me to forgive her." Guy turned to Magnus and said, "I will have that drink, after all."

Tessa burst into laughter. "You're incorrigible, aren't you? You've got the devil's own nerve." She mocked his tone, " 'I will have that drink, after all.' You're not a friend of ours, you know. You're not a friend of this family. You forced your way into it God knows how many years ago and we've been trying to get rid of you ever since. You never seemed to understand: *You've no place among us, you're not our kind of person.* To be perfectly frank, no matter how much money you've made, you don't belong in our class. Basically, you're still an Irish yob, a street toughie. It'd be an insult to the working class to say you're working class, you're not, you're an erk from a slum and you always were."

There was a tap on his shoulder and he looked up to see Magnus's death's head above him, a glass of something held out in the papery, slightly tremulous hand. He hadn't been asked what he wanted. Something Magnus thought suitable (or something he'd got most of or didn't himself like) had been brought. Medicine. A remedy for shock. In fact, it was whisky, slightly diluted with water. The taste of it brought Guy the faint nausea whisky always did, then the beginnings of a surge of energy.

"The absurd thing," Tessa was saying, "is that you ever supposed my daughter might marry you, might be *allowed* to marry you."

"She's of age, Tessa," said Magnus, legal as ever. "No doubt she could make her own choice about that. She *had* made her own choice, in point of fact."

"No, she hadn't," Guy said. "Not in point of anything. Others made it for her, and that's the real point. Your wife was right when she said that about not being allowed. You lot, you Chisholms and whatever else you are, you didn't allow her to do what she wanted."

"What utter nonsense! I honestly wish I'd made a tape recording of the things my daughter said. I honestly do. The number of times I asked her why she bothered with you and she said seeing you was the only possible way. She played along for the sake of peace, for the sake of being free to do what she liked for the rest of the week, that's what she did."

"If only she'd seen the perfectly reasonable step of applying for an injunction as feasible . . ."

"Well, she didn't, Magnus. She didn't want to, I quote, 'hurt his feelings.' She was always far too soft-hearted for her own comfort. Unlike our guest here, she put others first. She would have done anything to avoid hurting him. But it doesn't matter now, it's all in the past, it's over. She's married. And when she and William come back from—er, Samos, they're going straight up north. They won't be coming back to London. And if you imagine I'm telling you my daughter's new address, you must be even more mad, disturbed, whatever they call it, than I thought."

Guy felt for his cigarettes. They were in the pocket that the gun wasn't in. He put one in his mouth and lit it, watching her. She reacted predictably.

"I don't allow smoking in this house."

"Too bad," he said. "If you want me to put it out you'll have to do it by force. D'you want to have a go? You or him?"

"It's outrageous," she said.

"You shouldn't make rules like that if you can't enforce them."

"Magnus," she said, "make him put that cigarette out."

Magnus's reply was to produce an ashtray, which he set at Guy's elbow. Guy said, "Your ex-husband got Newton that job through his brother. Leonora as good as told me that. He introduced Newton to her and then he pulled all the strings he could to get him a job in the north."

Tessa began to pantomime coughing. She covered her mouth, shivered a little. "That may be. I know nothing about that. I haven't seen Michael Chisholm for years." She put out a hand to her husband. "I think I'll have a drink too, darling. I notice you didn't ask me. Gin and ginger ale, and why don't you have one too? Since," she added, "we're apparently saddled with a protracted discussion about his—well, what would you call it? Paranoia?"

"Frankly, Curran," said Magnus, "don't you think it's time you left? My wife's told you a great deal more than you could reasonably have expected in the circumstances."

"I'm not going yet. I want to know whose idea it was to set me up."

Tessa said in a bored voice, "I'm not sure if I follow you. How were you 'set up'?"

"Deceived, then. I was led to believe the wedding was next Saturday." Guy hesitated, rephrased it. "No, I was led to believe there would be no wedding." *I love you, I'll come to you, anything you say.* He remembered her kiss on the night when his arm was wounded, and he touched his arm, touched the silky stuff of the scarf. If I sob when I start speaking, he thought, I will kill them both. "Who," he said, and his voice was steady, "put her up to that? Who made her tell me the wedding was on the sixteenth and then made me think the wedding was off? Who was it?"

"I told you, I don't know." Tessa took the glass her husband held out to her. She held it up as if for a toast, was going to say something, but thought better of it and drank. "It doesn't matter who it was, we all approved."

"She shouldn't have told him untruths," Magnus said unexpectedly. "I mean, if he's right about her saying she told him she wasn't marrying William, she really shouldn't have done that."

"*What?* Whose side are you on, pray? Let me tell you, she

was entirely justified in telling him anything. Anything. And if you say another word about an injunction I shall scream."

Magnus took no notice. The creases on his face ironed themselves out a little, like screwed-up paper smoothed by painstaking fingers. He was smiling. He said, "I recall perfectly whose idea it was. I was quite taken aback. It seemed so—well, audacious."

His wife made an impatient gesture with her hand. "It's quite unimportant who thought of it. The thing is that it worked and all that miserable business in the past *is* the past." She began staring hard at Guy, looking into his eyes, into both his eyes. He could tell she wasn't in the least afraid of him, and he wondered at that. She was observing him quite coolly, even clinically, like a state torturer she would ask him briskly if he had anything to say before she started with the thumbscrew, but she didn't. "That's it then," she said, "all out in the open. And now I think you should go."

"Oh, I'm going. I don't want to stay here. Why would I? Guy stubbed out his cigarette but left it smoking a little. He looked at Magnus. "Okay, whose idea was it?"

"Idea? You mean, who thought of that business of the wedding date? There ought to be a name for the relationship. I ought to be able to say something like my 'stepwife,' but that wouldn't quite do, would it? I'm simply obliged to call her by her name—that is, Mrs. Chisholm, Susannah Chisholm."

The man enjoyed saying all that, Guy thought disgustedly. He enjoyed spitting out all that pedantic rubbish. Then he realized what the man had said. "Susannah thought of it?"

"We were at some family gathering. Very civilized. It couldn't have happened when I was young, ex-husbands and ex-wives all matey together. But it's very pleasant, I'm not complaining. Mrs. Chisholm—that is, Susannah—came out with it. It certainly appealed to my wife, didn't it, darling?"

"Yes, it did. Of course it did. I was thrilled." Tessa, who had said she couldn't remember, now seemed to have acquired total recall. "I was tremendously grateful to Susannah. I was only too happy to help work out the details. I played my part in it, don't you remember? I'm sure you remember my coming round to that house of yours and making a point of telling you the wedding was on the sixteenth. If I'd had my way, you'd have been sent an *official invitation for the sixteenth.*"

Her husband nodded. He nodded and nodded like one of those wobble-headed dogs drivers have in the rear windows of cars. "Leonora didn't care for it, though. Wouldn't do it at first. She said it was wrong, but I said to her, 'There's nothing illegal in telling a white lie.'"

"I don't remember that, Magnus. I think you dreamt that up." She coughed again, reached over, and with a shudder ground out Guy's cigarette end. "It was wonderful for Leonora, it took away all her worries."

"Needs must when the devil drives," said Magnus, his eyes gleaming, leaving little doubt as to whom he meant by the devil.

Guy got up, patting his pocket where the gun was. Tessa's eyes followed his hand. The telephone was beside her on a low table, within easy reach. He had no sword to cut the wires. With his wounded arm, he lacked the strength to pull them out of the wall. He wouldn't have wanted to anyway, but he put his hand into his pocket and felt the smooth cold metal.

"Where have they gone?"

"Where have who gone?" Tessa had got up too.

"Anthony and Susannah. They've gone away on holiday." Or was that a lie too, put about by the sister? "I was told they were away."

"Only for a few days. I wouldn't dream of telling you where. It's been quite bad enough our having to put up with this interrogation, but I took that on myself. I volunteered. I said to send you here and I'd be the one to face you. That was to save the others. I felt it was the least I could do, so you can be sure I'm not going to drop poor Anthony and Susannah into it at this stage. Anyway, they can't tell you any more than I've told you."

He felt the gun and thought again of killing them. If he did that, he would spoil his chances of finding Anthony and

Susannah. He took his hand out of his pocket. Breaking the place up, even kicking the vases of flowers over, would spoil his chances of finding Anthony and Susannah. Magnus Mandeville was the kind of man who wouldn't hesitate before getting on to the police. He was probably on to the police about something or other every couple of days. Guy looked from one to the other of them and then he looked away, sickened.

He thought, she is married. While I waited for her in that restaurant, at the very moment set for our meeting, she was getting married. I tried to make those phone calls, I went from house to house, I saw myself as her rescuer. All the time I was doing that, she was at a party, her own wedding party. She was drinking champagne and laughing and being congratulated. The flowers in this room had been in that room, she had probably smelt them, touched them, perhaps even carried some of them as a bouquet.

He walked out of the room and across the hall, opened the front door, slammed it and walked down the long path to the gate.

They were watching him, he knew that, but he didn't look back. They had won, all of them. Tessa and Magnus, Rachel, Maeve and Robin, Anthony's brother and Susannah's sister, Anthony and Susannah. They had done what they had set out to do four years before. It had taken four years to accomplish it, but they had done it, and the instigators, the leaders of the plot, were Anthony and Susannah.

He sat in the Jaguar. He switched on the engine and saw the digits on the clock light up: eight fifty-two. All these things had happened, his life changed, he himself changed, and it was still only ten to nine. It wasn't believable, so he looked at his watch. Ten to nine. He drove a little way and parked the car again. He parked simply because there was a space at the kerb and no yellow line. The cigarette he lit was so comforting it nearly made him cry. How could he have considered giving up smoking? He would never give it up.

When his head cleared and he could think again he would

remember where Anthony and Susannah had gone. Susannah had *told* him where they were going. She had told him that day when he called in at Lamb's Conduit Street. He had forgotten, but it would come back. On the other hand, he could phone the sister. What was her name? Laura Stow. He could phone Laura Stow. It was only ten to nine—well, five past now. He could be home by a quarter to ten. That wasn't too late to phone someone. He wouldn't be himself on the phone, he would think of some tale—an urgent message for Anthony, a package to be delivered express . . .

All of them were guilty—Magnus and Tessa, Rachel, Robin and Maeve, Laura Stow and Michael Chisholm, but most of all, Anthony and Susannah. It had started with Susannah's opening that letter from Poppy Vasari. That was the beginning of their vendetta against him. Then Anthony had set to work, forbidding her to go on holiday with him, preventing her from borrowing the money for the flat in Portland Road from him. Negative moves, all of them, but the next one had been positive. The next one had been finding a husband for her, introducing her to William Newton. It was as bad as Indian immigrants arranging marriages, he thought.

The husband secured, all that remained was to get a job for him in the north of England, far away from the man she really loved. And the final step was Susannah's plan to get her married in secret, a week in advance of what he had been led to expect. Anthony and Susannah had master-minded the whole thing, made the plans, carried out the operation, brought it to a triumphantly successful conclusion. The others were no more than their servants, willing and obedient, awaiting instructions. And Newton was their pawn, an innocent nonentity. How much had they paid him to fall in with their plans?

Guy started driving home. On Battersea Bridge he stopped, left the car and looked down at the brown, gleaming, dirty water of the river. He took the blue leather box with the sapphire engagement ring in it out of his pocket and, after a very small hesitation, threw it into the water. His thoughts reverted immediately to Anthony and Susannah Chisholm. The world was not big enough to hold within it himself—and them. He wouldn't rest while Anthony and Susannah were still alive.

CHAPTER TWENTY-ONE

It was normal for the lights to be on. There was a timer arrangement that switched them on as dusk fell. He left the car in the mews, let himself into the house, and went straight to the phone in the living-room. The directory in his brain that held a list of Chisholm numbers came up immediately with the one for Lamb's Conduit Street.

A man answered. Laura Stow probably had a husband. Guy said he was Wing Express Carriers of South Audley Street with an urgent packet for Mr. Chisholm, and where could he reach him? If Laura Stow herself had answered he would have disguised his voice, but with the husband it wasn't necessary. The man wasn't suspicious. He gave Guy the name of an hotel in Lyme Regis.

Guy fetched himself a drink, a very large brandy, a triple. On the table, where he had left them, lay *The London Review of Books* and *The Guardian*. He thought he had left *Cosmopolitan* magazine there too but he couldn't have because it wasn't there now. Other things came to mind, the Paloma Picasso perfume and bath essence he had put in the bathroom, the house he had arranged to view on Monday. Rage that was as much misery as anger took hold of him and he seized the two papers, pulling them to pieces, tearing the sheets. He cursed as he did it, holding his head up, shouting at the ceiling—or God. He could hear his own voice raving as if it were someone else's. He kicked the table, drummed with his fists on the wall.

"Guy," someone said. "Guy, what is it?"

He turned round. Celeste was standing in the doorway.

"Sweet Guy, what's happened?"

"Oh, God. Oh, Christ." He had forgotten their date, or rather forgotten that he hadn't succeeded in cancelling it. They had arranged for her to come here and she had come. How long ago? It was almost ten. "Celeste." He simply spoke her name, his voice all ragged and rough from the shouting. "Celeste."

"I thought something had happened to you. I thought, Guy's had an accident."

As if it were not himself but another man seeing her, as if he saw through that other man's eyes, he thought how wonderful she looked. Her long dark chestnut hair hung loose, but still in the ripples made by plaiting. An inch-wide gold band held it off her face. She wore a black silk sweater and a black skirt densely embroidered in turquoise and blue and pink and red. Everything was perfect, from the tiny gold studs, snail shells, in her ears, to the bracelets of gold wire, to her flat gold-embroidered blue-and-green silk pumps. He closed his eyes and saw Leonora in navy-and-white washed-out cotton and dirty running shoes. The pain of it made him wince.

"Are you hurt?" she said. "Is it your arm?"

"Celeste, I'm sorry I wasn't here. I forgot you were coming. I'm sorry." If he used those words and asked her to forgive him ("forgive me"), he would start crying. "Awful things," he said carefully, trying to be careful, "have been happening."

"What things, Guy?"

He lit a cigarette and gave her one. He tasted the brandy. It was good but it made him shudder. "I've got to go out again. I only came home to make that phone call. But I've got to go out soon. I'll drive through the night."

"Can I come with you?"

"No. I have to go alone. You stay here and sleep. Okay?"

"I'd like to come with you. I could drive you." She didn't say he soon wouldn't be fit to drive but that was what she meant. Still looking at him, she knelt down and began picking up the pieces of torn newspaper.

"Oh, leave that." He put his hands up to his head. "Celeste, she didn't come today. She's married. She got married while I was waiting for her in the restaurant."

"What?"

He said it all again. It was easier the second time. She sat beside him and he told her all about the Chisholm conspiracy. Celeste listened in silence. When he had finished she was still silent, then she said, "That was a terrible thing to do."

He nodded. He had always liked the way she spoke, with that faint touch of accent that is Caribbean, the stress on the last syllable of words. "Teri-bull" was what she said. He looked at her affectionately. It came to him that she understood, she had always understood.

"They ganged up against me," he said. "They set out to turn her against me and they succeeded."

"I meant what she did was terrible. What *she* did. It was wicked, Guy. A good person wouldn't do that."

He jumped up and stood a few paces from her. The warm feelings he had a few minutes before were gone. She continued to look at him.

"She's twenty-six years old," she said. "She does her own thing. She does what she wants. You have to face that she wanted it. No one could make her, she's not a child or an animal, she's intelligent, she's got a lot more brain than me and I'm younger, but I'd never do what people told me, never, never. And she didn't. She did what she wanted. She enjoyed it, I really think she enjoyed it. You said she stood there and watched you fight William. She liked you fighting over her and making a goddess of her and not asking for anything in return."

His body trembled. He would have liked to kill her. His right arm itched to rise and his hand to strike her a swinging blow. Something stopped him, an old gallant shibboleth that you don't strike a woman. You may kill her but you won't hit her. He held his hand in the other hand and the scarf touched it, the silky scarf that was Leonora's. All that he would ever have of her, he thought.

"You're jealous," he said. "You always have been."

She shook her head. He didn't know if she meant yes by it or no. "Leonora's in love with William, Guy. Her father didn't find her a husband, she found him. She loves him."

"How would you know?"

"She told me. That day in the restaurant. She said, "I'd like to think of Guy loving someone the way I love William and them loving him back."

"It's funny you never mentioned that before."

"I tried to tell you. You wouldn't listen."

He went to pour himself another drink. The night had become very quiet, though it was Saturday and early yet. He heard her say, "Where are you going?"

"A long way. To Dorset." The brandy nauseated him. It had never had that effect before. "I want to see Anthony and Susannah."

There must have been something in his eyes to tell her. "I've hidden the ammunition for your gun. When you didn't come I had a sense, a premonition." By gun, she meant his .22. She didn't know about the Colt. "I'll never tell you where it is. You'd have to kill me first."

"You can stop interfering in my affairs, Celeste. You're not my wife. You're not even my girl-friend. You're just *a* girl-friend. Isn't it time you got that straight?"

He wanted to hurt her. Sometimes, in the past, he had seen her wince and he wanted to see it again. But her face was calm. She was still. "Have you ever thought," she said, "that if you hadn't been chasing that dream, you had what was best for you right here at home? You and I, we've got everything in common, Guy. We like all the same things. We want to do the same things. We've got the same tastes. You don't love me but you would one day if you gave it half a chance. I love you. I don't have to tell you. We've been good lovers, haven't we? We've been good to each other there, haven't we? There's never been a better for me—has there for you? Has there? Be honest, Guy. Have you had a better, more loving lover than me?"

"I told you," he said, "from the first I was in love with Leonora."

"I know what you said. What you say and what really is, they're not the same. D'you know your life's one hundred per cent illusion?"

"You're talking about things you don't understand. Leonora is the great love of my life. She *is* my life." He remembered that utterance Leonora had denied, had attributed to a character in some book. "I *am* Leonora," he said. "We were one person." The brandy was making him wild and slurring his speech. "I'm dead without her. Life's meaningless without her."

For a moment he thought Celeste was going to laugh at him. She didn't. She said softly, "How many times did you actually make love to her?"

It struck him as a monstrous impertinence. "That has nothing to do with it," he said stiffly.

"From that first time you told me about, on a grave or whatever, all those years ago—how many times, Guy?"

It was like one of those anti-Catholic jokes, priests in the confessional and the little Irish girl kneeling. "How many times, my child?" Celeste was looking at him very seriously, though. She wasn't joking. He thought back to those early years, but he could only remember Kensal Green, the long summer grass, and the butterflies.

"Does it matter?"

"I should think it matters to you."

"Five or six times," he muttered.

"Oh, Guy," she said. "Oh, my sweet Guy."

He shrugged his shoulders, looked away. Suddenly he was aware of tiredness, heavy and dark, covering him like a blanket. He reached for the brandy and drank what was left. The cigarette he lit tasted ashen from the first draw.

"She liked it," Celeste said. "You were right when you said she wanted to meet you on Saturdays and have you phone every day. She liked having you on a string. What did it cost her? Nothing. It was flattering, having you hanging after her, you so handsome and rich and nice, Guy, and her not wanting anything from it but people knowing you were in love with her. She could get herself another boy-friend and fix up to marry him but you'd still be there, phoning her every day and taking her out to lunch on Saturdays, and her not having to pay a thing, not even sleeping with you."

"It wasn't like that," he said, but it had been. "Get me another drink, would you?"

"Aren't you going to drive through the night?"

"Get me another drink, please."

He would go to Dorset first thing in the morning. That would be best. When Celeste was asleep. He always woke early. Fresh, revived, he would make a start at eight and be there by midday. It occurred to him that he had had nothing to eat all day except that bread and cheese in the afternoon, but he didn't want anything. For the first time in years he hadn't gone out to a restaurant or someone else's house to eat his dinner.

In the Chinese bed he lay for a little while apart from Celeste. He was thinking about his plans for tomorrow. It would be better to have a night's rest first. When he got to Lyme he would walk straight into the hotel and ask for them. The clerk in reception would tell him they had gone out and he would go in search of them, along the cliffs maybe— Were there cliffs at Lyme? There must be. He could see them in the distance, walking along the beach at the water's edge. The

Colt was still in the pocket of his leather jacket. Let it stay there. In the morning he would put on his jacket and go. How would they feel, what would they do, when they saw him in the distance, walking along the sands to meet them?

The wide empty beach, the vast sea, no one else there. Nowhere to run to, but they would run . . . An image came to him of Leonora's smile, coquettish, controlled, secret, Vivien Leigh's smile in *Gone With the Wind*. It was her wedding night. Not that this meant much, she had been living with the man on and off for weeks. How cruel she had been to him! He had never supposed he could think of Leonora as cruel, but he did now and with self-pity and wonder . . .

Celeste's slender hands touched his face and she brought her lips to his, very soft and warm. She could speak through a kiss, he had never known anyone else who could do that.

"Sweet Guy, I love you. I want you to make love to me."

He did. He thought that in order to do so he would have to conjure up Leonora, never difficult for him, but this time she refused to appear, or Celeste's presence was too strong to admit ghostly intruders. It was as if Celeste were determined to dispel by her love everyone but herself and him. This was Celeste in his arms and no one else, her eyes open and shining, her voice silenced. He could feel emanating from her a curious concentrated power, and the word "witchcraft" came into his mind. Inside her body, her self, was a healing white magic.

•   •   •

It was a kind of boast of his that he could never sleep late. He had hardly expected to sleep at all, only to rest. But when he woke up, the hands of his carriage clock told him it was after nine and Celeste still lay wrapped in sleep, as deeply burrowed into sleep as if it were still the small hours.

This way it was better, he could make his escape without her knowing, go without her. He showered. It struck him as absurd that a man should bother to wash his body all over, soap himself and stand under these power-driven cascades of hot water, before going off on a killing mission. Why bother with anything? Why stand here making tea, waiting for the kettle to boil? Why consider, wrapped in his towelling robe, what clothes to put on? There should be nothing between his determined aim and its accomplishment. He should already have been on his way.

A light mist lay over the little garden. The sun's rays had already begun to pierce it. All summer long the lilies had bloomed on his pond, they were still in bloom now in the autumn. He had a ridiculous absurd desire, immediately suppressed, to go out there and stroke the bronze dolphin's head. But he opened the French windows and felt the mild breath of the morning.

His head ached, but normally. Most mornings his head ached. It didn't amount to the monumental, hammer-ringing, bone-splitting wrenching-apart of brain fibres he called a hangover. Housework wasn't something he ever did, not even washing a cup, but he knelt down now and began picking up the torn pieces of paper from the floor and carrying them to the kitchen. The kettle boiled, its light went out. He made tea, a tea-bag in each mug, then decided against waking Celeste.

Silently, so as not to disturb her, he put his clothes on—jeans, a black T-shirt, the most sombre pullover he had, a plain navy thing with a polo neck. It came to him that he dressed like that because this most resembled the garb of an executioner. He put Leonora's scarf round his neck, took it off again and pushed it into a drawer. In the mirror he saw himself as Anthony and Susannah would see him, approaching them along the beach. He imagined the jacket, the heavy pocket, and he mimed reaching into it for his gun. And then he said to himself, "You're playing games, stop playing games, you know you're not going to Lyme, you're not going anywhere and you're not going to kill anybody."

Last night he had been. Hot with angry pain, he had cared for nothing but his revenge, nothing else mattered. There was no future. A night's sleep had changed that, Celeste had changed it. He would have gone, he thought, if she hadn't been there. He would have gone last night. And Anthony and

Susannah would be dead by now and he arrested or else dead by his own hand.

I don't want to die, he thought, I don't want to be imprisoned. I want to be free. He *was* free. By what Leonora had done she had freed him. There would be no more enslavement to the phone, no more Saturday lunches that brought as much suffering as pleasure. The idea was so novel that he sat down to think about it, sat down outside in the pale sunshine on one of the white chairs.

He wouldn't stop loving her, he couldn't. He would always love her. In a cool, sane, very grown-up way he knew he would be in love with her all his life. That was the way it was. It sounded melodramatic, but it was true that he'd met his fate that day in the street when he was there with Danilo and Linus and she had come along, a little girl, and stood there watching them.

But she was gone now, she was lost to him. He had thrown the ring he bought her into the Thames. She had married someone else, and if they ever met again it would be in the company of others and with all of them there: Tessa and Magnus, Anthony and Susannah, Robin and Maeve, Rachel Lingard and Uncle Michael, maybe Janice and her husband. And he would be there with Celeste.

Why not Celeste? She had saved him last night. She always saved him. It was true what she had said about the way they were together. They were good together, they had everything in common, they could *talk* to each other, they could be silent together, there was between them no shame or pretence. She loved him the way no one had ever, all his life long, loved him, and he was fond of her. Even he, tough as he was, street-wise baby grown up, one-time dealer in Class-A drugs, gangster, entrepreneur, and sharp businessman, even he needed to be loved.

Why don't we try? he thought. Why don't I try to make a go of it? What can we lose? He felt an extraordinary hollow lightness at the thought of no more phone calls, no more fantasies, no more sick longings. If he had exacted his revenge he would have lost everything . . .

"Oh, Leonora," he said aloud as he went back into the house. It had been such a long haul, so long for someone of his years, only twenty-nine years old but for fourteen of them in thrall to love. "Oh, Leonora."

Passing into the hall, he had a look at the Kandinski. He had never liked it. No matter what people like Tessa Mandeville said, it was hideous. Having it there was all pretence. He would sell it. He took the Colt out of his jacket pocket, sat down on one of the Georges Jacob chairs, and emptied it of its ammunition.

From upstairs Celeste was calling to him.

"I'll bring you your tea," he said.

If it were Leonora lying up there, in his bed, his wonderful Chinese William Linnell bed, waking to put up her arms to him . . . The time for these fantasies was past. He carried the mug of tea upstairs. She said, "Sweet Guy, thank you. Did you sleep well? Do you feel better? Ah, yes, I can see you feel good this morning."

He sat on the bed beside her. He held her hand as he might hold the hand of a sick person in a hospital bed. Celeste wasn't ill, she was young and healthy, glowing with health and vitality. Her dark hair shone like a tiger's-eye jewel. He thought he would buy her a necklace of tiger's eye. I will try to love her, he thought, oh, I will try. If willing it will do it, I will do it.

The doorbell rang.

He couldn't help remembering how once, when that had happened, he had been sure it was Leonora. It couldn't be Leonora now. It couldn't be any of her family either. He let go of Celeste's hand, said to Celeste, "We'll do something nice later. We'll drive out to the country. We'll have a nice day."

The bell rang again when he was half-way downstairs. Someone was very insistent. He opened the door and saw two men standing there, the older one, a white man in a suit, looking like an accountant. The black man, who was about his own age, wore jeans like his own and a polo-necked sweater also like his own. He looked like an executioner, and there was also something familiar in his face. The man in the suit said, "Mr. Curran? Mr. Guy Curran?"

Guy nodded.

"I'm a policeman, we're policemen. I expect you'd like to see our warrant cards, save you asking. I'm Detective Inspector Shaw of the Serious Crime Squad, and this is Sergeant Pinedo. May we come in, please?"

It was Linus. He must know Guy, recognize him as his old street companion, but he gave no sign of it, and Guy said nothing, only looked at him. So that was what had happened to Linus, he wasn't a down-and-out or a drug bandit executed for smuggling, but a policeman. The dark face, fuller now, less handsome, seemed rigid, fanatical. They said a knife edge separated the policeman from the criminal, while the affinity between them was strong. Linus had chosen to hunt rather than be hunted.

Guy backed a little to let the two men in, and the light from the open door fell on his Colt, which still lay on the little table. Shaw said, "Do you have a firearms certificate for this weapon, Mr. Curran?"

"Yes, of course." But he hadn't and they would ask to see it. "For a rifle, yes," he said. "For a twenty-two."

"This isn't a rifle," said Shaw.

He didn't touch the gun. He walked down the hall and into the living-room, Linus following him. Linus still walked with that pimp roll, hips stiff, thighs together, shoulders on the move. The thin man in the grey suit sat down on the sofa in Guy's living-room, having looked neither to the right nor the left, having ignored the Kandinski.

"What is it you want?"

"We're making inquiries into the death of Mrs. Llewellyn-Gerrard."

"I don't know any Mrs. Llewellyn-Gerrard."

Guy felt enormous relief. This must be some neighbour. They were inquiring at every house in the mews. It was one of those cases of a woman found stabbed in a bedroom or dead of an overdose. It happened all the time. Shaw was looking narrowly at him.

"Mrs. Janice Llewellyn-Gerrard," said Linus. "Of Portland Road, West Eleven."

"Janice," Guy said, all wonder. "Yes. Yes, I suppose I do know her. If it's who I think it is. But Portland Road? I know some other people in Portland Road."

He sounded confused and breathless, he could hear it in his voice. Shaw was looking at him. Linus was looking at him. "She's dead?" he said, trying to make things better. "What did she die of?"

"She was murdered." Linus's gold tooth gleamed.

He was all innocence. He didn't understand, he said, "How was she murdered?"

"It went wrong," Shaw said. "The man was seen. He's in custody." Guy thought he sounded proud of himself. "He's been in custody since an hour after it happened at eight last evening."

"You mean she was mugged?"

"No, I don't mean that. He rang the doorbell, but the entry-phone didn't work, something like that, so she went down. He shot her at point-blank range, through the chest and the head. She died immediately, she can hardly have known what happened to her. But her husband had come down behind her and seen it all. He was able to make an identification."

"We'd like you to come with us, Mr. Curran," said Linus. He had lost the accent, Celeste's Caribbean. He talked like any policeman on his way to the top. The first black Commissioner, thought Guy. "Down to the station. We'll do better down there."

"Me?" said Guy. "Why me? You've got someone for this, you said so. You said you'd got him in custody."

"Charlie Ruck, yes. Would you like to see this card we found on Charlie Ruck? It's got your name and address on it."

Guy read the card, though he didn't need to. He had recognized it. He had given it to Danilo in the Black Spot when arranging for the "wasting" of Rachel Lingard: "Short, round-faced, fat, glasses, dark hair scraped back, about 27 . . ."

"I can explain this," he began, and then he understood that he couldn't.

He had forgotten, but now he remembered, that one of them had mentioned how Janice and her husband would be staying in Portland Road. Perhaps it was Leonora who had mentioned it. Always he could remember when Leonora told him something, but he couldn't now and knowing this, he felt a bitter pang.

The two policemen were watching him.

"Come 'long then, Curran," Shaw said. The "Mr." had been dropped. That was the beginning.

He called out bravely to Celeste, "See you later."

"I doubt it," said Linus.

They went out into the mews. One of Guy's neighbours gave them an indifferent glance. Guy got into the car and they took him away.